I'm No Angel Copy Copy

SINGLE TITLE SERIES BOOK #14

MIMI BARBOUR

SARNA PUBLISHING

Contents

Also author of...

Together for Christmas (Book 6)

Together Always (Book 7)

~*~*~*~

Angels with Attitude Series

— Angels Playing Cupid! —

The Angels with Attitudes Anthology (Books 1-3)

My Cheeky Angel (Book 1)

His Devious Angel (Book 2)

Loveable Christmas Angel (Book 3)

A Wonderful Life (Book 4)

Mischievous Christmas Angel (Book 5)

~*~*~*~

Elvis Series

— Make an Elvis Song a Book! —

She's Not You (Book 1)

Love Me Tender (Book 2)

Don't Be Cruel (Book 3)

~*~*~*~

Vegas Series

— Action–Packed Thrillers!—

Vegas Series – Complete Boxed Set

Partners (Book 1) **FREE**

Roll the Dice (Book 2)

Vegas Shuffle (Book 3)

High Stakes Gamble (Book 4)

Spin the Wheel (Book 5)

Let it Ride (Book 6)

~*~*~*~

Undercover FBI Series

One of the series will be put on sale every month.

— Popular & Compelling!—

~*~*~*~

Holiday Heartwarmers Series

— Truly a Christmas favorite! —

Christmas, Puppies & Romance (Book 8)

Santa's Gifts of Romance (Book 9)

Christmas is for Everyone (Book 10)

Flamingo Christmas (Book11)

Christmas Tempest (to be released Fall 2024)

~*~*~*~

Her Sweet Revenge Series

— She's unstoppable! —

Retaliation (Book 1)

Justice (Book 2)

Resolution (Book 3

Endings (Book 4)

Faith (Book 5) **FREE**

Leni (Book 6)

~*~*~*~

Single Title Series

He's My Baby (Book #1)

Christmas Runaway (Book #2)

Because You Cared (Book #3)

Daddy's Mine (Book #4)

Her Hero (Book #5)

You Make Me Happy (Book #6)

Sweet Christmas (Book #7)

You're the Boss (Book 8)

Young Love Strikes Again(Book 9)

Dear Hottie (Book 10)

Born a Hero (Book 11)

Get Serious (Book 12)

Sexy, Sassy & Not Available (Book 13) to be released in Sept 2024

The Surrogate's Secret (Book 14)

Big Girls Don't Cry (Book15)

~*~*~*~

The Best in Romance Series

Red Hot Divas (Book #1 BoxSet)

Hot and Handsome (Book #2 Box Set)

Too Hot to Handle (Book #3 Box Set)

~*~*~*~

Other Titles

I'm No Angel

Hotshot Cowboy

Mimi's Mix (Box Set)

'Tis the Season (Box Set)

Hearts, Flowers & Romance (Box Set)

~*~*~*~

***All Mimi's books can be found on her
website at - http://mimibarbour.com

Dedication

I want to dedicate this book to my beautiful and gentle-hearted young niece, Jenna. This lovely girl is at that terrifying age right now where she's no longer the little girl of the family but she's still not quite a self-reliant woman of the world. During these last couple of years, she's had to make a lot of difficult choices. Hard ones that most teens face when they're growing up and moving into their twenties. Jenna faces these challenges in such a brave way that she has made me so very proud.

Chapter One

Angelina shot to her feet, forcing her office chair to thud against the back wall. It couldn't be! The ear-splitting crack and the escalating rumbling convinced her that it could be... and it was. Born and raised in a country where earthquakes were a common phenomenon, she recognized exactly what was happening.

But how? This is Victoria... Canada, for heaven's sake. But the earthquake didn't seem to care.

Frantic, she scanned the various files scattered over her desk and began scooping them together. Commitment overpowered her fright. Just this morning, her dreams had come true. Her most important client to date had brought over his business and hired her to be his company's accountant.

However, old-fashioned, the guy didn't live in the twenty-first century. He still believed in hard copies, and it was up to her to protect his property. Since Angelina's life now operated on a timetable, in two months, the sentimental old fool's business would help her realize her goals.

The disruption escalated, lights flickered, and the noise intensified. By this time Angelina had tossed the files into a heap, then begun awkwardly stuffing them into the nearest metal cabinet. Suddenly, she remembered the disk in the computer. Her trembling fingers pushed the button. The wait felt interminable. Who knew seconds were so hellishly long when terror controlled the time clock? Finally, the CD popped out. She grabbed it. Threw it with the files. And slammed the drawer shut.

Shock whitening her face, Coralee, Angelina's assistant, turned back. Screams for her boss to hurry sounded like a shrieking alarm and further galvanized everyone else. People were scrambling to and fro, vying with each other to get to the doorway and down the stairs to safety.

"Dammit! Run, Coralee. Get out." Since Angelina occupied the farthest office from the outer doorway, she understood her chances were slim that she'd make it. It was possible for the rest of them. Not for her.

Barely functioning, Angelina gripped her desk. Shaking feverishly, a piece of advice slammed into her consciousness. Get near an outside wall, find a big piece of heavy furniture and curl up beside it.

Panic clawing at her senses, she grabbed her cellphone and crouched down on the floor, snuggling as close to the side of her large old wooden desk as she could get. She pushed her cheek against the coolness of the solid wood and covered her head. She made it just in time.

Walls and ceilings began crumbling and ripping apart, while furniture either tipped over or rocked wildly. Stunned, she kept her head down and prayed.

Brass-bottomed desk lamps plunged and broke into shards of glass and clanking metal. The horrible sounds of her property's destruction forced her to peek. Paralyzed, she watched as computer screens crashed onto chairs, plummeting to join the debris below. Filing cabinets shifted, battering into walls, while desks pitched back and forth on undulating floors. She heard a crash overhead and felt the air sucked from her space. The closest filing cabinet fell sideways to land on the edge of the desk, covering her like a roof, missing her by inches.

The worst hazard was the glass from the shattered windows: small deadly needles flew willy-nilly, stabbing and slicing, cutting unprotected skin.

High-pitched sounds like those in an action movie reached a crescendo, and she felt a deep throbbing throughout her body. Oh God... is that gas? A stench filtered through the surrounding plaster dust and added another dimension of dread.

Sweat pooling, barely able to breathe; she sobbed her fury to the one presence she'd believed was in her corner. "Why now, Dios? How could you wait until after I'd signed all the papers and started renovations? Just to destroy everything in an earthquake? I've worked so hard..."

As she ranted her disillusionment, tears and saliva mixed and dripped from her chin. Swiping at her face, anger stiffened her backbone and buried the dread. Fury helped. It made her stronger.

Suddenly, she sensed a change. The noise lessened and the shaking slowed. She breathed a sigh of relief, until she became aware of her personal circumstances. Trapped, stuck in a very small, dark, suffocating space, her claustrophobia kicked in with a vengeance.

It was nearly impossible to move from side to side, and moans accompanied her every breath. Very carefully, she stirred, but there were only inches to spare. Biting down hard on the soft skin of her lower lip helped her marshal her willpower. After all, panicking could be fatal and shift the ceiling of rubble suspended over her cave.

No! Please!

The action started up again. Angelina's heartbeat tripled and jolted her fear into pure unadulterated terror. Used to earthquakes, Chilean citizens were well-aware that aftershocks could be worse than the initial trembler.

Sweat dripped from her neck down into her cleavage. Her hands hid and protected her face. Crazy as it seemed, by covering her eyes, she shut out the evil.

Due to the tension in her crunched muscles, agony sprouted in her spinal column. Her jaw clenched so tightly that her face shook from the force of keeping her screams inside.

Finally, the aftershock waned and eventually came to a shuddering stop. Black loneliness clawed at her nerves. She sensed the pandemonium holding, like a call waiting. As the sounds of the monster dissipated, she heard the hoarse cries of another hostage

"Coralee, is that you? I can hear you. Are you hurt?" Angelina waited, taking deep breaths. Calm down, be cool...

"Yeah, it's me, boss. I'm kinda injured and totally pinned down. Are you okay?" Coralee's shaky voice sounded nearby."

"What do you mean, kinda injured, how kinda?" A sobbing chuckle broke loose when Angelina replayed the words to herself.

"Something clonked me on the head. I feel a bit wonky."

"Coralee, por favor. Speak English. What does wonky mean?" Coralee's habit of making up words normally amused Angelina, but not today. When Angelina had first met her, she'd believed that Coralee was getting back at her for her own frequent lapses into Spanish. But over time, she'd had to accept that it was Coralee's way, and all part of the ditzy redhead's charm.

"Don't pick on me. I have a headache. There's a bit of blood. What about you?"

"How much blood?"

"Some—not too much, don't worry. You haven't answered me. What about you? Are you hurt?"

"I can't move and my heart's beating so fast it feels like it'll shoot right out of my chest." Her voice wobbled and she cleared her throat, pretending that dryness, and not fear, was the culprit.

"Hang in there, sweetie. I can't move either or I'd come to you. But I'm right here, so don't lose it."

Angelina could tell by Coralee's remarks that she remembered her boss suffered from claustrophobia. Not long ago, she'd seen her panic in a small elevator.

"Someone will come soon." Coralee soothed.

"As long as I'm not alone, I'll be okay."

Just then, debris shifted and gave way. A horrendous crash split the quiet of the room. Angelina screamed and again hid her face. Every bone in her body stiffened in resentment at this further torture. She wheezed in a breath, held on and then groaned in a continuous melody of defiance.

It stopped! The monster was teasing.

Seconds later, she called out. "Coralee, that sounded like it came from your direction."

She waited; her ears primed for any sounds...anything at all.

"Coralee?" This time she yelled.

Silence.

A feeling of hopelessness washed over her. Curling into herself, sniffles and hiccups were the only sounds she made. Please, please let Coralee survive! She couldn't have persevered over the last two years without her best friend's help. Coralee worked almost as hard as

Angelina did toward her dream of owning her accounting firm. How could she manage without her?

"Coralee? Can you hear me?"

Nothing.

Sick and tired of feeling like a victim, Angelina took stock of her situation. Knees shaking, she unlocked her fingers and rubbed knuckles that were sore from being twisted and squeezed. The voice of reason gave her hell. Do something!

She wiggled around carefully and realized that the huge old desk had sheltered and saved her. Rather than crawling under something that could have collapsed on top of her, it had been smart to crouch beside a strong piece of furniture.

In the darkness, she blindly extended her hands to the smooth feel of the overturned filing cabinet that had imprisoned her. It had formed a slanted roof from the desk to the floor. Thankfully, purchasing the strongest type of steel-lined cabinets, she'd chosen strength and fire safety over frugality.

Trying to shift her legs from the sideways position they'd slid into, her hands reached out again and felt her slender naked thighs. Wetness from blood spotted her legs and the cuts burned. Her skirt, a good portion which had somehow wrapped itself around her waist, wouldn't come loose.

Frightened to shift anything, it still seemed important she cover herself. Whimpering, she tried gently yanking and tugging. Her hands encountered a solid object near her left knee. Oh God...my cell phone!

Suddenly, wailing sirens pierced the deadly silence, bringing instant relief. So did the light when she opened her small pink phone and frantically pushed the numbers.

"Nine-one-one! State your emergency."

"Hello! Thank God! Listen, my name is Angelina Serrano—"

"Could you speak louder, Angelina?"

Swallowing the dryness, she raised her voice. "We're trapped on the third floor of my building at 7211 Fort Street."

"Who's we? Do you know who else is with you?"

"Yes. My assistant, Coralee Becker, is here. There could be others confined below that I don't know about. Please! My friend is hurt. Since the last aftershock she hasn't spoken. We need help! I heard the sirens outside. Can you send in someone to get us out?"

"Yes, the emergency crews will be with you shortly. Are you injured?"

"No... no. I suffer from claustrophobia and being trapped is killing me. But I'm mostly just scared."

"Don't be, we'll be getting to you as soon as possible. I want you to stay on the line. Okay? Don't hang up."

"I'll try, but my battery is low. I don't know how long it has left." Her voice broke. Pressure from smothering her sobs and exasperation at her oversight of not plugging in her phone made talking almost impossible.

"Okay. Don't worry. Someone will be in contact as soon as they're ready to come in for you. I have your number. I want you to hang up and stay calm. Try calling to your friend periodically to wake her up."

Just then, the blood-chilling horror started again. She screamed, "I will. Hurry!" Swallowing, she gathered whatever moisture her parched mouth could find, at least enough to lick her lips. Then she counted the seconds.

And she waited.

Startling her, the Macarena – her dial tone – rang into the stillness. The racket buoyed up Angelina's spirits like nothing else could have.

Manipulating her talk button, she heard a soft-spoken male voice. "Hello. Miss Serrano? Angelina Serrano? It's Dr. Joe Davidson. I'm with Search and Rescue." The man spoke soothingly, and his calmness beguiled her into uncharacteristic chattiness.

"Dr. Davidson, can you come and get us? Hurry! Please! Everything here is unstable. It could all come crashing down any moment, and my friend Coralee is hurt. She needs medical attention." A sobbing gasp escaped. Connecting with another person had filled her with hope.

"We're coming, Angelina. I understand you have a low battery so hang up now, and we'll call you right back as soon as we're set up to come into the building."

Hang up? Dios, not again! Slowly, she ended the call. Darkness surrounded her once more.

Praying for an answer, Angelina took a deep breath and cried out, "Coralee, can you hear me. They're coming for us."

"I hear you, Angelina. What happened?"

"You're back? Thank God! An aftershock is what happened. You stopped talking, and I came close to losing it. Where exactly are you?"

"In hell," answered Coralee.

"Okay then, where in the hell are you?" The wisecrack made her grin, and from out of the darkness the answering chuckle cheered her as nothing else could have.

"I'm under Johnnie's desk and seriously trapped." Coralee coughed harshly.

"They're on their way, Cara. The sexy voice of a Dr. Joe Davidson promised me they're working on it."

Coralee groaned. "Well, Dr. Joe needs to work faster." Another bout of coughing ensued. Then she croaked. "I need the ladies' room!"

Chapter Two

Joe Davidson wrapped the messy waves of his hair behind his ears and rubbed his aching eyes. Taking his hand from the steering wheel, he brushed stiff fingers over his day-old beard and massaged his weary face. Today had been a long shift, on top of a late night playing hard to get: his sister-in-law, Mary's, latest choice of "a-wife-for-brother-Joe" had ruined the previous evening for everyone. With her non-stop chatter, sly innuendos and birdbrain opinions, this candidate had caused more eye-rolling than anyone had ever done before.

A blunt chat with his brothers sat first on his to-do list. No more Mr. Nice Guy. No more set-ups or blind dates.

Zoning out on the day's stresses, Joe thought about his situation.

Married friends and family sabotaged him constantly, and set him up every chance they got. His being single and happy really seemed to bother the hell outta them.

A few years back, he'd had a close call—almost joined their ranks. At the time, he'd thought he wanted to get married more than anything in the world. Then his fiancée, Sara, had met Cody, one of his older brothers, and sparks had ignited. Within a short time, Cody's ring had replaced Joe's, and the wedding had gone ahead. To show there were no hard feelings, Joe had offered his services as best man. But erased pain was still a lesson inflicted, and in his case—well learned. Neither women nor love were to be trusted.

Now, pathetically, rather than watching his back, or standing up for his right of bachelorhood, his brothers—all older than him—were crumbling under their partner's demands. The sad, ass-chewed cowards were falling in with their obsessive wives' plans to mend his damaged heart, and find him someone to replace Sara.

It was a real pain to be the youngest of the six Davidson boys. And to make matters a thousand times worse, there were five sister-in-laws attached like conjugal twins to those poor saps. Just thinking about it caused shudders and a nauseating aggravation.

A shrieking horn snapped Joe out of his reverie and back to the present. After dropping his tired crew off, he'd taken his turn to drive the Search and Rescue vehicle back to the parking bay, his last chore before he could claim the rights to a cold beer and a long hot shower.

Stretching his length and flexing his muscular frame as much as he could while wedged in the space behind the wheel, he thought back over the horrendous day.

Many times, volunteering for the Victoria Search and Rescue Special Services Unit could be hectic as hell. In the last two days, he'd had call outs to three major situations. Being a part-time doctor, albeit of Chinese medicine, and taking umpteen lifesaving courses in land and sea rescue created huge demands for him to undertake the worst accidents.

The pealing of the dash phone tweaked him out of his trance.

"Yeah. Joe here."

"Hi Joe, it's Lee. We need you downtown. An earthquake has demolished some sections of the city—"

"An earthquake?"

"Yep, a 7.3! Crazy, eh? It hit mid-island, west of Nanaimo. It's a mess down here. We have some folks trapped in a building on Fort Street and we'll need you to get here as soon as possible."

"On my way." Wheeling the special vehicle in the direction of the downtown area, Joe hit the lever on the dash. Light bars flashing and sirens blaring warned other drivers to beware.

How could he not have known an earthquake had erupted northwest of the city? Obviously, it hadn't registered where he, along with his crew, had saved the lives of three people stranded on a capsized boat off the south coast. Working on the water was one facet of his job he found severely frustrating. Today the helicopter rescue had been cold and wet, grueling and treacherous.

The city of Victoria, situated on the southern tip of Vancouver Island, was a tourist haven for a variety of incautious visitors who didn't understand the dangers of coastal waters. They took terrible, heedless risks in the turbulent seas. At times, situations ended tragically. On the good days, because of the Coast Guard and the Search and Rescue, they didn't. Thankfully, today's success reaffirmed Joe's choice of livelihood.

But earthquakes on the island were rare—especially ones that strong. Being a high-risk zone due to underlying geological pressures, small tremors often occurred and were treated as normal. The earth's plates in this region were conducive to seismic activity, and Joe knew the geologists expected some movement, but this event was astonishing.

Chapter Three

Once Joe arrived at his destination, he saw that chaos ruled the scene. Piles of rubble from broken buildings littered the sidewalks. Damaged vehicles flung helter-skelter looked surreal. Dislodged overhead wires, hanging and swaying from lopsided telephone poles, were dangerously shooting sparks.

Looking like aliens in their gear, Joe spotted several workers cordoning off the area for safety. Flung from pressurized windows, pieces of glass were still raining down in every direction. In the sparse light they looked like floating chunks of crystal, but in actuality were a deadly menace.

Ear-splitting sounds reverberated from the huge screaming dozer working down the middle of the street, opening up a path for the special vehicles. The horrendous noise added to the atmosphere of unreality with bizarre, movie-like intensity.

Waving him down, Joe's partner, Lee Nivens, anxiously awaited him. A retiring, likable fellow and Joe's best friend, dependable Lee was always available for an evening out with the boys.

First things first; Joe inspected his buddy to make sure he wasn't injured. As usual, Lee's uniform hung on his string-bean body. Having worked with him for a number of years, Joe knew those loose folds hid muscular wiriness. Lee's overly large ears evoked Joe's grin; tactless maybe, but a reflex nonetheless. And his warm grey eyes, always cheerful, had Joe unconsciously reacting with a smile.

Still behind the wheel, Joe questioned, "What's up, Swift?" Gesturing to one of the younger workers to take the vehicle away, he stepped out and gave his full attention to Lee.

Calm and composed, Lee gave him the lowdown. "It's a standalone building, Joe, with three floors. They've recently renovated the first two. Guess it's their good luck that the bulk of the damage is on the third."

"Where people are trapped?"

"Yep...up there." Lee grimaced.

"Figures."

"The landlady, Angelina Serrano, called Emergency. As far as she knows, there's one other woman with her for sure. Seems that victim is injured and floating in and out of unconsciousness. Miss Serrano says she's personally okay, but she's trapped, in the dark, frightened and slightly claustrophobic."

"How slightly?"

"Emergency says she's making sense, but the strain is starting to tell in her voice. We'll have to get to her quickly before she completely loses it. One other thing: her cell phone power is low. They had to limit the use."

"Shit! Why me, Lord? Why do I always have to get the tricky cases?"

"Because you're a good man." Grin splitting his face, Lee connected with Angelina and passed the phone to Joe.

Chapter 4

"I can hear you grumbling, Angie. Something's wrong?" Coralee's voice seemed to come from far away.

"My hair's come loose and it's all over my face. I hate this mess!"

"Girlfriend, how many times have I told you to get it cut? You complain about it all the time. I can send you to my hairdresser, she'll doll you up."

Not sure what Coralee meant by getting dolled up, and knowing she'd never let the same hands touch her hair that created the multi-colored, crazy-modern styles her assistant often wore, Angelina ignored the offer. "I told you; I promised my father I wouldn't cut it."

"So he's in Chile, and you're in Canada."

"Yes, well the promise flew over with me."

"Ha! You're so not funny. Stop letting that old tyrant rule your decisions. You've worked like a maniac for the last two years because of him. When are you going to live your own life?"

Realizing that Coralee was keeping her talking so she wouldn't panic, Angelina gladly kept the conversation going. "He's not an old man, he's barely sixty. I've told you before, because of his hard work and perseverance, Serrano and Sons is the biggest and best accounting firm in Santiago."

"Don't forget your two brothers. Surely, they've helped?"

"Yes, but they only joined recently. He alone started the company and, as he likes to brag, owned it outright after two years."

"Is that why you've been working day and night like a lunatic with that big red X on your calendar for the end of March?"

"I never told you the full story, did I? Before I left Chile, he and my brothers had decided that I should marry Fernando Regaldo, who they thought would suit me perfectly. When they called me to the office, I had mistakenly believed that my receiving honors from the University for completing my CGA degree would be my entrance into the family business. And the invitation to come to the workplace was to offer me a position. You won't believe how angry it made me to think that, after all my accomplishments, they wanted me to meet their hand-picked gigolo, get married and have bambinos. Bah!"

"Ahh,... now I get it! I've seen you in a Spanish snit a time or two, so I'm surprised they weren't taken to the ER."

"I know you joke, Coralee, but it was a very bad time for me. I demanded to know what it would take for them to offer me the position in Serrano's that I had earned and deserved."

"Don't tell me. You had to accomplish what your father had done? Right?"

"They said the office was no place for me. I needed to get serious about my future. Stop trying to be a rebel and do what the other young girls of my station did, provide their papás with grandchildren."

"Oh ho! I would love to have been a fly on the wall to see what you did then."

Angelina felt herself flush and had to swallow a few times before she could bring herself to admit to her total meltdown. "I guess I lost it. Told them I was leaving, going to Canada, and I'd start my own firm and... do it in two years. I made them promise that if I succeeded, they would give up their old-fashioned views and allow me my place in Serrano's. They laughed and agreed."

"Bastards! But why come all the way to Canada? Weren't there other cities in Chile you could move to?"

"Not where their reach couldn't sabotage my efforts. I needed to be completely away from them. So I moved to Victoria."

"Not fair. They forced you to come to a strange country to prove what your credentials had already proven, that you're a brilliant accountant."

"Not so strange. Remember I'd visited this beautiful city to see my grandmother every year and came to love the place. Thanks to her, my English is flawless. And, as you know, accounting principles are the same everywhere."

"Still! I'm pissed off at your family. I just pray we can get out of this situation and back to work. Now you've got me wanting to show them how wrong they were."

"It's what's kept me going these last two years. Though after this, I don't know." Angelina had to stop, or completely break down and maybe scare her friend into thinking she wasn't stable.

"Don't worry, babe. We'll get it done. You, me and Johnnie, plus the other girls in the office. We'll all help you..."

Her phone's noise made Angelina jump, and quickly swipe at her nose and cheeks.

"Dr. Davidson, is that you? Can you hurry? Coralee desperately needs attention—"

Interrupting, he replied, "Copy that! Thought you'd like to know, Angelina, it seems the rest of your people managed to get out safely. Right now we're trying to locate the floor plans for the building. We've notified your contractor, who will be arriving shortly. Before I forget, do you want me to call anyone for you? Your family, a husband or a boyfriend, someone who can come and look after you when you're released—maybe take you home and stay with you?"

"No, don't bother yourself. My people are on holiday in Las Vegas right now, so I'm alone at home for a short time, and there is no husband or boyfriend."

As soon as she said the words, she wished them back. Why the hell did she add on that last bit? Now he'll get the wrong impression—possibly decide his victim couldn't attract a man.

"Okay! Good! Relax and pay attention. Be careful, it's dangerously unstable up there, and any shift could upset the whole mess." In her emotional state, Joe's tone began sounding condescending.

Is he for real? "No kidding!" Angelina couldn't believe it. Joe Davidson was another bossy male control-freak, like the men she'd left Chile to avoid. At a time like this, after all her prayers, God chose to have a sense of humor.

"Angelina..."

Cutting him off, probably, another be careful, don't move, don't panic order, she took a deep breath, calmed her voice, and added what to her signified the most important information of all. "Coralee Becker's in the main office, close to the stairs. She has a head injury. Says it's bleeding, and I know for a fact that she lost consciousness earlier."

Silence lingered on the other end, as if he was waiting for her to finish. So, she continued. "I'm in a small office against the far south wall, and I'm trapped beside my desk but uninjured." She'd finally run out of steam. He still remained silent. Was he paying attention?

"Dr. Davidson?"

"I'm here, Angelina. Is there something else you need?"

Si! To get the hell out of here for starters! "Was the earthquake widespread? Do you know if any of the residential districts were affected?"

"Not from the reports coming over the radio. The worst hit area is downtown and only certain ill-fated streets were involved. Look, your building contractor, Mr. Ray Armani, has arrived and he'll figure out how he can get us safely into the first-floor office to retrieve the blueprints. Utilizing those, and following his directions, will help us to find you much quicker."

In the background, Angelina could hear Ray earnestly talking. "Joe, Miss Serrano is an angel, and her people are special. Me, I'll help, and we'll get 'em out."

Joe? For her it was Dr. Davidson. Unfortunately, the click from his phone shut down her snooping. She would have liked to hear Joe's answer.

The black void engulfed her once more as she hugged her cell phone to her chest. Through the exposed open windows and walls, she became even more aware of the screeching noises and loud voices over the abrasive grinding of operating machinery. The periodic crashes from other parts of the building were, to her, the most upsetting sounds.

"Cora, mi amiga, they're coming for us. Cora?" Oh no! Please be okay...

The answering silence made her sink into meditation. Giving thanks for the great news about her other employees escaping injury; she forgave her guardian angels their insensitive joke in acquiring the mysterious, controlling Dr. Davidson as her savior. No doubt, putting up with her sprightly, affable Italian contractor would tax his patience.

For months, she'd been working all her wiles on the crusty, old-school builder. Neither prodding, coaxing nor threatening had forced him to speed up the work on her building. In frustration, she'd glowered at him, and he'd glared right back saying, "Angelina. If I do the work, I'ma gonna do it right. This beautiful old building—she deserves nothing but admiration and lotsa respect."

Having met her match in stubbornness, Angelina had finally acknowledged her plight and backed off. Resuming her normal, good-natured attitude, she'd switched her battle plans to support Ray instead of fighting, and they'd become good friends. Most mornings had her stopping at a fast-food restaurant to pick up Ray's favorite double-double coffee with a side order of a cinnamon and raisin bagel, topped by strawberry cream cheese.

She never doubted her building would be perfect. However, paying for it concerned her. And now, she didn't know how she would accomplish that.

"Angelina, what's up? Why are you so quiet?" Coralee's voice had sharpened with worry.

"Thank God, you're back, Coralee. You had me worried. I called and you never answered."

"I must have slipped out for a while. I'm back now. I heard you talking to someone and then muttering in Spanish."

"It seems we have a know-it-all on our hands. Not that it'll matter if he gets us out of here, but why is it that every man I meet has to be so bossy?"

"What men? There aren't any except Johnnie, and he doesn't count. He acts more like your babysitter than I do. And the lucky bum got to miss today's excitement. After all our prodding, him taking little Jeremy to see Mickey Mouse turned out to be a good thing. But—let's get back to the subject of all the men in your life. What men? You're always with women."

"Women are safe. They don't make demands. And they don't try and change me or make me bow to their wishes."

"Angelina, men aren't all that bad. You just have to meet the right one."

"Tell me, Coralee, you've had how many boyfriends since I've known you? I've heard your incessant complaints, so go ahead and enlighten me—where are the right ones?"

"Still looking, my friend, still looking. I've met some geeks and idiots, true. But I've also met a lot of really nice guys, Angelina. Just not the one! You know, the man I'd want to be the father of my babies."

"You and babies. You're a mom waiting to happen. I've never known anyone who wants children as much as you."

"I do want kids. And I'm beginning to think test tubes shouldn't be scoffed at. Who needs a man nowadays, anyway?" A chuckle followed and then Coralee asked. "Seriously, don't you want a family?"

"One day, maybe. Right now, I have too much to accomplish."

"Right! The... agenda. We'll win, babe! See if – if we don't." Coralee sounded tired, as if her words were difficult to form.

Angelina's anxiety for her assistant pounded at her almost as much as the darkness and the cave-like surroundings. Her palpitations increased as agitation ignited once again. Taking shallow breaths helped her budding headache, however with impending disaster hovering, possibly waiting to strike; the solitude was eerie as hell. Where were they? Should she call Joe back? Would he think her weak? She shifted her cramped legs, and arched her tired back, trying in vain to find a comfortable position.

"Angelina, you're quiet? Don't freak out," Coralee whispered. Her voice had lost all trace of its usual vitality.

"I'm holding on, Coralee. I was just sitting here remembering my childhood. The day my brothers left me trapped in a chest for hours when I was around four years old." Her voice began fraying noticeably so she stopped.

"Don't think about that." Angelina's statement had woken up her friend. She sounded stronger. "Close your eyes. Imagine the beach on a hot, sunny day, you in your bikini and all the guys around you with their eyes bugging out."

Laughter was good medicine, and it worked on Angelina, just she suspected Coralee knew it would. "Right! Me in a bikini. I've never even worn a two-piece."

"You should. You have the sexiest body of anyone I know."

"You are one crazy lady. Do you know how often my so-called, sexy body has been my curse? I've thought a lot about my operation. It's only since the breast reduction that I've enjoyed shopping and wearing nice clothes. Before, I hated me."

"And I'm too small. Always have been. So don't think I'll feel sorry for you. I wished I had more of a chest, so men would look at me like they do at you. Not that you ever pay attention." Coralee added the last sentence under her breath.

"Men! Bah! Who needs them?"

She heard Coralee moan, and then cuss.

Trying to lighten the mood, Angelina said. "Dr. Davidson sounds like an overachiever and his ultimate goal tonight is us. I have no doubt we'll get out of here safely. No doubts whatsoever!" The noise made by workmen now came from inside the building. "They're getting closer, I can hear them."

The cheesy ringtone pealed again and jolted Angelina. She clutched the phone nervously and, in the act of swiping the screen, her cramped fingers refused to work and she dropped it instead.

"Hello? HEL-LO? Miss? Angelina, are you there? What the hell!"

Hearing the frustration in Joe's voice shouting out in the dark helped her to locate the tricky, slippery object. The stupid thing was almost out of reach, and by the time she'd wiggled her fingers to coax it nearer, the fool's voice on the other end was all but deafening.

Using his own words back on him, Angelina crooned, "Calm down, Joe. Don't panic. I merely dropped the phone."

First there was an electrified quiet, and then loudly, sarcastically, he answered, "Don't lose the phone, girl. It's our only means of communication at this point."

Oh! He was getting to her!

"We're working hard to get to you."

Trust me–you are!

"If you get scared, call through to Emergency and they'll link us up. Otherwise, try to stay calm and we'll be there before you know it. We now have the floor plans and we're clearing our way to you. We'll have to shore up a lot of the weak places, and the stairs might take a while to clear out, but the first two floors aren't that badly damaged. Seems the top floor where you are took the worst of it."

Cooling down, she answered in the same finicky, blunt tone as he used. "I understand. We'll be here waiting."

"Yeah! I kinda figured so. Stay calm. It shouldn't be too long." Then he hung up.

In a bit of a nasty copycat whisper, she mimicked, "Stay calm, don't panic." Got it!

Guilt set in quickly. What was wrong with her? Her attitude stank, and it wasn't like her at all. She really did feel thankful knowing Dr. Joe was coming for them. He was her connection to reality and safety—even if he bugged the hell out of her.

Chapter Four

"I can hear you grumbling, Angie. Something's wrong?" Coralee's voice seemed so far away.

"My hair's come loose and it's all over my face. I hate this mess!"

"Girlfriend, how many times have I told you to get it cut? You complain about it all the time. I can send you to my hairdresser, she'll doll you up."

Not sure what Coralee meant by getting dolled up, and knowing she'd never let the same hands touch her hair that created the multi-colored, crazy-modern styles her assistant often wore, Angelina ignored the offer. "I told you; I promised my father I wouldn't cut it."

"So he's in Chile, and you're inCanada."

"Yes, well the promise flew over with me."

"Ha! You're so not funny. Stop letting that old tyrant rule your decisions. You've worked like a maniac for the last two years because of him. When are you going to live your own life?"

Realizing that Coralee was keeping her talking so she wouldn't panic, Angelina gladly kept the conversation going."He's not an old man, he's barely sixty. I've told you before, because of his hard work and perseverance, Serrano and Sons is the biggest and best accounting firm in Santiago."

"Don't forget your two brothers. Surely, they've helped?"

"Yes, but they only joined recently. He alone started the company and, as he likes to brag, owned it outright after two years."

"Is that why you've been working day and night like a lunatic with that big red X on your calendar for the end of March?"

"I never told you the full story, did I? Before I left Chile, he and my brothers had decided that I should marry Fernando Regaldo, who they thought would suit me perfectly. When they called me to the office, I had mistakenly believed that my receiving honors from the University for completing my CGA degree would be my entrance into the family business. And the invitation to come to the workplace was to offer me a position. You won't believe how angry it made me to think that, after all my accomplishments, they wanted me to meet their hand-picked gigolo, get married and have bambinos. Bah!"

"Ahh,... now I get it! I've seen you in a Spanish snit a time or two, so I'm surprised they weren't taken to the ER."

"I know you joke, Coralee, but it was a very bad time for me. I demanded to know what it would take for them to offer me the position in Serrano's that I had earned and deserved."

"Don't tell me. You had to accomplish what your father had done? Right?"

"They said the office was no place for me. I needed to get serious about my future. Stop trying to be a rebel and do what the other young girls of my station did, provide their papás with grandchildren."

"Oh ho! I would love to have been a fly on the wall to see what you did then."

Angelina felt herself flush and had to swallow a few times before she could bring herself to admit to her total meltdown. "I guess I lost it. Told them I was leaving, going to Canada, and I'd start my own firm and... do it in two years. I made them promise that if I succeeded, they would give up their old-fashioned views and allow me my place in Serrano's. They laughed and agreed."

"Bastards! But why come all the way to Canada? Weren't there other cities in Chile you could move to?"

"Not where their reach couldn't sabotage my efforts. I needed to be completely away from them. So, I moved to Victoria."

"Not fair. They forced you to come to a strange country to prove what your credentials had already proven, that you're a brilliant accountant."

"Not so strange. Remember, I'd visited this beautiful city to see my grandmother every year and came to love the place. Thanks to her, my English is flawless. And, as you know, accounting principles are the same everywhere."

"Still! I'm pissed off at your family. I just pray we can get out of this situation and back to work. Now you've got me wanting to show them how wrong they were."

"It's what's kept me going these last two years. Though after this, I don't know." Angelina had to stop, or completely break down and maybe scare her friend into thinking she wasn't stable.

"Don't worry, babe. We'll get it done. You, me, and Johnnie, plus the other girls in the office. We'll all help you..."

Her phone's noise made Angelina jump, and quickly swipe at her nose and cheeks.

"Dr. Davidson, is that you? Can you hurry? Coralee desperately needs attention—"

Interrupting, he replied, "Copy that! Thought you'd like to know, Angelina, it seems the rest of your people managed to get out safely. Right now we're trying to locate the floor plans for the building. We've notified your contractor, who will be arriving shortly. Before I forget, do you want me to call anyone for you? Your family, a husband or a boyfriend, someone who can come and look after you when you're released—maybe take you home and stay with you?"

"No, don't bother yourself. My people are on holiday in Las Vegas right now, so I'm alone at home for a short time, and there is no husband or boyfriend."

As soon as she said the words, she wished them back. Why the hell did she add on that last bit? Now he'll get the wrong impression—possibly decide his victim couldn't attract a man.

"Okay! Good! Relax and pay attention. Be careful, it's dangerously unstable up there, and any shift could upset the whole mess." In her emotional state, Joe's tone began sounding condescending.

Is he for real? "No kidding!" Angelina couldn't believe it. Joe Davidson was another bossy male control-freak, like the men she'd left Chile to avoid. At a time like this, after all her prayers, God chose to have a sense of humor.

"Angelina..."

Cutting him off, probably, another be careful, don't move, don't panic order, she took a deep breath, calmed her voice, and added what to her signified the most important information of all. "Coralee Becker's in the main office, close to the stairs. She has a head injury. Says it's bleeding, and I know for a fact that she lost consciousness earlier."

Silence lingered on the other end, as if he was waiting for her to finish. So, she continued. "I'm in a small office against the far south

wall, and I'm trapped beside my desk but uninjured. "She'd finally run
out of steam. He still remained silent. Was he paying attention?

"Dr. Davidson?"

"I'm here, Angelina. Is there something else you need?"

Si! To get the hell out of here for starters! "Was the earthquake
widespread? Do you know if any of the residential districts were affected?"

"Not from the reports coming over the radio. The worst hit area
is downtown and only certain ill-fated streets were involved. Look,
your building contractor, Mr. Ray Armani, has arrived and he'll figure
out how he can get us safely into the first-floor office to retrieve the
blueprints. Utilizing those, and following his directions, will help us
to find you much quicker."

In the background, Angelina could hear Ray earnestly talking. "Joe,
Miss Serrano is an angel, and her people are special. Me, I'll help, and
we'll get 'em out."

Joe? For her it was Dr. Davidson. Unfortunately, the click from his
phone shut down her snooping. She would have liked to hear Joe's
answer.

The black void engulfed her once more as she hugged her cell phone
to her chest. Through the exposed open windows and walls, she became even more aware of the screeching noises and loud voices over the
abrasive grinding of operating machinery. The periodic crashes from
other parts of the building were, to her, the most upsetting sounds.

"Cora, mi amiga, they're coming for us. Cora?" Oh no! Please be
okay...

The answering silence made her sink into meditation. Giving
thanks for the great news about her other employees escaping injury;
she forgave her guardian angels their insensitive joke in acquiring the

mysterious, controlling Dr. Davidson as her savior. No doubt, putting up with her sprightly, affable Italian contractor would tax his patience.

For months, she'd been working all her wiles on the crusty, old-school builder. Neither prodding, coaxing nor threatening had forced him to speed up the work on her building. In frustration, she'd glowered at him, and he'd glared right back saying, "Angelina, if I do the work, I'ma gonna do it right. This beautiful old building — she deserves nothing but admiration and lotsa respect."

Having met her match in stubbornness, Angelina had finally acknowledged her plight and backed off. Resuming her normal, good-natured attitude, she'd switched her battle plans to support Ray instead of fighting, and they'd become good friends. Most mornings had her stopping at a fast-food restaurant to pick up Ray's favorite double-double coffee with a side order of a cinnamon and raisin bagel, topped by strawberry cream cheese.

She never doubted her building would be perfect. However, paying for it concerned her. And now, she didn't know how she would accomplish that.

"Angelina, what's up? Why are you so quiet?" Coralee's voice had sharpened with worry.

"Thank God, you're back, Coralee. You had me worried. I called and you never answered."

"I must have slipped out for a while. I'm back now. I heard you talking to someone and then muttering in Spanish."

"It seems we have a know-it-all on our hands. Not that it'll matter if he gets us out of here, but why is it that every man I meet has to be so bossy?"

"What men? There aren't any except Johnnie, and he doesn't count. He acts more like your babysitter than I do. And the lucky bum got to miss today's excitement. After all our prodding, him taking little

Jeremy to see Mickey Mouse turned out to be a good thing. But – let's get back to the subject of all the men in your life. What men? You're always with women."

"Women are safe. They don't make demands. And they don't try and change me or make me bow to their wishes."

"Angelina, men aren't all that bad. You just have to meet the right one."

"Tell me, Coralee, you've had how many boyfriends since I've known you? I've heard your incessant complaints, so go ahead and enlighten me — where are the right ones?"

"Still looking, my friend, still looking. I've met some geeks and idiots, true. But I've also met a lot of really nice guys, Angelina. Just not the one! You know, the man I'd want to be the father of my babies."

"You and babies. You're a mom waiting to happen. I've never known anyone who wants children as much as you."

"I do want kids. And I'm beginning to think test tubes shouldn't be scoffed at. Who needs a man nowadays, anyway?" A chuckle followed and then Coralee asked. "Seriously, don't you want a family?"

"One day, maybe. Right now, I have too much to accomplish."

"Right! The... agenda. We'll win, babe! See if – if we don't." Coralee sounded tired, as if her words were difficult to form.

Angelina's anxiety for her assistant pounded at her almost as much as the darkness and the cave-like surroundings. Her palpitations increased as agitation ignited once again. Taking shallow breaths helped her budding headache, however with impending disaster hovering, possibly waiting to strike; the solitude was eerie as hell. Where were they? Should she call Joe back? Would he think her weak? She shifted her cramped legs, and arched her tired back, trying in vain to find a comfortable position.

"Angelina, you're quiet? Don't freak out," Coralee whispered. Her voice had lost all trace of its usual vitality.

"I'm holding on, Coralee. I was just sitting here remembering my childhood. The day my brothers left me trapped in a chest for hours when I was around four years old." Her voice began fraying noticeably so she stopped.

"Don't think about that." Angelina's statement had woken up her friend. She sounded stronger. "Close your eyes. Imagine the beach on a hot, sunny day... you in your bikini and all the guys around you with their eyes bugging out."

Laughter was good medicine, and it worked on Angelina, just she suspected Coralee knew it would. "Right! Me in a bikini. I've never even worn a two-piece."

"You should. You have the sexiest body of anyone I know."

"You are one crazy lady. Do you know how often my so-called, sexy body has been my curse? I've thought a lot about my operation. It's only since the breast reduction that I've enjoyed shopping and wearing nice clothes. Before, I hated me."

"And I'm too small. Always have been. So don't think I'll feel sorry for you. I wished I had more of a chest, so men would look at me like they do at you. Not that you ever pay attention." Coralee added the last sentence under her breath.

"Men! Bah! Who needs them?"

She heard Coralee moan, and then cuss.

Trying to lighten the mood, Angelina said. "Dr. Davidson sounds like an overachiever and his ultimate goal tonight is us. I have no doubt we'll get out of here safely. No doubts whatsoever!" The noise made by workmen now came from inside the building. "They're getting closer, I can hear them."

The cheesy ringtone pealed again and jolted Angelina. She clutched the phone nervously and, in the act of swiping the screen, her cramped fingers refused to work, and she dropped it instead.

"Hello? HEL-LO? Miss? Angelina, are you there? What the hell!"

Hearing the frustration in Joe's voice shouting out in the dark helped her to locate the tricky, slippery object. The stupid thing was almost out of reach, and by the time she'd wiggled her fingers to coax it nearer, the fool's voice on the other end was all but deafening.

Using his own words back on him, Angelina crooned, "Calm down, Joe. Don't panic. I merely dropped the phone."

First, there was an electrified quiet, and then loudly, sarcastically, he answered, "Don't lose the phone, girl. It's our only means of communication at this point."

Oh! He was getting to her!

"We're working hard to get to you."

Trust me – you are!

"If you get scared, call through to emergency, and they'll link us up. Otherwise, try to stay calm, and we'll be there before you know it. We now have the floor plans, and we're clearing our way to you. We'll have to shore up a lot of the weak places, and the stairs might take a while to clear out, but the first two floors aren't that badly damaged. Seems the top floor where you are took the worst of it."

Cooling down, she answered in the same finicky, blunt tone as he used. "I understand. We'll be here waiting."

"Yeah! I kinda figured so. Stay calm. It shouldn't be too long." Then he hung up.

In a bit of a nasty copycat whisper, she mimicked, "Stay calm, don't panic." Got it!

Guilt set in quickly. What was wrong with her? Her attitude stank, and it wasn't like her at all. She really did feel thankful knowing Dr.

Joe was coming for them. He was her connection to reality and safety—even if he bugged the hell out of her.

Chapter Five

Another hour of anxiety and discomfort passed, leaving Angelina dazed, dozy and thirsty. The noises of the workmen below were like a magical salve to her panic; that and the fact that the aftershocks were waning to short rumbles with no real force.

Finally, her phone rang again. This time, prepared, she answered without any mishaps.

"It's me, Angel. How are things on your end? Did you feel the last couple of aftershocks?"

This gringo had a lot of nerve making free with her family's pet name for her, the one she hated. She'd never met the man. On the other hand, he was her rescuer, and upsetting him at this time probably wasn't such a good idea.

"Yes, but they were relatively light ones, and changed nothing in here. I've not heard anything from Coralee for a while. I'm very worried. I keep calling, but she hasn't answered. Please hurry, Joe. I am afraid she's hurt worse than she let on." If he could call her by her first name, she could repay the compliment.

"We're almost to her now. It won't be long; you can bet on it. Hang in there, sweetheart. Be with you soon. Bye!"

Sweetheart? Was there no end to his audacity? The deep timbre of his voice zinged along her nerve endings, tantalizing them. Intrigued, she began to look forward to their meeting.

Sometime later, Angelina woke from a doze to the distinct sounds of the workers in action, filtering through the murkiness. She glowed as she heard Coralee chatting with her rescuers. Hearing their laughter brought immediate relief. It would be just a matter of time before they'd come for her.

Fluttery palpitations exploded in her chest. She wriggled her hands and took deep breaths. The anxieties she'd suffered throughout the ordeal had taken their toll. Bravery be dammed, she could relax now.

A longed-for voice came to her from the darkness, "It's okay, Angel. We're almost with you," Joe reassured her.

Shaking out of a momentary stupor, she cleared her throat, and in a raspy voice answered, "Good," and a few seconds later, "thank you."

Another aftershock gave one last good shake as if to warn of the still powerful possibilities. It gentled at the exact moment Angelina looked up into a brilliant, riveting light. Like a doe caught in approaching headlights, the glow all but blinded her. The light moved closer, and then was raised so it stopped shining in her face.

"Hello, Angel." A man smiled, white teeth gleaming in the dimness.

Joe, her savior in rescue gear, had the most wonderful piercing green eyes she'd ever seen beyond those of her grandmother's rangy, slumming tomcat.

Chapter Six

The unexpected brightness stung Angelina's eyes, and she reached up to cover her face protectively. Without meaning to invade her privacy, Joe got an eyeful. Gorgeous naked legs, curled into her body like those of a small resting forest animal, were dotted here and there with bloody lacerations.

And her hair...whoa! She had masses of black curls cascading over her slumped shoulders, her drawn-up knees, and dusting the floor.

He saw her trancelike expression as she slowly lowered her shaking hands. Watch my heart! Eyes simply shouldn't be that intensely grey—no—blue, a mixture that tantalized and held an unconscious invitation that read: take me to bed. Their slanted affect—pure sexy South American—had his heart accelerating like an engine revved up at the start of a high-speed race.

He took his gloves off and laid them aside, and then reached out a gentle hand in her direction. "Hi, Angel. It's me, Joe."

"I'm no Angel! Please, it's Angelina," she whispered huskily from a throat that had gone too long without liquid. "I knew you'd come, Joe. Is Coralee safe?"

Her firm belief that he'd rescue her softened his hard core, and warmth penetrated his normally brisk tones. "She's doing just fine, Angelina. My partner, Lee, is taking good care of her."

Unwrapping a thermal blanket as best he could in the small space, he tried to cover her. Then taking the initiative, he lifted her limp hand and sneakily took her pulse. He held it long enough to assure himself of her state. Then shook it slightly, feeling her quiver from the effect of his touch. He opened and passed her a bottle of water. She greedily drank, coughed and drank more.

"Not too much all at once, honey." Meanwhile, he eyeballed the situation around her. The clearing was a pretty tight squeeze, but he figured they could take their time. It was a big plus that she had such a tiny frame.

"Okay? Ready? Let's get you out of here."

He knew the workers had cleared behind the filing cabinet which had her pinned down. It made his job easier for sure.

"I'm going to lift this furniture away from you so we can get the back of your skirt loose. When I say ready, you pull it out from under." Because her movements were so pitifully awkward, he had to help her gather the material and soon she was free.

"I don't think I can move," Angelina told him candidly. She collected her hair with one shaking hand to push it back over her shoulders and lifted her bottle of water to finish it. "My legs have been in this position for so long, they're numb."

With immense care he sufficiently cleared the area in front of her in order to straighten her legs. Agitated, she shoved her skirt down to cover herself.

He did a quick survey of her other vital signs, and decided she was suffering mostly from dehydration and exhaustion. She'd perked up after finishing the water and that was a good sign.

"Angelina?"

"Yes?"

"I'm going to massage your legs, so you'll be able to move easier. The pathway we've opened isn't large enough for me to carry you out, so you'll have to crawl some of the way."

"Yes, I understand." Her hesitant tone made him aware she was rattled. She acted as if no man had ever touched her body before. "Relax Angelina, I'm a doctor," he said to calm her agitation.

With the utmost care, he uncurled her legs in order to rub them soothingly with his warm, hypnotic hands. His smooth palms circled tenderly as he gently kneaded first her feet, then her ankles, up her calves, and over her knees to her thighs.

"I can't believe how painful the tingles are," she said, her husky, sensual accent, leaving him with tingles of his own in an area that he knew had no business in alerting him.

Man! Her beautiful little body enthralled him. Naturally tanned, her skin felt smooth, and her well-toned muscles were apparent as she tensed repeatedly. Wanting to keep his hands on her body and explore all of her secrets, he had to force himself to let her go.

"How's that? Feeling better?"

"Yes. I think can move now, Joe. I just want to get out of here." There was a fine sheen of dampness on her forehead and her gaze flickered everywhere, never focusing on him at all. With jerky movements, she gathered all her hair over her left shoulder and braided it into one thickness. She tossed it towards her back and out of the way.

He'd noticed how shaky her hands were. "You're not panicking, are you? Everything is going to be fine. I'll back out and guide you.

There'll be enough light to see the way. Just stay with me, and we'll be okay."

"I'm good, Joe." She nodded at his suspicious, intense look. "Honest!"

Within minutes, she was cautiously following his lead, crawling, and slithering along the tiny passage. He relaxed a bit, thinking she was beginning to move easier. She marveled out loud at the hideous mess around her, highlighted by the light on his hardhat, and from distant floodlights.

In fact, she could see what he couldn't.

"Stop right where you are, Joe," Angelina ordered, her voice cracking from dryness and anxiety. "Don't move."

"Don't panic, Angelina, everything's fine now." Joe didn't realize how silly those words sounded.

"No! You don't understand. Stop!"

But he didn't listen. The surrounding wreckage, braced by one lone timber which had shifted slightly in the last aftershock, exploded over his back. In the last second of realization, he instinctively drew her under him protectively and threw himself over her body.

"Estupido! Imbecil! Dios—why is it that so much of your attention was wasted on men's egos, and not on their brains?"

Spanish invectives flowed from under him as the noise of the wreckage finally abated. Sounded like she was pretty mad! God, he loved her voice. It was his last coherent thought.

Chapter Seven

Pummeled and cold-cocked by a huge section of wall that somehow had shaken loose after the last aftershock, Joe's body wasn't stirring. Dust, drywall, and timbers blanketed them. The big man shrouded Angelina to the point where she couldn't move. Stunned but unhurt, she lay there pinned down and more furious than she could ever remember feeling. Now what?

"Help" she called out. She called again louder, but there was no reply. Not surprising, since her voice sounded more like a croak than anything else.

His warmth settled into her and seeped through to her bones. It was one thing to be thankful for. Unfortunately, his weight also crushed her, making breathing difficult. His abrasive whiskers, scratching her cheek, caught her attention next. He was so close she felt his breath on her cheek. A faint odor of coffee was noticeable, and she wished he'd brought some of it with him. She sighed with relief at the strong rhythm of each inhalation.

Her hands, trapped under her skirt, were difficult to loosen, but she clawed this way and that until they were free. It was obvious to her that she needed to be in charge of their destiny. She couldn't afford to wait around for someone to come and find them. But, on the other hand, she had to take care not to bring another barrage down on them either.

Go slow, she thought. Stay calm and don't panic. Hearing those words in her own mind made her giggle, insanity too close for comfort. Joe would be so proud! More giggles...

What a stupid time to laugh, but she just couldn't help it. I think I'm losing it!

Carefully, she wriggled, pushed, and shoved her way out from under his body, a little at a time, until she was free and lying next to him. Then she stole his headgear so she could use his lamp to check the area. Removing the debris that covered him, taking the smaller pieces first until she'd freed him and cleared the space, she gave thanks that the timber that had initially dropped on them had rolled from his body, ending up wedged against the wall.

During this time, she screamed for help, but no one answered. The clamoring and crashing sounds from the machines outside must be hindering the rescuers from hearing her calls.

Maybe that last crash had left them stranded upstairs. She didn't know but couldn't wait. What if the unconscious man needed medical attention? She had to do something. If he'd made it to her, it meant they'd cleared a path. She had to find it and go for help, and he had to come with her. Scanning her surroundings, she realized only half the roof had collapsed. The rest could come down at any minute. She needed to move quickly.

With extreme caution, she unjammed the debris that blocked their route. Nails broken, hands and knees scraped and bleeding, she heaved with all her might, wishing herself another forty pounds heavier and three inches taller. Like her papa often said, she's stubborn as the devil even if she is my little Angel. Finally, she had an opening.

She turned Joe over with the utmost care, all the while sobbing and ranting under her breath. Then she tucked his arms over each other on his chest and scurried over his body to his feet. Hefting his boots in her small hands, she dug in her heels and pulled him slowly, from side to side. Lugging him inch by inch towards where she knew the stairs were hurt like hell. Her back and arms throbbed, as did the returning headache. The man was a deadweight, and she was bone weary, but fear pumped her adrenaline and gave her strength. She knew she had to get them out of the building before another aftershock struck. He was hers to save, and she would if it killed her.

"It's okay Angelina, I'm right here." A gentle voice spoke softly from behind her.

"You're almost to the stairs, and from then on it's clear. Let me change places with you so I can pull him the rest of the way."

Her hands clutched Joe's pant legs so tightly she had to send a message to her brain to let go, but it wasn't listening. Tears of fury stained her cheeks and dripped from her chin. Her hair, which had worked itself free from the braid, hung over everything, curtaining Joe.

"Miss, you can let go now."

Leave him? "No, we're almost there. Here, grab his other leg." She held onto one and moved to let the rescuer get the other, and then they pulled simultaneously. Within seconds, they were free. Many hands were waiting, ready to help, to take over, and to pry her fingers from Joe's pant leg.

Once on the street, the stranger solemnly wrapped a blanket around Angelina and introduced himself. "Miss Serrano, I'm Lee Nivens."

Twisting frantically and half-crazed, Angelina pushed at Lee's restraining hands and tried to follow Joe's stretcher to the ambulance.

Chapter Eight

Lee held her back, his voice firm. "Angelina, it's over. You're safe, and Joe will be fine. His breathing and color were good. I think he must have gotten knocked out." Passing her a bottle of water, he intimated that he wanted her to take a drink.

After a few sips to moisten her mouth and clear away some of the dryness, she said, "I tried to warn him, Lee. I really did. The stubborn fool wouldn't listen when I told him to stop. Then the wall collapsed on top of him." Her glazed eyes stared fixedly into Lee's. The bottle fell from her nerveless fingers.

Lee chuckled and turned her toward the area where they'd parked an ambulance. "Joe's hard-headed, so it'll take a lot more than a wall to kill him. It's you I'm worried about. We'll get you checked over, and if everything's okay, we'll get you home."

Minutes later, he hustled her across the wet, blackened, partially cleared street and into the back of the waiting ambulance. The attendants did the usual checkup and found that she was slightly dehydrated, exhausted and had surface wounds, but nothing serious. They carried on with first aid, cleaning up the worst of her cuts and scrapes. After she'd wheedled permission to leave, she joined Lee.

Just then, her contractor, Ray, spotted her. He pushed his way forward to pat her hands. "Angel, are you okay? What did the doctor say?"

Automatically, she told him, "Don't call me that, Ray. You, more than anyone, should know I'm no Angel."

Ray grinned. "Were you hurt?"

"I'm fine, a bit tired, but otherwise good." She glanced past him, and sadness covered her expression as she spied her beloved building.

"Donna you worry your pretty head about the place. I'll board it tonight, and I'll be back tomorrow to check the damage. I know you have good insurance, I helped you choose it. So, go home and get some rest now, my girl."

Looking at the men as if they were imbeciles, Angelina sighed, "I can't go home, I have to go to the hospital and see how Coralee is."

"You go home," Ray all but shouted. He assumed a stance that everyone who knew him well was familiar with: his hands went to his hips, fingers to the front and thumbs to the back. Leaning into her face threateningly, fully prepared to get his way, he glared at her.

Muttering Spanish imprecations under her breath, temper flaring, she copied him. Dropping her blanket, she swung her head first one way and then the other to clear all the bulk of her messy locks out of her face. She stepped closer to him and with eight, maybe less, inches of space between them; she raised her small, pointed chin and stared him down. Then she spat out, "I am going to the hospital."

"No! You are not! You are going home."

Lee, trying to help, angled himself beside Ray and cleared his throat. They both ignored him.

"I am going to the hospital." Now, all but screaming, in her befuddled mind, Angelina knew her place. First she had to see to Coralee. Then, she needed to check up on the idiot who'd almost killed them both while trying to save her.

"Tomorrow, you go. Tonight, you go home and rest." The Italian contractor had crews of men who would have fled hearing his tone.

But it didn't even faze Angelina. "My friend is in the hospital, and I am going there." Following this shouted avowal came a sob, and then another, and inevitably out of her gorgeous eyes poured a gush of tears.

Galvanized, both men bobbed their heads up and down, and concurred.

"Okay, okay! So you're going to the hospital."

Lee, eyes full of contrition, spoke up. "I'll take you."

Chapter Nine

When Lee and Angelina arrived, they could see the Emergency ward verged on being a disaster area. The severely injured were stowed away behind curtains, and the more fortunate and superficially wounded took up space in the waiting room. All were frustrated, awaiting attention. Many were baffled by the delays; others were scared and angry.

Annoying reporters trolled for a story, and exhausted police officers deflecting questions, interviewed victims, getting their paperwork seen to. Frazzled nurses assisted overworked doctors, while lack of space and the dread of more aftershocks contributed to making everyone testy as hell. The smell of fear fought and won over the faint antiseptic odor most hospitals tried to hide.

In the midst of the turmoil, Lee asked, "Who first, Coralee, or Joe?"

"It doesn't matter, you chose."

He nodded and then guided Angelina's blanket-wrapped figure to the desk where the nurse recognized him and extended preferential treatment.

"Hey, Lee. What's up? We have your handsome partner in cubicle four, and he's giving us a hard time." The blonde nurse was middle aged, heavily made-up and slightly chubby. Her tired smile and cheeky facial expressions signaled she was joking.

"Hi, Christy. I'm not surprised. I bet you girls are scaring the hell outta him."

"Right! He's so terrified; he's already put his moves on two of my young nurses."

"He's my man! Can we go in and say hello?"

"Sure, as long as you don't encourage him to leave. He took a walloping, and his back is badly bruised."

"You girls just want to keep him here for your own nefarious purposes. Maybe I should stay with him to protect the poor lad." Lee's wink took the sting out of his words.

They arrived at Joe's cubicle, just in time to see a gushing, dark-haired nurse full of saccharin sweetness eyeing him hungrily while chatting him up. Her nametag, strategically placed to draw one's attention to her protruding breasts, read Gail Berg. She had riveting brown eyes, decorated with smudged purple eye shadow, and thickly-applied mascara on overly-long, curly eyelashes. They fluttered like moths caught under a lampshade.

A movement behind Gail caught Angelina's attention. She spotted Joe peeking around the nurse's well-endowed body. He saw Angelina and his face froze. Red stains surged over his cheeks. As chatty Gail turned to leave, Joe noticed Lee. Comically, instant relief appeared on his face.

Gail stopped at the curtain. "Behave yourself, you rascal. If I catch you trying to get up again, I'll have to use restraints. Come to think of it—that might be fun." She bestowed a come-on smile to Joe, and a less sparkling one to Lee. Angelina, she ignored altogether.

Angelina looked at Lee, the man whose arm supported her, and caught his grin. Instinctively, she grinned back.

Joe glared his annoyance her way and demanded, "What are you doing here? Good God, woman, after what you've been through, you should be home in bed."

Angelina visibly stiffened.

Obviously, Lee didn't like the tension that was spiraling between the other two. He intervened, smoothing troubled waters. "Joe, we wanted to make sure you were okay. We've come to see Angelina's employee, Miss Becker, but when Christy told us you were right here, we decided to say hi and see how you were."

***

Joe's eyes never left the bedraggled woman in front of him. She was dead on her feet. Instantly, he tuned in on what prompted Lee's attentive behavior. Her dainty frame looked pitiful inside the grey rescue blanket. He'd recognized her smallness during the rescue, but standing, she was so tiny, she looked like someone who needed to be taken care of. Then he remembered: her size obviously didn't match her temperament.

She'd formed another untied braid with her abundant coal-black hair and it hung over her left shoulder, almost to her waist. Her dazzling sapphire-like eyes, diluted from weariness and ringed with a greyish tinge, looked too large for her strikingly beautiful face. Dried tear-tracks on her pallid cheeks enhanced her look of misery.

He felt something move inside, a kind of tenderness mixed together with a load of responsibility. He had the urge to pick her up and cradle her, soothe away the cares burdening her slumped shoulders. Pamper her like he did with his favorite baby niece. He fought the impulse with everything inside him that warned he was in dangerous territory.

"Go home, Angelina. Come back when you're not weak on your feet, or better yet, call the hospital for information." Maybe the commanding tone in his voice suppressed his feelings of inadequacy. Whatever. The only thing he knew was that it came out sounding a lot tougher than he'd intended.

"Gringo! Quit giving me orders. Who are you to tell me what to do?"

"I saved your life."

"Ay caramba! It was I who saved you." Her hands shot into the air. He loved her accent.

"Children, please! Calm down. Don't panic." Lee repositioned Angelina's blanket and, as any parent would protect a young one, he patted her shoulders. Joe saw Lee's joking seemed to strike her as being funny because first she smiled, then erupted into giggles.

He looked at Lee, who shrugged.

"I appreciate your visit, but please–I'm asking you please–go home soon." Joe's voice was soft, coaxing. "When I get out of here tomorrow, I don't want to have to come back to visit you after you collapse."

He felt her look bore into him. Holding her gaze, he kept his face as innocent but caring as he could. She sighed deeply and then seemed to accept his advice.

"Okay, Joe. I promise I'll only pop up for a minute to check on Coralee."

"Don't take any longer. Lee is exhausted. He's had a couple of long, hard days." He figured to play on her sympathies for his partner, and, hot damn, it worked like a charm.

Angelina turned to Lee with a horrified look on her face, her exclamation heartfelt. "Lee, I'm sorry. I wasn't thinking. You must be beat. You leave now; I'll take a taxi home. Really, I'm fine with that."

Lee shot an angry glance at Joe, whose manipulation had backfired, but then he smiled at Angelina. "Sugar, I'm fine. I'll just go and find out where they've put your friend, and I'll be right back to get you." She stiffened and glanced warily toward the bed. Joe watched as Lee patted her reassuringly, and then left before she could voice her obvious disagreement.

Surprised to find himself gritting his teeth, Joe dismissed the idea that Lee's tender display had put his back up. He decided that what bugged him was that she seemed uncomfortable staying with him. "Angel..."

"Please don't call me that. I'm no Angel. Call me Angelina or Angie, everyone does. My papá is the only one who insists on calling me Angel."

"How about the special man in your life? What does he call you?"

Suspiciously, she peered at him through half-closed eyelids. Her blanket flared out as she turned her back, heading to the curtain.

"Miss Serrano..." Prickly little thing.

"You need your rest. I'll wait for Lee in the hallway. Take care, Joe."

"Angelina," he emphasized her name, "you get your sweet butt home soon. You hear me?" His voice followed her behind the barrier.

Chapter Ten

During the rescue, Lee had concentrated most of his efforts in clearing the debris from the stairs and coordinating the other volunteers. His brief glimpse of Miss Becker, Angelina's assistant, had happened only as she'd been carried out on a stretcher to the waiting ambulance. He'd heard her joking with the guys and had chuckled at her high spirits.

Now, approaching her bedside along with Angelina, there was no warning whatsoever. No indication that Cupid was busy tonight. And no way of knowing that the arrow would shoot straight and true and reside in his unlocked heart.

Stunned, weak-kneed, floored, were appropriate adjectives he'd use later to describe his feelings to Joe. From the very first glance, she became his one and only. It happened that fast. Like a twinkle of a star on a warm summer's night. He wanted her. Forever!

How the hell was he going to share this realization with her and convince her he meant it? He'd need fancy words to explain how he felt.

I'm so screwed!

His second look confirmed his plight. Even though the woman was a mess of cuts and scrapes, he still wanted her. Black and purple bruises indicated she was in a lot of discomfort, and he instantly experienced phantom pains.

Her eyes looked bruised. The unequal pupil size marked the probability of concussion, and their big brown softness indicated a kind soul.

While Angelina scooped her friend into a gentle, teary hug, Lee, still quivering from shock, lowered himself onto the one available chair hidden in a deep recess in the darkened corner.

"Coralee, what did the doctors say? God, I'm so glad you're not badly injured." Angelina spoke in a shaky voice, obviously reassured that Coralee was indeed in one piece.

"Angelina, what are you doing here? For heaven's sake, you should be looking after yourself, you goofball." Though her words were chastising, Coralee's battered face lit up like a touch lamp after getting swatted.

"You've had stitches to stop the bleeding?" Angelina continued, again hugging her friend gingerly. "Does your poor head still hurt?" She nattered on while gently kissing it. She was like a mother caring for an adored, favored child.

"Hey, I'm fine. After a facelift, my old mug will be as good as new." The twinkle in Coralee's eye should have tipped Angelina off, but she missed it. Quickly, Coralee seeing her distress said, "Angelina, I'm kidding. I'm fine. I'll be outta here tomorrow, or the next day, and I'll be back to help you at the office. Hey? Who's that skulking over there in the corner? I can hardly see him."

"In the corner? Oh, Lee, I'm sorry. This is Lee Nivens, who helped save us tonight and has been magnificent." Angelina beckoned him over.

No way he'd come closer. He didn't trust his legs to hold him. Instead, he called out from his hidey-hole and waved. "Hi, Coralee. Hope you're feeling better than you look."

What? You idiot! If he could have chewed his tongue off, he would have.

Coralee's comedic response rescued him from his colossal nervousness and the ultra-dumb remark. "If you think I look bad, you should see the freaking building that fell on me."

Their laughter brought a flustered nurse running. "Shush!" she said with a finger to her lips. Then the same finger pointed to the doorway, "Out!"

Chapter Eleven

Sometime later, after directions given by a drained Angelina, Lee drove up a curved driveway to a large, well-lit Victorian house. The antique black, hanging lanterns were a welcoming committee of brightness. All seemed to be in order.

Lee pulled up in front and stopped the truck. He stepped out and helped Angelina from the vehicle. She felt weary and unsteady on her feet.

After he steered her to the door, he said, "Is there someone who can come and stay with you? You didn't call anyone after the rescue, but maybe you shouldn't be alone tonight."

Angelina liked Joe's lean sidekick. Chivalrous described him well. This often-neglected quality reminded her of her countrymen. Chile was a place where men cherished and protected their women. As long as it didn't get into the realm of smothering—which in her case it had—the custom worked very well.

"I'll be fine, Lee. You've been very kind. If there's ever anything I can do for you, you have only to ask." She hoped her earnestness appeared in the look she flashed his way...

"Actually, there is one small thing."

His puppy-dog expression melted her heart. "What's that?"

"Will you help me get to know your assistant, Coralee?"

Chapter Twelve

Twice during her fragmented sleep, images of a distinctive male disturbed Angelina's dreams. The first time, she woke before she could make out the features of the man whose warm hands caressed her body. All she remembered was his gruff whispers of seduction. But the second time, his startling green eyes were recognizable.

Insatiable, his lips drugged her with passion, heating her body with delight and leaving her wet and wanting. It was a long, hot night.

The morning finally arrived. Against plump, feather-filled pillows crushed skillfully to form a back support, Angelina lolled in her extravagant canopied bed, lost in a haze of reminiscence.

The distant bong of the grandfather clock warned her that she'd spent too much precious time fantasizing. She groaned. "Enough with the laziness!" Aware that it was past her habitual early-rising hour, she flexed and stretched. Each aching muscle and bruised area of her body detonated, warning her that the soreness of yesterday's experience lingered on.

Coaxed by the idea of a shower long enough to drain the water heater, she dragged her sorry backside from its warm nest. Wincing, unsteady on her feet, she stumbled towards her luxurious private en-suite bathroom, which was a cunning mix of the best of the old and the comfort of the modern.

Directly in front of the exquisite stained-glass windows, crystal candleholders embedded in tall wrought-iron stands of various heights caught her eye. She liked to light the candles when it was dark and when she was in the romantic mood, or as romantic as she could possibly be without a man's lips to kiss, or his body to answer the cravings that overwhelmed her so often lately. Could be why last night's dreams of a certain Search and Rescue worker were so raunchy.

An hour later, she felt more like her usual perky self, and was ready to face the mammoth amount of chores she'd mentally lined up to fill the day.

The hospital was placed top of her list. Visiting Coralee was one duty she relished.

She bit her lip while she fumbled around her cell phone contacts to find the one for her insurance company, then arranged to meet with an adjuster later at the site of destruction.

She dreaded the stop at her office. But on the other hand, she couldn't wait to see what she was up against. It helped a lot knowing Ray would be there. He'd called earlier and promised his support.

She'd telephoned every one of her employees the night before to check up on them and told them not to come in until further notice. Some would show up, she knew, if only to give her a hug and show their support.

Eventually, she'd get in touch with Lee, and possibly Joe. He sat last on her list, but for some strange reason occupied first place in her thoughts all morning. Not comfortable with that concept, in fact downright overwhelmed, she shied away from seeing him too soon. Not today! Maybe tomorrow–tomorrow being one of the greatest labor-saving devices for today.

She dressed appropriately in hip-hugging jeans and a turquoise T-shirt with Believe scrolled across the front. Her hair, semi-tamed and gathered in a modern-messy French braid, would be out of her way during a day that she expected to be fairly physical. But she couldn't control or restrain the wispy curls that fluttered around her face. They had a mind of their own.

To boost her self-confidence, she wore her regulation high-heeled boots. Most South American young women wore heels everywhere, which added to their height and their need to be appropriately dressed. Packing her mammoth carryall, filled with the organizational tidbits she'd need, she braced her shoulders and stepped out to face the day.

A sauntering, six-foot-two-inch male-model-type perusing the winter gardens of peonies and fancy grasses diverted her from searching for her keys. He had a way of moving—hips grinding in a slow sway that made the moisture in her mouth dry up. She snapped her lips closed, making sure to trap her tongue inside.

Sexy looking in well-washed jeans, Dr. Joe Davidson considerably raised the number of beats her heart pumped. There was a bright Search and Rescue logo embroidered on the arm of his black jacket, and the dark material provided a startling backdrop to the large pot of bright pink azaleas nestled gingerly in his large hands. Prettied up with a huge silver bow, they drew her attention, forcing her to blink repeatedly.

It would be like trying to stop a ticklish child's giggle to prevent the well of gladness that was sweeping over her.

"Joe! What are you doing out of the hospital? You should be resting." He must have asked Lee for her address.

Startled, he whipped around to face her and smiled. "I wasn't sure if you'd feel well enough to venture out today. I figured since you were here alone, someone should check on you. Heck, Angel... Angelina, I worried about you all night. You went through a pretty dangerous experience yesterday, and I felt sort of responsible for some of it. I'm stunned you're up and around at all. Are you sure you should be?"

She approached him, stood up on tippy toes, and warily stretched to kiss his cheek in greeting, a custom ingrained from her Chilean childhood as the way one received a guest, and especially one bearing gifts. His head lowered as she approached—her intentions clear.

"You needn't have worried about me. I have a lot to do today and putting off the inevitable is plainly unacceptable. Thank you for the lovely flowers, and for caring," she answered, accepting the plant and hugging the pot to her chest.

"You're welcome." His eyes ranged over her body, though not in a disturbing way. "You sure are a little thing, aren't-cha?"

"Not at all! You're just too tall for me!" Soon as the words escaped, she wished them back. Like he can do anything about his height, dummy! To change the subject, she added. "I'm astounded your Florence Nightingales let you leave so soon."

"I escaped. They bugged me all night. I hardly got a moment's peace."

"From what I remember, you didn't look like an abused man to me."

"I'm a good actor." He grinned. "Truly, I was glad you stopped by to see me. When I regained consciousness in the ambulance, I was anxious about what had happened to you. Diving for you was the last thing I remembered—that and your voice."

"Do you speak Spanish?" Did her discomfort sound as clear to him as it did to her?

"Nope, but there is an international knowledge of languages when it comes to cussing, don't you think?" Sparkling green twinkles filled his knowing eyes.

Chapter Thirteen

Angelina's soft lips on his cheek floored Joe. He wanted to leave and return just to get more of the same treatment.

Slanted with attractive dark rims, her blue eyes undoubtedly added to her overall beauty. As did her pint-sized body and pretty hair. The few cuts and bruises she'd skillfully hidden didn't distract; quite the opposite. She was as precious as he'd envisioned during the long, sleepless night. Those few conscious moments he'd felt her trapped under him had replayed over and over, reminding him of just how damn good she'd felt.

With the best of intentions, he'd come to offer himself as an escort for the next few days—to assess her building and decide her options. Fully aware of the workload and the dangers facing her, he still hesitated. Her prickliness brought out the coward in him. Frankly, he was shocked that she was up and around already.

When he saw her looking positively radiant, and seriously focused to begin a day that for anyone would be stressful and difficult, his scornful opinion of women took a shaking. He felt his perceptions of her frailty break apart. Uncomfortable at having to accept that this female had a strong, tenacious character, her independence threw him in a tailspin.

His preconceived ideas about women, gleaned from the behavior he'd encountered with some of his apathetic, self-centered, demanding sister-in-laws, didn't fit the feisty woman in front of him at all.

Seeing her perplexed stare, he decided to go for it. " I'd like to tag along with you. I have to stop by your building anyway." He knew from experience the demoralizing shock people felt when they went back to the scene of an accident. For some strange reason, he wasn't about to let her face that wrenching turmoil alone. Why this had become so important to him, he hadn't figured out yet, but as his mom liked to say, "When Joe gets a notion in his head, nothing short of major surgery will remove it."

Angelina turned so he couldn't read her expression. "You don't have to. I'm not going to the office until later. And I have a list of things that have to get done now. Trust me, you wouldn't enjoy being dragged around all morning to different places."

"What kind of places?" He stood with his hands tucked into the front pockets of his jeans and his shoulders hunched like a youngster who felt unwanted but was too stubborn to give up. Her attitude seemed to soften, and she smiled.

"First the hospital to see Coralee, then to pick up some papers from the bank, and then I'm going to the office to meet up with Ray and the insurance agent. Also, I have to see if my car is still in one piece. It was parked it in the lot behind the building." She started towards her grandmother's Lexus.

He moved quickly, took her arm, and guided her to his old blue Ford truck. "Works for me," he said, giving her no chance to argue.

He spied the pout she tried to hide. What's with this woman? Try and help her and she gets her tail in a knot.

Once they were in the truck and moving, to pacify her, he began a conversation. "Before I came to your house, I drove to the worst hit areas in the city. I'm flabbergasted and very happy to report that the majority of the destruction centered around one location."

"I watched the news on television, both last night and this morning," she said, de-icing somewhat. "I had to phone a colleague, Johnnie Steele, who's in Disneyland with his son and assure him all was fine in most areas of the city and not to shorten his trip. Then, of course, I called to Las Vegas to reassure my grandmother who's vacationing with my mother and father for some time in her favorite playground."

He saw the guilty way she lowered her eyes when she talked about her parents. "You didn't tell them about your offices, did you?"

"Not in any detail! I didn't want to worry them or have them rush back to force their help on me."

"Did you ever think that maybe they'd want to help you? That we all might want to help you?"

Earnestly, she looked at him. "Please don't take this the wrong way, but I mustn't be distracted. My employees and I have a lot of work ahead of us in the next two months. Now more than ever, we need to focus. I talked to each and every one of them last night and they're all willing to pitch in."

"That was kind. I bet they're worried about you."

"Not once they knew I was safe." She shrugged. "Earthquakes in Chile are numerous, but I never expected to experience one here, on the island."

"We live on a system of thrust faults along the Pacific and North American Plates, and there are over two hundred small earthquakes recorded in our region every year. Therefore, it's not unimaginable to expect exactly what occurred last night." Shifting to his professional persona, he added. "It's human nature to ignore the signs but not too intelligent. Thankfully, the epicenter was below the surface, and not nearly as catastrophic as it could have been. I bet this will shake up the doubters, no pun intended, and our future preparedness will be an ongoing subject for many agencies—Search and Rescue included."

He listened to his own words and couldn't believe it. Joe Davidson, big shot, cool dude, babbling like a show-off idiot. What the hell was wrong with him?

He looked over to see if his rambling had bored her.

What he didn't see was the bus in front of them.

Chapter Fourteen

"I'm sorry about your truck, Joe. The bus shmucked the front bumper quite badly."

"Shmucked?" He glanced at her quickly but then jerked his attention back to the traffic in front.

"One of Coralee's words. It means—"

"I know what it means. Not to worry, Angelina. I needed a new paint job anyway, and now I'll just have to do a few repairs first. It's not as bad as it looks. More important, you're sure you weren't hurt?"

"I'm fine." She'd answered the same way all four times he'd asked.

"I can't believe I didn't see the bus stopping. Thank goodness you yelled at me when you did. It could have been so much worse."

"I don't think you hit it all that hard. At least the driver didn't seem to be very concerned, especially after you gave him your particulars and apologized so many times. Even your friend, the officer who stopped to help, accepted that nothing too serious had happened."

"I'm worried you'll begin to think I'm some kind of a klutz. I've put you in danger two times in as many days. And I've held you up from doing your chores."

All bad things come in threes! The saying popped into her mind, and a chill scurried over her back making her shudder. Shaking off the superstitious silliness, she replied. "You came through an earthquake for me, Joe. Without you— knowing you were coming; I'd have really flipped out. I consider that good luck. Plus, those chores will get done." They just won't be done on my time schedule. She groaned silently.

His wide, wonderful smile took away the guilt from her little white lie. She didn't need to share how often she'd cussed his attitude. After all, now that she'd met him, it seemed in keeping with his personality. She was just touchy about men and their need to rule.

At the entrance to the hospital, Joe stopped to let her out of the truck. "I can follow you in as soon as I park, or collect you later," he said. "I have some paperwork in Administration that I can catch up with if you want to see your friend alone. Your decision."

Strange choice of words coming from any man, she thought. Being gracious, she answered, "If you don't mind, I'd rather go in alone, Joe. She might not be feeling up to a lot of visitors. And listen, I can take a taxi from here. You don't have to collect me later. Honestly!" She made her tone as firm as she could without seeming rude.

"No problem!" he answered, grinning. "See you later." He waved at her and drove away.

She fumed, swore in Spanish and threw her hands in the air. He's like crazy glue!

As soon as she entered the hospital, she made her way straight to the gift shop, and latched on to a goofy floating balloon with a caricature of a grinning puppy and Get Well Soon scrawled from one side to the other. Then, she chose a gigantic bouquet of yellow roses to stick it in. Armed with her parcels of affection, she went searching for Coralee.

When she arrived at her friend's cubicle, Coralee was at her confrontational best, bothering her doctor to sign her release. As soon as the slim older woman in the white coat saw Angelina, she nodded and made good her escape.

Angelina approached, set the flowers on the windowsill, and leaned down to kiss Coralee's cheek. She perused her assistant's face closely and could tell Coralee wasn't going anywhere for a while. The visible cuts and scrapes on her cheeks and forehead appeared worse than last night. And her black eye, more prominent today, was downright appalling.

Angelina sat close to her on the mussed-up bed. "From the look of your face, I'd say they want you to stay in the hospital for a few more days."

"Actually, it's my sweet personality they don't want to let go of. I'm trying to be meek here, but what can I say?"

Angelina playing along said, "Right, meek—like a lightning bolt."

"Ha, ha! Sourpuss. That's just nasty."

"Look, my friend, you need to stay put until the doctors are satisfied you're one hundred percent fit."

"Yeah, yeah! Whatever! Are you going to check out the office today? I wanted to be with you when you go to see it for the first time. I know how much you love the old place. It'll break your heart when you're faced with the destruction."

"I'm not a baby, I'll be fine. You pamper me too much. I can handle this situation. What I couldn't have coped with was if anything worse had happened to you. So please, get better soon, Miss Doomsday."

Coralee grinned, making her poor face look even more grotesque.

Angelina felt a reaction throughout her body, nerves leaping in sympathy with the pain her best friend was trying to play down. She had to control her features so as not to upset Coralee further. "I'll miss you, but I'll survive." She caressed Coralee's left hand and held on when her friend's fingers tightened. "I promise to visit the hospital with updates and get my daily Coralee fix."

"Even still, I wish Johnnie or Grandma Evie was in town to support you through this." Coralee flipped her hair back from her face and held it behind her ears, a gesture she made when uptight.

"Stop it, worrywart! Joe's asked to go with me today, so I won't be alone. I'm sure he'll check out the safety issues before I get anywhere near the bad spots, so relax!" Angelina had to appease her.

The thought popped into her head that it might make more sense for her to be guarding Joe, but she quickly discarded it as being too cheeky.

"Oh—Joe is it? What about the formal Dr. Davidson?" Coralee's eyebrow lifted, which made her wince and smirk simultaneously from the cut above it.

Not comfortable with Coralee's inquisition, Angelina strove to appear indifferent. "He came by the house this morning because he knew I was alone, and thought I was without transportation. I pointed out that I could drive Grandma's car, but he wouldn't hear of it. He all but kidnapped me, drove me here and dropped me off; informing me he would be by later to pick me up. He's playing chauffeur and friend today, nothing more." She left out the part about the bus accident on purpose. That would really freak out Coralee.

"Too bad! If my memories from last night serve me right, he's a prime specimen. Of course, I only saw him for a few minutes, because as soon as he knew the others had freed me he went after you."

Wanting to get rid of the gleam in Coralee's matchmaking eyes, Angelina added, "I haven't paid much attention to his looks, just his domineering personality."

"Hell, your nose is going to grow at least an inch with that whopper, Pinocchio," Coralee gleefully teased.

Angelina left the side of the bed and pulled over the chair, her back turned to give her face time to lose its flush. Once settled, she opened a new topic and ignored the knowing gleam in Cora's blood-shot eyes. "I'm meeting with the insurance adjuster today as well."

The grin slid off Coralee's face and her expression became serious. "I was never sure about you signing up for that extra earthquake clause. It was expensive, and even though I know you experienced a lot of shakes in Chile, I thought those crazy things never happen to us here." Coralee snorted and nodded. "I should have known."

"This year, I almost didn't bother. Now I'm glad I stuck with it. Just hope it covers most of the expenses."

"I have to tell you, Angelina, I'm surprised your family aren't arriving today even without you asking. They must know about the earthquake."

"Grandma had already started making return flight arrangements last night when I called, but I nagged her into staying in the States, and coming back with the parents as previously organized. There's no need for her to hurry back, as there isn't anything she could do, or for that matter, anything I'd want her to do."

"Is that fair to her, or your parents, Ange? When they realized you've duped them, won't they be upset?"

"Between you and me, I truly want to take care of this crisis alone. I need to prove to myself, and to them, that I can."

Coralee looked comical with her thick, reddish bed-head hair sticking out all over, and her blackened eye half-closed. Thankfully, her taunting grin revived her looks astonishingly. "Boy, you're stubborn," she groaned. "Why are you so independent? It pleases people to help you, especially those of us who care about you."

"Yes, I know, but you have to understand. It pleases me to be able to stand on my own two feet. For years my father and two brothers tried to restrain me. They belittled my choice to follow in their footsteps and be an accountant. They scorned my dreams of working in the family business. They even tried to choose a husband for me. Every battle escalated into a war. To save my sanity, they forced me to be the independent person I am today. I knew they loved me, but it was suffocating. And don't forget, I'm claustrophobic."

Coralee groaned at the pun. Then she shook her head, obviously confused. "You're lucky to have all these people who care. I don't have a father or brothers, just an embarrassingly long string of miscellaneous dorky boyfriends."

"You think I'm lucky?" Angelina drifted off remembering how she'd had to battle daily for her independence. All that testosterone was unbearable. Especially to a girl whose greatest pleasure was in pleasing others. In South America, in traditional families, the men were endlessly spoiled from birth. Those men-babies, coddled and cosseted by their womenfolk, ultimately grew up adoring the opposite sex and became dream lovers.

On the other hand, the girls weren't nearly as fortunate. They were habitually petted, true, but over-protected from the complexities of life by their hawk-eyed menfolk. And for someone like Angelina, it was like trapping a butterfly in her own velvet cocoon.

Coralee broke into her reminiscences. "It's hard to imagine you being ruled or manipulated by anyone. I've only known you as a liberated woman. And... a woman extremely possessed by the calendar." Coralee stuck to the subject like a fridge ornament. "I've tried to ask you before about your obsession with your timetable. Angelina, please tell me. I want to help."

Angelina saw the love in the eyes of her best friend, and something gave within her. "You know I made that wager with my father—that I could own a business outright in two years. Well, that bet started from the time I opened my own office, which was exactly twenty-two months ago. Therefore I have only two months left before I win."

"Right! I get that. But what you didn't tell me... what's at stake?"

Angelina could see by the lightness of Coralee's features that she wasn't taking any of this seriously.

But she would.

"If I win, he agreed to let me work in the family business, right alongside him and my brothers."

A more serious expression flooded Coralee's face as she asked. "And if you lose?"

"I have to return to Chile, let him help me choose a husband, settle down and marry. Give him grandchildren, be a society wife—stop breathing."

Angelina had Coralee's full attention now. "No way! My God, Angelina! You're not serious. That's a bunch of hooey; it's like the Middle Ages. You certainly aren't going along with any this nonsense. Are you?"

"I have no choice." Angelina clasped her hands to still their habitual gesturing. "My entire life, our menfolk tried to slot me into the pattern they believed women belonged in. When I wanted to study at college, my father was angry, but mother blackmailed him into letting me go. I excelled and received honors at the best university in Santiago. I was sure he'd see how serious I was in wanting to work with him and my brothers, but he is domineering and stubborn. All he could see was his Angel. He spoiled me with affection and gifts and talked about how I should be like my society mother. Drove me crazy! I decided I either had to do something drastic or bow under and say goodbye to my vision of the rest of my life. He and my brothers saw a little woman, wife and mother. I saw a successful, fearless businesswoman."

"Does that mean you don't ever want to get married or have children?" Coralee looked away, her expression soft, her face sad. "Babies are all I think about."

Angelina smiled. "One day, sure." The image popped into her head of Joe holding a pot of pink flowers. Then like a zoomed-in TV shot, the azaleas became a curly, black-haired baby with devilish green eyes. No way!

Huskiness attacked when she tried to speak. Clearing her throat, she admitted shyly, "Only problem is, I'll have to learn how to talk when I'm around interested men. I have a habit of stuttering that's very embarrassing." Now why did I share that secret?

Wickedly, Coralee suggested, "The best way to control the stuttering is to keep your mouth occupied with something a whole lot more fun!"

Angelina followed her advice. Tongue sticking out and waggling, she crossed her eyes. "You mean like this?"

Coralee clutched her forehead, her face a picture of faked sadness. "Sure, right–fearless businesswoman! And you very well know that's not what I meant for you to do with your mouth."

Angelina recognized the moment when the wager's full impact hit Coralee. Her friend's grin faded and her face whitened noticeably, even under the bruising.

"Hold it, girlfriend. Either way, you'll have to go back to Chile. What about your business here? What about your employees? Angelina, what about me?"

"Right from the beginning, I intended for you to someday take over this office, Coralee. You're good. You'll do fine, and I can come back and forth periodically."

"Oh, Angelina. I can't take this right now. I never thought you'd leave us or give up what you've worked so hard for."

"I've struggled so long to make this dream come true, Coralee—for so many years. To belong! Be a part of our family business and take my rightful place. It's what I've always wanted. To make them proud. You have to understand how much it means to me."

"I'll try, but it breaks my heart. The thing is, can we still win? Do we have a chance now after the earthquake?" Angelina noticed that her friend had automatically kicked in on her side; it was why she adored her.

"I hope so. The profit we'd have made from the new Florist's account which arrived yesterday would have paid off the last of the money I owe. I was absolutely floating after they left, but now, I just don't know."

"If we can't pull it off, what'll happen?"

"I made the bet, and if we lose, I'll honor it."

Chapter Fifteen

Unknown to the two girls, Joe had arrived at the curtain in time to hear the last part of Angelina's impassioned speech about the Florist's account and how she needed it to pay back some of the money she'd gambled.

Her being a gambler shook him to the core. Right from the beginning, when he'd looked into her beautiful eyes, there'd been a kind of sweet connection, a yearning that had started tormenting him. She was different than anyone he'd ever met, and he'd felt a respect for the way she'd handled adversity. But he didn't have any respect for people who gambled. He'd seen too many lives broken up because of the addiction. In fact, one of his brother's wives was in a recovery program, and their relationship had suffered tremendously until she'd gotten help.

Nope, he couldn't deal with it. Better to back off now, he decided. Wait! You promised to take her to her office. He argued with himself. She didn't really want to come with me. She said she'd rather go by cab. Tough–you promised.

Back and forth he struggled, his thoughts conflicted. Finally, he pulled back the cubicle curtain and stepped inside.

Both women pivoted abruptly.

"Angelina, something has come up and I'll have to meet you at your office building later—after lunch. Sorry about the ride." He couldn't look her in the face. But he did wink at Coralee as he said, "Hi there. Hope you're feeling better."

"Hey, Dr. Joe. I feel a lot better than I look."

"You're gorgeous, and don't let the wozos in here say otherwise." He waved and was gone.

"Wozos? A new word for me," Coralee chuckled.

"Do you believe that?" Angelina's voice was many octaves higher than usual. "First he forces himself on me after I tell him not to bother." Her hands were waving ferociously. "Then, when I'm glad he'll be there, he leaves skid marks on the floor to get away. Gringo loco!" she seethed; disgust evident in her voice.

At first, Coralee laughed. Then she added. "Don't be mad at him, Angelina. He looked weird, like he'd had a shock, or lost his best friend. Don't you think he looked kinda pale?"

"Pale?" Angelina's head swiveled in the direction of where Joe had disappeared to moments before. "Well, he did have a concussion last night. And then he had a slight accident with a bus this morning. Maybe he's had a relapse. Now I feel terrible for getting so huffy. It's just that when I tried to talk him out of bringing me to the hospital, he wouldn't take no for an answer, all but dragging me into his truck. Now he dumps me." Her hands kept time with her voice, up in the air, then down, then waving around to start their journey yet again.

"The man came to tell you that something came up; he didn't just dump you."

"I guess. But he was overly friendly this morning, and I got the feeling just now that he couldn't wait to get away."

"What happened last night for him to get concussed?"

Discomfort kicked in while Angelina searched for the right words. "We were crawling, zigzagging out of the cleared passageway he'd made for us, when some of the debris fell on him and knocked him out. Because I could see the tottering wall he was backing in to, I tried to warn him to stop, but the stubborn mule wouldn't listen. At the last second, he dove to cover me and took the full brunt of the crash."

Angelina didn't want to remember how panicky she'd been when she'd thought that Joe could be dying right there in her arms. She pushed the horror away and continued, "They brought him to the hospital in an ambulance, soon after they took you away."

"And today he's on the loose. For heaven's sake, he should probably still be in bed. And what was that about an accident?"

"It was nothing—a slight bump to the front of his truck."

"Nothing? Holy mackerel, were you in the truck with him?"

"Uh huh! Seems to be a pattern starting up here. Sharing accidents!"

"It doesn't look good, Angelina. No wonder the guy seemed disturbed."

"This morning, he told me the hospital cleared him. I have to admit, he did look healthy enough earlier. I guess his back took the worst hit, or so the nurse said last night." Angelina was beginning to feel ridiculously guilty. She was being bitchy. After all, the poor guy just got out of his sick bed and came straight to help her.

"Who took you home from the hospital last night?" Coralee interrupted her musings.

"Lee Nivens, the fellow who came with me to see you."

"I thought I remembered someone here with you. What's he look like? Is he nice?"

"He's wonderful. One of the nicest guys I've met in a long time, and a real gentleman. You'll like him, Coralee."

"He must be gay."

"Now why would you say that?"

"If he didn't come on to you, he's either gay or blind. And if he had come on to you, then you wouldn't be singing his praises."

"He's not gay, you goofball. He's a nice single man who's a sweetie, so there." Angelina crossed her fingers hoping that her comment about him being single was true. After all, if he had a crush on Coralee, he'd better not be hooked up with anyone else, or he'd answer to her.

"Know what?" Coralee was back on the earlier train of thought. "I'm still intrigued—curious about your life in Chile. Joe interrupted us, but since you're in the mood to talk, tell me more. You realize that for me this is a no-win situation. If you succeed, you go back to Chile, and if you lose, you still go back. Did you specifically move to Canada to accomplish this goal?"

"Yes. You know I was born in Canada?"

"You were? How did that happen?"

"Mama was about five months pregnant with me, and came to spend time with her mother, Grandma Evie. Some serious health problems pestered her while she was here, and the doctors put her to bed for the rest of her pregnancy. They wouldn't allow her to fly home, so Papá went back and forth, and had to leave my brothers with the nanny in Chile. I was born here in Victoria, and after a month or so, we went back. Being a Canadian citizen helped when I decided to move here and open my own business. There was a lot less paperwork and fewer permits to deal with."

"Did you spend a lot of time here on holidays while you were growing up?"

"Oh yes. I loved it here. Grandma was a spoiler, and as kids we knew whenever we came here, she would take us all over the island. My brothers especially loved to go to Long Beach and surf, but my favorite was the Butchart Gardens. Those spectacular, showy flowerbeds were a joy for Grandma Evie, and so they were for me also. Victoria was like my second home."

"I've always liked it here too. It's a pretty city full of nice people. What's your home in Chile like? You live in the capital city, don't you? We've talked about it before."

"Yes. It's called Santiago. Chilean people are warm and friendly, and we have a huge network of friends and family on my father's side. My brothers are bachelors who are very much sought after. Sebastian only recently became engaged and will marry in the spring. Rodrigo is still on the prowl."

"I met them a few times, but I must admit I was pretty intimidated. They're way too handsome for my comfort."

"You know what's funny? They both thought you were pretty, but shy. I laughed when they told me, and now I see why they thought so."

"I have to admit, if I feel like I'm out of my league I clam up. Hard to believe, eh? I love Grandma Evie though. She's a pet."

"When the wager started, she was my savior. I didn't quite trust my family to play fair if I stayed in Chile, and so she invited me to come to Canada. Right from the start, she's been good for me. Without her influence I probably wouldn't have gotten up the nerve to have my breast reduction operation, and I needed it desperately. Those big babies were embarrassing, uncomfortable and were the cause of some my worst moments. Since she'd lived with a similar problem all her life, she was deeply aware of how they curtailed my activities and held me back. She coaxed me, saying if she'd had the chance at my age, she would have jumped at it. She's been a wonderful mentor, an example of how to stand on my own two feet, and I love her dearly."

"She is a sweetheart. You're lucky to have her."

"Thank goodness, she lets me make my own decisions, not like my family's bossy men."

"I wouldn't mind some man being my boss if he cared about me."

"You think you wouldn't mind, but, trust me, it's crippling. You, on the other hand, I've always admired. You are level-headed and full of self-confidence."

Angelina had no idea why Coralee snorted or looked away.

Chapter Sixteen

Without cattiness, Coralee's thoughts took over. Poor little lucky rich girl doesn't know how fortunate she is. Try a life where a father, soured from living with a mean-hearted woman, only stuck it out for two years of his daughter's childhood. Try putting up with a mother who was more interested in her own love life than caring about the traumas and troubles her mixed-up child might have been experiencing.

Coralee's mother's way of parenting had been to ignore or belittle. Later, because she was never around, the teenaged Coralee grew up streetwise. The street became her teacher and the neighborhood her callous school of life.

She tried to explain to Angelina without divulging too much of her past. "Growing up was a never-ending struggle for me. I left home when I was very young, drifted in and out of trouble, and finally smartened up after a few good scares and one disturbing incident that I've put behind me. I worked a couple of jobs for three years and lived meagrely in a one-room basement suite. During that period, I saved every penny I could get my hands on to pay for my education. When I think back to my wild teenage years, the only bookkeeping I ever visualized myself doing then was as a bookie in some sleazy joint." Coralee grinned unselfconsciously, not realizing how much she'd given away.

Angelina's spoke softly, her hand gently caressing the agitated one in front of her. "Is your family still alive? Do you ever see them? You never talk about them, and I've been hesitant to question you in case there was a tragic happening you don't like to speak of." She had noticed that whenever family was brought up, Coralee became evasive.

"I dislike being in a bad mood. Thinking about my childhood always does that to me. You know those young kids on the street corners, the panhandlers I always catch you sneaking money to? Well, when I was younger, that would have been me. Now, I neither know nor care where my parents are. They never gave a hoot in hell about me. They left years ago, first my old man when I was still a baby and then her. When she left, it was at the worst period in my life. A time I don't talk about—ever. I just want to forget." Coralee's cynical voice had risen dramatically, and Angelina became worried.

"Coralee, you better know you're loved now. If you ever do want to talk, I'll always be here for you. You know that?"

"You'll be in Chile, you mean."

Chapter Seventeen

Angelina sat beside Coralee's hospital bed and held her hand while her friend slept. Coralee's long, amber-toned lashes held the only natural color on her face. The other shades were caused by yellow and mauve bruises with black and blue highlights. Tenderness welled up inside for this big-hearted, child-like girl, so smart and full of goodness.

When she returned to Chile, she'd miss Coralee terribly. Just thinking about it left an ache twisting and gouging inside her. A massive depression enveloped her that had her squirming in her seat.

She heard footsteps and twisted to face the gap in the curtain. When she saw the man with a spray of mixed flowers gripped tightly in his hands, she nodded and smiled at the brilliant red rose in the middle of the bouquet.

She put her finger over her lips and motioned for him to follow her outside the curtain and into the hall. As soon as they arrived, she turned and put her hands on her hips. "Are you single?"

"Yes," he answered, "but if I'm lucky, not for long. How is our girl today?"

Angelina's face changed instantly; her suspicions disappeared. She grinned at Lee, her sparkling blue eyes alight with affection. Gazing at him like a proud mama, watching her son take his first step, she said, "I'm so glad."

"I'm glad you're glad." His lips curled in a sweet smile. "Is Coralee better?" The tips of his oversized ears tinged to red.

"She's snoozing. I tired her out. It's probably best for only one of us at a time to stay with her, so it's your turn now. Tell her I'll be back later."

Angelina whirled around and returned to Coralee's area, scooped up her bag of goodies and wiggled her fingers as a goodbye gesture toward the man who paid her absolutely no heed. His eyes were for one person only.

***

Later, after taking care of other business, Angelina arrived close to her office. The street and sidewalks were clogged with repair vehicles and piles of debris, waiting to be collected. The smell of smoke still permeated the air. Cracked walls, missing plaster, damaged bricks and open gaping holes where once there were windows disfigured many of the neighboring edifices.

Walking toward her building, she decided the mutilation wasn't too apparent. Except for the boarded-up windows, the exterior walls looked to be fairly intact.

What worried her was seeing the mess inside for the first time. She wanted to be upbeat and put on a good show, but her hazy memories of yesterday's devastation warned her to be prepared.

Gladness shocked her when she stepped through the doorway and saw Joe perusing the blueprints with her contractor, Ray. Stop it! He's not for you!

"Hi, guys. I finally made it. Sorry I'm late."

Upon seeing Angelina, Ray teared up, stepped forward and wrapped his big arms around her slight body. Hugging her, he rocked her from side to side. "It's gonna be okay, bambino."

Angelina laid her head on his shoulder. Sliding her arms around his wide back, she clung for minutes, absorbing his strength. When she looked over his back and caught Joe's gaze, she couldn't stop her smile.

Strangely, he closed down and turned away. His rejection made her feel numb and sad. What's wrong with him?

Ray continued to pat and rub her back which ramped up her affection for the man. It pulsated throughout her whole body and when she pulled gently away, it gave her a reason to smile.

"I'm ready to see the damage. If I keep telling myself that it could have been worse, do you think it'll help?" She turned to Joe, her eyes glittering with the tears she fought to hold back. "I'm glad you're here." She was being honest, though it made her feel uncomfortable, which steadied her.

Looking nervous, he cleared his throat and wiped both hands on the sides of his jeans. "Me, too. It's not so terrible, Angel...ah, Angelina. The top floor is the worst, but Ray, who by the way has a good handle on this place, told me he hadn't yet done the renovations up there. If he'd have finalized the job, all his work would have been destroyed. At least you haven't already paid for those repairs, and that's a blessing."

"I'll take all the blessings I can get." She grinned and began feeling cautiously optimistic.

Ray interrupted. "Angie, I'm gonna leave you with Joe and start clearing debris on the staircase so you can check out the damage from the top landing. You're probably anxious to see how bad we got hit."

"Thanks, Ray. We'll be there soon."

Joe watched the contractor stomp out and turned back to Angelina. "The sad thing is much of the cosmetic work that had been finished on the first two floors will need some repairs. Since you were intelligent enough to recognize the beauty of the original hardwood floors, moldings and other architectural gems, it won't be a major do-over. With some refinishing, those wooded areas will look new again. It's mostly a cleanup from all the dust, fixing the cracked walls and so on that's needed. Many of the windows will have to be replaced, but I can give you a name of someone I know who specializes in restoring old frames."

"Oh, Joe, I already have most of these windows on order with a genius artist who works in stained-glass. They're to be delivered in a few days. Imagine how unthinkable it would have been if they had already been installed." Hands held instinctively in a prayer-like position; she breathed a sigh of relief.

"That's wonderful. More good news."

Angelina had the feeling that Joe was working hard at coaxing her into an upbeat attitude for a reason. Now, more than ever, she dreaded going upstairs.

They examined the rest of the first floor and moved on to the next level. "Because areas of the roof and the flooring on the third story collapsed, the second floor sustained a little more damage." Joe spoke soothingly.

"Thankfully, in relatively small sections," Angelina said, muttering out loud. Still, it looked to be mostly a case of a cleanup and minor repairs, which she observed with a sigh of relief.

The rooms, other than the ceilings in some places, needed various touch-ups in the same way as the first floor, not so much structural repairs but repainting and refinishing. Knowing Joe would've stopped her if there'd been any danger, she felt perfectly safe as she wandered through the offices making mental notes of the major problem areas.

"You're not saying too much, Angelina. Look, don't be upset. You've gotten off relatively lucky so far." Joe came over to her, speaking consolingly.

"Yes, I know. I'll admit, what's waiting for me upstairs scares me." She instinctively slipped her fingers into his, in the same way as she would have with any close friend. As they walked one flight up, side-by-side, she felt him stiffen, but then near the top his hand squeezed hers before letting go.

The third floor was utterly destroyed, an unholy mess. From the safety of the stairs, she could see smashed desks and broken computers, felled filing cabinets and destroyed office paraphernalia. Mixed together with the rubble from the walls and roof, it created an unimaginable clutter.

The unmistakable odor of damp plaster prevailed, while the cold left her shivering. Tarps were positioned over openings in the roof and offered some protection from the birds and the weather; signs Ray had been at work either the night before or early this morning.

"We can't go any further." Joe held his hand across the railing at the top step of the staircase. "I don't believe it's safe past here."

"My goodness, it's a miracle we weren't killed. I can't imagine what the outcome would have been without the reinforcements Ray put in when he restructured many of the inside walls. I guess my building got hit pretty badly in comparison to others in the area."

"When I go to work at the Search and Rescue office later this evening to catch up on filling in the various forms, I'll have a much better idea of the outcome. It seems to me this block suffered immense damage in comparison to what else I witnessed while driving around. At the hospital earlier they were happy to report that, though there were a few major injuries, there were no deaths because of the earthquake. That alone is great news."

He leaned into her and smiled. The whiff of his cologne made her imagine a forest full of tall grass and velvety moss, and that reminded her of his eyes. The same eyes that were now full of affection. Without knowing she would, she reached up to stroke his cheek and watched as discomfort replaced the fading grin. She dropped her hand like a hot coal. What is wrong with him?

Tentatively, she asked. "Do you have a few minutes for me to make a short list of plans for the next few days? It'll help to do it while I'm here, and I can see what all has to be done. Also, would you mind checking it over to see if I've missed anything?"

"Sure, go ahead and take your time. If you need any help, I'm all yours," he said, not realizing what images the words brought to her conjecturing mind.

Stomping down on her instinctive gladness, she made up her mind. I don't want you with all your moody ups and downs.

Chapter Eighteen

Retrieving a pad and pencil from in her purse, Angelina returned to the first floor. Wandering from room to room, surveying every little corner, she reeled in her emotions. Concentrating, she began writing down her strategy for the next few days. Totally involved in her list, she worked her way over to a closet area at the back of the staircase. After opening the door, a strange noise caught her attention. Something's there!

In her stubborn standalone way, she forged ahead to see what the lump concealed. Breath abated, Angelina snuck forward and drew back the ragged blanket from a curled up sleeping form. She stopped—poised to take off, even scream for help if the need arose.

Squeezed together were two bodies. One looked to be a teenage girl still out cold and the other a pitifully small, very soiled and matted puppy. Only the pup looked up. Fear emanated in waves from his shaking fuzzy body and his weepy blinking eyes. Almost as an afterthought, there came a noise, supposedly a growl but sounding more like a disgruntled whimper. The somnambulant girl woke instantly and shushed the puppy, patting him gently and embracing him closer. Suddenly, she froze and peeked out from one very slightly open eye.

Clearly, Angelina, a lone woman, posed no real threat therefore she tried the offense is the best defense policy and hissed, "Hey, what are you doing?"

"I'm inspecting my building after the earthquake. What are you doing?"

"Duh! Sleeping. What does it look like?" The girl sat up, snaking back against the wall, clutching the pup reassuringly.

"It could look like a B&E to the police I'll be calling real soon if you don't lose that attitude," Angelina sarcastically answered, using the same inflections as the ragamuffin.

"Go ahead and call. I haven't touched a thing," Raspy and hard to hear, the teen's voice was still querulous and scrappy. "It rained last night, and the puppy had nowhere to go. So, I brought him in here to keep him out of the wind."

As the girl labored to her feet, Angelina noticed her painful grimace. She also noticed the well-worn, black cloth backpack the girl clung to and threw over her thin shoulder. Amazingly colorful, decorated with beads, embroidered dragons and carefully stitched edging, it evidently held her precious possessions. All the street people carried one or more totes and were very protective of these articles. Like any person would be if everything you owned fitted inside.

Losing the autocratic demeanor, Angelina reached over and gently helped the girl out from under the enclosure. Deep wrenching coughs broke out as she clutched her chest.

"I'm not on drugs," she promised, sounding as if she hoped to escape without getting into trouble.

"Well, you should be," Angelina said, putting a helping arm around the thin shoulders, and guiding her to the stairs where she could sit. "At the very least, decongestants and cold medications." The puppy, still nestled safely in his protector's arms, stared at Angelina and she saw intelligence mixed with apprehension—watching and waiting. "What's the pup's name?" She reached over and caressed her head.

"Don't know. I found him last night. Some losers had tied tin cans around his neck. The noise terrified him." The girl's voice croaked and squeaked at the same time.

"You realize that you need to see a doctor immediately, don't you? That's an appalling cough and your chest seems to be congested. You could end up with pneumonia."

"Okay! I'll look right into it!

The gutsy little twerp, still pushing buttons, made Angelina shake her head. "Don't be a smart-ass. I mean it."

"Look, now that it's daytime we'll take off." The abrasive cough came again, harsh, and surely painful. The girl forced herself upright and went over to retrieve her blanket. Putting the puppy down for a second, she efficiently folded the thin material and stuffed it into her pack. Quickly, she gathered the little one back into her arms.

"Where will you go?" Angelina couldn't help but ask.

"Not your problem. Things were freaky last night. Black as hell, the streets were full of weirdoes, crazy dangerous. So, I figured to wait it out. The door in the back was loose." Shrugging, she continued, "I came in and closed it down best I could. You should be paying me night-guard wages instead of hassling me." A crafty look appeared, and her hand shot out, palm open.

"I don't think so," Angelina grinned, taking the waif's hand and shaking it. "I'm Angelina Serrano, and this is my building. What's your name?"

"Tee—short for trouble," the teen shot back, jerking her hand from Angelina's as if it had been burned.

Getting a closer look at the girl now upright on her wobbly feet, Angelina saw a slim but well-muscled adolescent, of medium height and sporting the uniform of today's youth—low-rise, stonewashed jeans, surprisingly clean, and topped with a layer of multi-colored t-shirts that suggested warmth more than style. Her plum-colored, almost pink hair, in drastic need of a cut, hung shaggy to medium length.

It was her eyes that caught the imagination. They weren't brown, as brown was too paltry a description. They weren't green or gray either. But all three colors combined. And they were eclipsed by ridiculously long reddish eyelashes that enriched her eyes with a distraction and density that caught the attention of anyone looking and would have most people looking twice. Teary, shifty and wearily sad was the poignant haunting impression they left with Angelina.

"Okay, Tee-for-trouble, how about donuts and coffee? Seems we have a guardian angel by the name of Ray who, if my nose isn't lying to me, has thoughtfully provided us with morning refreshments."

Chapter Nineteen

"Either I'm hearing voices or there's someone else with you, Angelina. Ray sent me to tell you he has coffee and goodies." Joe appeared from behind a cracked and buckling wall on the far side of the rounded staircase.

"Joe, meet Tee. She's my new friend, and so is this ferocious baby whining in her arms who has no name as yet. Seems like Peewee might suit. Whatcha think?" Angelina laughingly petted the head of an obvious mutt, Terrier being the breed most favored in his scraggly little face.

"Tee, meet Dr. Joe Davidson. Tee has a horrendous cold, and I thought maybe you could help her. I'll gladly cover the cost as she looked after the place for me last night, so I owe her."

Guiding Tee to an area where she'd earlier spotted a mock table set-up, she waved her hand. "Help yourself."

Head on a swivel like a plastic hound dog in a car's back window, Tee seemed shocked by the realization that there were more people in the building she'd considered her sanctuary. She looked first at Joe, then back to Angelina, then at Joe again, then to Ray who now appeared and nodded amicably. Lastly, her glance fell on the food. Angelina heard her stomach growling and listened as the pup all but sobbed with hunger.

Joe spoke to Tee. "I'll be glad to help you, but just so you're aware, I'm not a western Doctor. My specialty is Chinese medicine."

Not too stupid, the youngster obviously understood about acupuncture. "No way, no needles for me," she said, the words muffled by a mouthful of donut.

"I wouldn't have to use needles, Tee. There're other methods to cure your cough and help with the congestion. One is totally non-invasive and will relieve the burning you must be experiencing when you breathe deeply. It's called cupping and it takes very little time. There are also some herbs, which will go a long way towards helping you." Passing a card over with his clinic's address he gave her directions. "I can meet you there in an hour. No charge! You're welcome to come, but it's your call."

"I can drive you over, if my car is still intact," offered Angelina.

"I'll be leaving soon; she can grab a ride with me." Ray suggested.

"It's very close; she can walk from here," confirmed Joe, trying to be helpful. Perturbed by the glares now directed at him from both Ray and Angelina, he shook his head and shut up.

"Ah… thanks." Tee took the proffered card and stuck it in the front pocket of her sack, and then soothed the whining puppy. "I need to take killer here outside. I think he has to go." Snagging a couple of donuts, she bolted.

While the probable runaway was outside occupied with bathroom detail, Angelina whispered to Joe, "We should keep her with us until we can get help for her. I don't believe she's a day over fourteen or fifteen. It's too dangerous for her on the streets."

"I'll call Lee Nivens to help us. He's a social worker; that's his regular line of work. He helps run a shelter for wayward kids and is wonderful with them." Joe's cell phone appeared immediately.

"Funny thing about Tee," Angelina said, looking perplexed and thoughtful. "She seems familiar to me."

"Me, too! It's strange..." Ray's hand cupped his cheek.

"Under all those dirty curls, that tomboyish manner and sarcastic attitude, she's surprisingly pretty." Angelina mused.

"You're right. Seems to me she's like somebody I've seen recently, but I can't place her at the moment. It'll come to me, inevitably in the middle of the night." Joe shook his head and chuckled.

"Must be someone I like, because I had the overwhelming urge to hug her and not to let her get away." Angelina blushed after the she heard her own words. Why did she always blurt out her feelings?

"You're a softie." Joe beamed his approval, until something else clouded his expression. "In case she's bad news, maybe it's better if you don't get too attached. No telling what kind of a kid she is, or what sort of trouble she's in. I don't want you to get hurt. Undoubtedly, we should hand her over to the police." Obviously rethinking his previous support, Joe became protective, bossy, and in big trouble with Angelina.

She shushed him, imagining she heard the door opening. Then she glared her disapproval. Just who does he think he is, warning me like I'm a child?

As they helped themselves to coffee, time passed. After a short while and with still no sign of Tee, Angelina called for her, and then searched the outside of the building, front and back.

The men joined in the hunt, but the girl had vanished. Finally, with Angelina's prompting, Joe contacted Lee, who knew most of the hanging places and hideouts for runaways. Lee made some phone calls on their behalf but had no luck. Apparently, she'd disappeared, which wasn't surprising. Street kids found places where most other people never went. Even with the three of them searching the surrounding neighborhood, it eventually became clear that she'd split.

Inevitably, Angelina gave up and returned to her office in time to meet with Joe and Ray, who was heading home. Her heart felt heavy with recriminations for letting the girl get away. She glanced over at the green-eyed devil and felt anger build over his highhandedness. Just when she'd begun to appreciate him, he'd gone and blown it.

Chapter Twenty

Lee gazed longingly at the sleeping woman. She was silhouetted by the weak light oozing through the panels of vertical blinds that covered the large window to her left. Another huge bouquet of yellow roses with a floating Get Well balloon prettified the scene, their pungent scent fighting with the sour hospital smells and adding even more color to the otherwise bland space. The area was undersized, especially with the floor-to-ceiling curtain wrapped around it.

Coralee looked small and sad, that is until her eyes opened. Vivacity flowed in and she lost her vulnerable appearance. Instantly she became the gutsy girl from last night.

"Hi!" Lee said. His drawl was soft. She took his breath away.

"Hi, yourself."

"I'm looking for Joe." He needed some excuse for being there. Shuffling from foot to foot, he finally leaned on the room's only chair and clutched the knobbed top like a paranoid mother clinging to her child in a crowded store.

A slightly agitated edge to her voice, Coralee answered, "You missed them. Angelina visited, but that was before I fell asleep. Joe left her here and said he would meet up with her later at the office." She stared at the flowers; her confusion obvious.

"These are for you." The hand clutching his gift sprang out in front of him.

"For me? Thank you. Do I know you? You seem very familiar." Her arms reached for his bouquet, and he was forced to move closer. He stumbled over the chair leg and caught himself before he took a header and landed on top of her. Then pretending it was always his intention, he perched his butt on the end of the bed.

"I was with Angelina last night. We came to see you. I sat there on the chair. But it was dark. You probably didn't see me. I'm Lee Nivens." Staccato sentences emphasized his nervousness. He sounded as if he was giving a report.

"Right! Angelina told me about how good you were to her. Thank you. It was a bad time, and I'm glad she had someone there to help."

"Angelina's very brave. She hung in there and looked after Joe last night. I owed her."

"She might be brave, but today is going to be tough, even for her. She's worked like a demon to buy that old building and has spent all her time and every bit of spare change she has fixing it up. I hate having her inspecting the damage without me. I wanted to be there."

Captivated by her caring attitude, he turned his head at an angle. "You're not ready to leave the hospital yet. Look at your face."

"Hey, watch it. Not an intelligent remark to make to a lady who's hurting something terrible, and I might add, in a disgustingly foul mood. Not smart at all."

Slow maybe, but not too stupid, Lee caught on to her teasing tone and grinned, "Sorry."

"Yeah! Me too. Seems I'm a tiny bit cranky this morning. Must be the absence of bagels and cream cheese."

"I can get you some. It would only take a few minutes." Lee feigned a movement as if he meant to jump up.

"You'd do that? Go and get me food?"

Her question stopped him.

"Just say the word."

She chuckled. "That's so cool. I really don't need any, but thanks for the offer." Her tone changed–became less irritated. He saw her good nature creep through the façade of a woman not at her best. Then he saw the sharpness in those same eyes click in and her gaze intensified.

She was closely inspecting him, and that made him nervous. He hoped she didn't remember him sitting with her throughout the night, soothing her troubled sleep. After taking Angelina home, he'd headed right back to her bedside and sweet-talked the nurse into allowing him to stay.

"At first, I couldn't remember you, but I have this strange feeling picking away at me. Were you here alone last night, later, after Angelina left?"

Coralee sensed a familiarity about him. As though he'd been with her in the dark hours. Through the mist of her dreams, he'd soothed her and petted her back to sleep—over and over again. His profile was achingly recognizable, and she thought she remembered at one point reaching up to touch his kind and caring face.

Oversized, his ears were red-tipped, and she would swear in later years they'd wriggled like those of an excited puppy. She fell for them long before becoming infatuated with the man they were attached to.

He shot to his feet, and her eyes traveled a long way up his thin, wiry frame before resting on his soft gray eyes, which were enhanced by the color of his dusky blonde, naturally curly hair. He had large gentle hands and a nice aura surrounding him. Nice was good, she decided. I like nice.

Cheekily, she reached out her hand, forcing compliance, and said, "I'm very happy to meet you, Lee Nivens."

He bowed as he shook her hand, treating it like that of a lady, not like some men who had a need to flex and maul with intimidation, as if to validate their masculinity.

She clung to his strength, loving the feeling of another person's skin next to hers. She pulled, forcing him to sit closer to her, so she could watch his expression.

Her loneliness disintegrated.

Nervous and needing to talk, Lee began. "I volunteer with Joe. We usually pull the same shifts at the Search and Rescue, and I like that. He's good to work with. My regular job is counseling kids though. I'm a social worker, and I run one of the shelters here in the city."

He seemed stressed, and she noticed his hand trembled in hers.

"Do you like kids?" She held her breath.

"They're my life. It's what I do, helping kids in trouble. The work is hugely rewarding." Taking a chance on sounding corny, he continued, "I don't even consider it work, it's more a privilege. Joe feels the same and helps us out a lot at the shelter. The kids get off on him. He has the knack of making them trust him."

"I bet they like you as much. Is your first name really Lee? I've never heard a man called that before."

"It's actually Rylie, an old Irish name, but I've always gone by Lee."

"It's strange. Our first names are so close. Mine is Coralee and yours is Rylie. Maybe it's an omen."

"Makes it easier to name our firstborn," he shot back.

His temerity shocked her until she saw him swallow. But he smiled shyly and stared right at her. One of her eyes was still swollen and half-closed, but with the good one she gave him an audacious wink. He was daring her to play with him and little did he know that she majored in playing.

"How many children are we going to have?"

"Oh, three or four would about do it."

"To start with."

"Sold," he returned, beaming.

Bingo! Here was her man. She knew it as well as she knew her real name wasn't Coralee.

Laughing, he made his way closer. She cleared a space for him by moving her feet and reaching down to shift the rolling bed table. But she'd moved too quickly and was rewarded with dizziness. It left her blinking and grabbing for something stable. Hard and muscular, but also gentle, his hand reached out and became her support.

"Something's not right with me, Lee. I feel nauseous when I move, and my body has no strength. Could it be from the concussion?"

"Of course. Your head took one heck of a hit. It'll take a few days before those symptoms disappear."

"Dammit to hell and back! I can't stay in here that long. Angelina needs all the help she can get right now, and she relies on me."

"Don't worry. She won't be alone. Joe and I will help her. Right now, it's best for you to concentrate on getting your strength back."

"But she's always been there for me, and now when she needs me, I can't do anything." Coralee's hands pummeled the blanket, obvious frustration in her tone. "You don't understand. It's huge for me to be able to help her."

"Why? Why is it so important?"

"I'm indebted to her. Years ago, when Angelina was first starting out, she visited the real estate office where I was an overworked, bullied, and underpaid secretary. She was the vision of a gracious, classy businesswoman. Long after, I found out it had taken her humongous hours to strike that look but she wore it so naturally, I just assumed it was who she was."

Lee passed her the nearby glass of water when her voice broke. She took a sip and fell back against the pillows.

"My boss was a – a chubby bullshitter whose brain, I suspect, was formed into the shape of a woman's privates, since every off-color joke he told was linked in some way to that very area. To him, women were only good for one thing. What a slimebucket! I was sick to death of the toad. In fact, I was actively searching for another job. I mean, don't get me wrong here, I like men and their hands, but I couldn't convince that thick-headed waste of space it was his particular hands which were the hang-up. The day Angelina arrived; I'd had enough. Screw the roof over my head, the savings account, and the reference I would need to get another job. Him, I wouldn't screw, which of course was the problem. Anyway, Angelina watched him come over to my desk and, in plain sight, maneuver his knuckles over the side of my breast while he leaned over to get the day's new listings. The dirty slob copped a feel right in front of her. It was the last grope he made for a while, let me tell you. Angelina spotted his antics and must have seen my disgust. She picked up the metal ruler off his desk and before anyone could move, she whapped him over the knuckles, not once but two or three times. The stunned idiot's mouth hung open, and he didn't have the brainpower to multitask—move his hand and close his mouth at the same time."

Lee laughed, his face showing interest and humor.

Coralee drank a bit more water and continued. "Señor," she said in the iciest voice I've ever heard. "I wouldn't hire you if you were the last real estate agent in this city. I was dumbfounded, and on the verge of laughing out loud. Then she looked at me. Are you a good worker?

she asked. Before I could answer, the toad spat out that I was lazy and good for nothing, and for his audacity she whacked him again right across his protruding fat gut. I lost it! Laughed and I told her, 'I'm a great worker.' She smiled and hired me on the spot. Man, I couldn't get out of there fast enough, but I have to admit to grabbing the ruler from her and getting a few whacks in myself, and with foresight, I also grabbed the morning sheets of the new listings. Her building was on the first page. Cool story, eh?"

He was enthralled but she seemed shy about holding the floor for so long. Then, like all savvy women, she turned the tables on him.

Chapter Twenty-one

Coralee started in on her questions. "Tell me something about yourself. Are you seeing anyone? Do your parents live close by? Do you have any brothers or sisters? Are you seeing anyone?"

His spontaneous laughter filled the empty space in her heart with joy. He went along with her silliness. "My parents live in Miami for most of the year. No, I'm not seeing anyone. I'm an only child, which was great in some ways, and not so great in others. I got all their attention. That was great. But they were both workaholics. That was the not so great. Spent a lot of time by myself. No, I'm not seeing anyone. As soon as I was old enough, I joined the Search and Rescue. Since then, I've met a lot of caring people—guys like Joe. He's one of the best. Like me, he spends most of his spare time with young people, encouraging them, helping them make good choices. He's a hard worker and a great guy. Nope, not seeing anyone I care about right now."

Other than playing along with her, she noticed he spent little time talking about himself and how quickly he changed the topic of conversation to his friend. "Is he good enough for our Angelina?"

"You mean in a serious relationship? Undeniably they'd make an awesome twosome, except Joe has a hang-up about lasting relationships."

Oh, oh! This didn't sound good to Coralee. "What do you mean?"

"He doesn't have any! Won't get involved past the first phase. Never wants to get married."

"Hmm, I'm kinda getting nervous here. Angelina's weird about men. She's ridiculously shy; not a man-hater or anything like that, but she's focused entirely on winning a bet she made with her father about establishing her own accounting business. I guess you could call her a workaholic, an ambitious woman with a goal."

Lee's head twisted to the side, like that of an inquisitive child trying to figure out what the flood of words meant.

"Sorry, I'm thinking out loud. You'll get used to it."

"I'm sure I will. Why are you so worried about Angelina?"

"It's Joe I'm worried about. The little I saw of him today; he came across as a heartbreaker; dangerous and with a subtle deviousness in his makeup."

"If you mean, do the women like him, then yeah, they do—lots of them. But he has this thing about getting serious. Something to do with his five older brothers who are all married. Hitched to misery, or so he's always telling me."

"Is that how you feel?" Coralee decided it was time to bring the conversation back to the important subject.

"No! Of course not. My parents might not have been around that much, but there's no doubt they love each other, and have a good marriage. I think my birth was just a mistake and never supposed to have happened."

"I, for one, am glad they screwed up. And I mean that literally." The gleam in her eye ignited a twinkle in his.

He leaned towards her, looked closely and saw her unhealthy pallor. Her tired lashes were fighting a losing battle.

"Hey, doll, you need your beauty sleep, no slight intended," he grinned. "I'll be back later." Leaning over he gently kissed her forehead. Her eyes gave up the battle and she became immersed in a wonderful, healing sleep. Her dreams were full of a soft-eyed man with unique ears.

Two bagels and cream cheese on a tray, wrapped in cellophane, with a red rose nestled to the side, lay waiting when she woke up.

Chapter Twenty-two

"Angelina, I'm sorry if the kid overhead what I said. Trust me, I'm not usually so insensitive around teens, but then again, she shouldn't have been snooping." Joe felt justified in his explanation. After all, he'd only been trying to protect her.

Face, angled to the side and wearing a peevish scowl, she had him backing up his thought processes. This time, the words passed through his brain. Shit!

"Okay, you're right. She's a kid on the run. I should have known to be careful. It's just that you're susceptible right now and I didn't want to see anything more happen to you."

"I can look after myself. I wish everyone would trust me, instead of trying to take care of me." Angelina wasn't backing down. He got that. He just didn't like it that he was in trouble for caring.

"Right! Got it!" He held up his hands protectively in front him, which made her relax and even coaxed a smile.

"I had a feeling about her, Joe. I'm sorry she left. I truly wanted to help her."

"Maybe she'll come back. I'll keep my eyes open for her in case she takes me up on my offer to treat her. In the meantime, you mentioned your car earlier. Do you want to look and see if we can salvage it from the lot in the back?" I need to get away from her. She's addictive.

"I completely forgot about that, what with everything else going on. Thanks, Joe. I'd appreciate your help, especially since I seem to be holding you up."

She's too intuitive; I'll have to be more subtle. "Not at all. I just thought I'd check the clinic and see if your Tee might be waiting."

That brought another smile. "Good idea."

Together, they went outside to where the destruction in the back had them both groaning. There were piles of debris everywhere and pools of dirty water to step over. As they approached the end of the lot, Angelina saw her car. It was the only one left in the rubble, as the others had been cleared away, probably the night before. Her habit of parking the furthest from the building, in order to allow others to get in closer, might have been her saving grace

Stepping over puddles and piles of rubbish, they approached the vehicle. Quickly, he verified that, other than needing a cleaning, the hood seemed to be intact.

"Joe, she looks pretty good. What do you think?"

"She? Your car's a female?" he teased.

Angelina held out one hand and pointed to one finger at a time as she counted off. "She always goes where I want her to go–no arguments. She looks good and purrs like a kitten. She always runs efficiently. She waits for me—"

"Enough! I get it."

Her giggles were infectious and, before he knew it, he joined in the merriment. God, she was beautiful. Laughter lit her face and showed off dimples that he'd love to kiss. The sun shone on her hair, turning its black to a shining mass of ebony. Her braids added an innocence to her features that in some strange way had him questioning his own common sense. After all, how many women today weren't as sexually active as men? Not very many! None he'd been fortunate enough to meet. But, from the first time he'd met Angelina, he'd sworn she lacked experience.

Abruptly, he turned and rushed to get to the car, clearing the mess from the wheels. I need to stay away from her.

Without looking into her face, he turned in her direction and held out his hand. "Do you have a key?"

As she searched her bag, he stifled the grin and instead sighed and feigned a bored expression. It caused a shrug and another self-conscious giggle that turned his insides to pure mush. Her laugh wasn't at all annoying, just the opposite.

"They're here somewhere." Angelina hefted the large carryall onto the hood, and began shifting through all the paraphernalia inside, lifting out five or six large objects to be able to see into the bottom. Finally, an exclamation of success proceeded her flinging the keys into his waiting palm.

Joe unlocked the car and slid in behind the wheel. When he turned the key in the ignition, it didn't exactly purr, but after a few tries, the engine started. Muttering, he began to ease the gearshift into reverse.

At the same time Angelina, who'd moved out of the way, bent over to retrieve some of the objects which had fallen from her purse. The outline of her tantalizing derriere captivated him and his foot came down harder than he'd intended. The little car responded abruptly, careening backward.

Chapter Twenty-three

It missed a telephone pole with only inches to spare.

The screech of hastily applied brakes caught Angelina's attention. First, she spotted how close the pole was situated to the side of her Mustang and shuddered. Then, for some strange reason, she glanced upwards.

Leaning at an odd angle, the post had one line haphazardly draped over another twisted cable, which was still attached but just barely. Both clung by a whisper and a prayer, as her Grandma Evie was heard to say, and Angelina wasn't taking any chances. In a soothing voice, she cajoled the shaken, red-faced man swatting angrily at the wheel.

"Joe, stay still."

"I'm sorry, Angelina. I can't believe I just did that. I'm a good driver, never had any accidents." Until I met you. "Now, all of a sudden, I'm a walking disaster, or should I say a driving disaster." He reached to open the driver's door, but her shrill voice stopped him.

"For God's sake, don't move, Joe. I mean it this time. Stop and look up."

"Look up? What? You want me to thank God for missing the pole?" He joked until he saw the scowl on her face wasn't nearly covering the fear.

"Madre de Dios, listen to me." This time, the strident yell caught his attention. "Don't move at all. The cable above your head is barely clinging to another. I have no idea if it is a live wire or not. If you move, it could come down and hit you, or drop into the water and kill me." She knew that would get his attention.

Voice full of authority, Joe resumed command. "Don't pan...."

"Basta!"

His index finger pointed in her direction. "I won't move, but you—you back away, slowly. Get to safety. I've got my cell phone and I'll call for backup. They'll be here in a few minutes. You're right about us not knowing if the wire is live, and after what happened last night, we can't take any chances."

Expecting her to follow his instructions, he slowly reached into his shirt pocket for his phone and, like the professional he was, began issuing orders and giving instructions. When he'd finished and saw her still standing there, he bellowed, "If you don't move that pretty little ass of yours, I'll get out of this blasted car and move it for you. You hear me, Angelina?"

Recognizing a time where stubbornness could be detrimental to one's health, his and hers, she moved her pretty little ass.

Chapter Twenty-four

In no time at all, the Fire Dept. along with a Search and Rescue vehicle pulled up, and the trained volunteers followed Joe's every suggestion. They contained the danger, freed him, and soon had Angelina's car parked in front of the building.

"Quick thinking, Joe! That wire was live and could have created a whole lot of damage. It's a good thing you noticed it and called us." Treating Joe with respect, the older man placed an arm over the younger but taller man's shoulders. "Would hate to see you charbroiled, son. You coming back to the office?"

"I'll be there soon as I see that Angelina gets home safely."

Two of the fellows called goodbye, and one called out ciao, as they piled into the truck. Waving, they drove off, this time with their lights dull and the siren silent.

Joe approached her warily. "I'll see you home, Angelina. I think your car is fine to drive, but it's still not running smoothly. After you saved me—again, it's the least I can do."

"Joe, please don't take this the wrong way. But I think I'd rather take my chances and drive the Mustang home myself. My plans are for a car-cleaning, car-washing evening. I couldn't stand any more of your kind of excitement today. But I do thank you." Her soft expression took any sting from her words, as did her reaching fingers, which fleetingly brushed over his clenched hand.

"I guess I can't blame you, sweetheart. It's been pretty hectic. But I promise you this isn't the norm for me either. I'll be seeing you soon. Take care."

Angelina didn't know whether to be glad or sad to see the tall man walking in the other direction. Her eyes never left his swaggering hips, moving with a rhythm that had a person wondering if he could hear music no one else could. Grimacing, shaking her head from side to side, she sent another thought winging upwards. *Dios, you know my schedule, right? So... why now?*

Chapter Twenty-five

"I feel like I'm on an emotional roller coaster. I need to get back to work," Coralee whined, sounding like a manipulative juvenile. "My brain is atrophying from lack of use. I'm gaining weight with hospital food being my main source of nutrition, and that's just plain scary. Okay! The chocolate everyone generously contributes isn't helping either. Plus, I'm lonesome away from you guys; talking about it makes me weepy. And maudlin women are pathetic." She sniffed and mopped at her leaking lashes, then blew her nose loudly.

When Angelina had appeared, Coralee had been crunching oodles of notepad paper into crinkled missiles and hurling them into the corner garbage can. Evidence her aim was way off was the amount of littered pages scattered all over the nearby floor.

It was three days after the earthquake, and Coralee was a basket case. She sensed Angelina's patience was rapidly deteriorating. Understanding that her crabbiness was due now to pure terror—that she'd been wrong, yet again, about another man—had her acting opposite her normal self. But this time if she'd made yet another mistake; her heart would take a real shit-kicking.

Sulking, she self-analyzed out loud. "That he's attracted to me is a plausible concept? Right?" Even she heard her disbelief but forged on bravely. "If he cared, truly cared, he'd have called me today. Wouldn't he?" She sank into silence but Angelina, who knew her mind was like a revolving door, sat near her quietly and waited.

It was pitiful to be this distrustful, and so transparently needy. If she and Lee had had a history, Coralee would know what to expect. But they'd only met a matter of days ago. How could she be sure what he felt was real?

All the circumstances surrounding their meeting were clearly "unreal," and for that reason, it was hard to accept the miracle of his caring. Add to the fact she'd never looked worse in her life—and her experience of healthy commitment was nil—left her feeling vulnerable. She admitted most of her so-called beauty came from makeup, plus oodles of creams, dieting and meticulous nit-picking at her image. That the end product turned out pretty well only proved what miracles one could do with some help. Only Lee had never seen her at her best, and if he saw past the bruises, the scars, and her pathetic fear, then the result could be mind-boggling.

Notorious for having had numerous crushes, way too many pointless dates and meaningless hollow love affairs which had turned out badly, she was terrified that once again, she'd misread the signs. Comparing those previous feelings to what Lee aroused in her brought reality home dramatically. For her, this time, it was the real deal.

Hell, she pined for him and constantly ached for him to call. Hearing his voice made everything right in her world. Dammit, why didn't the bum call?

"Oh, Angelina, I'm scared. What if I'm exaggerating the moments we spent together, imagining his feelings were genuine, and not just my sappy imagination? We both know it wouldn't be the first time." Coralee had confided to Angelina about her romantic interlude with Lee.

"Now you stop it, querida. He's smitten. Crazy for you, like you are for him. When I talked to him, he asked me so many questions about you, I teased him, asking if he was a cop. He laughed and apologized, said he needed to learn everything he could. He didn't say he wanted to, but that he needed to! Do those words sound like a guy who's not interested?"

Glowing, Coralee muttered, "I guess not. He didn't come last night, though he said he would. And I didn't hear from him again today."

"Don't worry; he'll be here to see you as soon as he's able. You know he gets called out on Search and Rescue missions, and he doesn't always have the time to contact you when those calls happen. Now relax and tell me what the doctors are saying. Your bruises are healing, but your overall color is still not good."

"Seems the tests they've been performing have shown a problem with my heart. Now don't get that goofy look—I'm fine." However, grabbing Angelina's hand she clung.

Angelina's eyes ignited. "I'm not gullible, so don't place me in that role. Of course, I'm worried. Tell me what tests have been done, and why didn't you say anything about this before? I would have been here with you."

"You have enough on your plate right now. Until they gave me the results from the electrocardiogram and the lab tests, I didn't know myself. The cardiologist just told me a little while ago."

Seeing Angelina pale with fear, Coralee, now contrite, reassured her comfortingly, "Don't look so panicky, Angelina. It's really not bad news. I was only advised this afternoon, and I wanted to wait to tell you in person." Sheepishly she grinned. "I sorta forgot. Guess Lee is first on my mind. Anyway, no biggie! They'll soon be performing coronary angioplasty surgery with some kind of a balloon, a stent—whatever that is—will be inserted somewhere in there." She pointed offhandedly towards her chest. "It'll open up some thinga-majiggie—"

Pale and shaken, Angelina began trembling, her hands waving frantically. A torrent of Spanish continued until Coralee took control.

"Shush, it's okay. I don't understand what it's all about, but they've frankly assured me, it's not considered risky. Unless I don't have the procedure. That could be dangerous. The anesthesiologist is coming early in the morning to brief me. Seems this old ticker of mine has been acting up now and again for a short while. My interpretation for the burning sensations was heartburn. The palpitations I explained away by thinking I was moving too fast or standing up too quickly. The pain I put down to doing too many sit-ups, exercising too hard. What can I say? I'm an idiot! The doc calls it percutaneous coronary intervention."

"Oh, Coralee, I'm awfully sorry. It's probably the stress from working all those hours at the office. We've been busy lately and you've put in scads of overtime."

"Now cut it out. It has nothing to do with the stress from work. If anything's to blame, it's gotta be the stress from the lack of mind-blowing nooky," Coralee deadpanned.

Predictably cracking up, exactly as Coralee intended, relaxed Angelina. "When will they operate?"

"Tomorrow morning. It seems they consider it necessary before I leave here, and since I've been such a pain in the ass, I guess they can't wait to see that exact part of my anatomy walk out the door. My doctor, Gail Robbins, is a wonderfully understanding woman, and has assured me it's not such a long or intricate operation, In fact, I can be released soon after. I can't drive for a while, but as long as I don't overdo it, I can be back at work in no time. It's the only bright star on my horizon right now. If Lee would call, then my whole galaxy would explode."

Angelina broke in. "I'm glad you two have hit it off so well. If it matters to you at all, I like him. He's been wonderful trying to help me find Tee, the homeless girl I told you about who I found hiding in the office. He's called to all the most likely places and has even checked at the police station with her statistics for possible identification, maybe as a missing person. But so far he's hasn't found anything. It's hard when we don't know her name, and only an approximate age and a description. I'll keep asking and praying for a miracle."

"Tell me more about this Tee girl. You've told me how you found her, but what was it about her that drew you in so deeply? I know you care about people like her who are homeless and live on the streets. I've seen you stop and talk to them and give them money. But you're positively obsessed with her for some reason. Why?"

"I can't easily explain it, except to say she reminds me of someone. When I looked at her, she seemed so darn familiar, and frankly, as foolish as this sounds, I had the overwhelming urge to take her home and keep her like a stray kitten or the puppy that was with her. In hindsight, I wish I had been more welcoming. She was desperate, and sickly, and so very young."

"Don't get your heart too involved, Ange. Be careful! Okay? I'll pray too, I promise. Maybe the power of two will do the trick."

Just then, a shrill ring made Coralee dive for her nearby cellphone.

***

At that exact moment, downtown, a bedraggled young figure, cradling a wiggling bundle could be seen huddled, crouching near the back door of a partially destroyed building.

Chapter Twenty-six

Intently, Ray preached the usual sermon to Angelina, his accent coming through strongly because of the depth of his concern.

"There was a degenerate wanderin' around here earlier, Angie, one of your strays. They come in dumb waves. Every time I turn around, another one is at the door, looking for handouts. Cara mia, you've got to stop donating, especially here at the office. I know it's only toonies you give for coffee and a muffin 'cause you're a softie, but these people are getting too pushy. They strut right into the place, cocky as all get out. Maybe you should back off, huh? Some of these characters, they're so far gone, they could be dangerous wackos." In his zeal to get his message across, Ray's arms were waving with every word, and his final gesture of circling his finger around his ears had her all but breaking up.

"You've made your point, Ray. I'll try, but it's tricky for me to refuse. I feel so fortunate in my life that it's hard to say no to a human being who is hungry and wretched. But I'll try. I promise."

"Speaking of hungry characters, any sign of your bambina from the other day? Her name, it was actually Tee?"

"I doubt it. She told me it was Tee... short for trouble."

"Get outta here!" Ray's grin was infectious.

"Serious! I liked her, amigo, and I'm worried about her. She was sick—had a terrible cough. I've been keeping my eyes open, but so far no luck. Do you think I should have called the police?"

"She'd not thank you for it."

"That's what Lee said when he called today. Joe asked him to put the word out on the street, and to keep his eyes and ears open. Since he's a social worker, an administrator at the center, and a counsellor for street kids, under these circumstances, he was the perfect person to go to for help. Unless she's in trouble, he's promised to keep things to himself. In the meantime, my belief is that she's simply an unhappy runaway with nowhere to go. And it frightens me to death."

"All your problems—you need more? Angelina, let it go. She donna wanna be found, especially if the police are looking for her, or if she thinks you'll call them. Most runaways take off 'cause they can't stay in the abusive environment they're living in. And they sure as heck don't wanna go back."

Angelina nodded; sadness etched over her face. "You're probably right, Ray. The poor girl acted tough, but I got the feeling all she wanted to do was hide."

The older Italian carpenter patted her cheek, his touch tender. "Lookie here now... I got good news to cheer you up. The crown moulding we ordered six weeks ago has arrived and we can pick it up tomorrow. The painters, they are lined up, and my own guys are all ready, willing, and waiting for the go-ahead. Your ladies—they did one hell-of-a job helping with the cleanup, so... we're all set to start the refinishing, probably sometime in the morning."

"For the main floor? Can you have it repainted and ready for early next week? I have all the new furniture and computers arriving on Friday and I'd love to start back up next week. What do you think?"

"No problem, Bella. I'm sure Johnnie will be a big help since he'll be back in a few days. We can use the extra hands and we'll put him to work."

"Don't fool with me, Ray. Are you serious?"

"You betcha, Cara."

"Ti voglio bene, Signor." Using his mother tongue earned her a beaming smile. In turn, she wrapped joyful arms around his neck and kissed his cheeks, both sides.

Happy again, she wandered through the first floor. While she and her workers had been cleaning over the weekend, Ray and his crew had been dry walling, patching and in some cases repainting the offices. The molding around the windows was almost ready, and the plywood boards would be coming off the broken panes as soon as delivery of the previously ordered stain-glass windows came about. It would be good to see daylight bring the place to life rather than the bare hanging bulbs scattered everywhere.

"Hey! Cut that out," Ray scolded when he rejoined her. "You wanna get me started? My boys—they say I'm amotionally unstable. Big words they use, showing off for their old man. What do I know? You cry? I'ma gonna cry too."

His words, along with his arm-waving antics and comic expressions, were too much for her. She giggled. "I don't know what I would do without you and your boys. How can I ever repay you for looking after me so well, dealing with all the extras, the paperwork with the district, ordering all the supplies, and for getting the work permits and well... for everything?"

"Aha! Wait till you see the bill, Señorita." He cut her off, lowering one bushy eyebrow comically to cover the twinkle. "Now, go visit Coralee and tell her to quit callin' here alla time. She's-a drivin me nutzo!" With that final comment, his hand flicked up to his forehead and then further upwards, his favorite mannerism.

Blowing a kiss, she turned and went to pick up her overloaded purse that she'd left hidden behind the stairs where she'd found Tee and the stray. Her stomach clenched as a well of sadness battled with her earlier joy. How could she be happy wondering if that poor, sick child wandered out there on the streets with nowhere to go? Cold, wet nights and rainy days, the island's normal weather for this time of the year; Angelina hoped that Tee had found a safe place to stay away from the nasty elements. If only she had gone to see Joe.

Just thinking his name brought a strong reaction. Anger surfaced because of the way he seemed to have dumped her. The fact that tears clogged her throat just made her swing her bag so hard; it all but knocked her off her feet.

Chapter Twenty-seven

Coralee was regaining her old drive and blossoming under Lee's attentiveness. Seems Angelina had hit the nail on the head when she'd surmised only emergencies would keep him away from the hospital and her friend.

Then there was more good news: Johnnie had returned early in order to help out at the office. One would find him either manually working with Ray—up close and personal with a paintbrush—or at his desk, ready to take on his accounts.

Days had passed since anyone but Lee had seen Joe. The missing jerk had called to inquire about how things were working out, but that had only left Angelina wanting more. Impersonal and brisk, his tone had hurt her feelings. After all they'd gone through together, shouldn't they have gotten past the insecurity of strangers?

Being as he lived in her thoughts constantly, either getting silently berated for not returning, or hungered after so she could experience the same tingling his presence evoked, Angelina was either up or down.

And she was sick and tired of it. Working like a demon to exorcise him didn't really help. Throughout her daily routine, she carried him with her—from home to office, from office to hospital, and then back to the office where she stayed to work until the grit in her eyes made focusing impossible.

Unshakable, the man invaded her mind with X-rated fantasies and strange yearnings. Annoyed she berated herself repeatedly. *All I am to him is another accident victim. One that ended up rescuing him three times in less than twenty-four hours! No wonder he'd written her off.* Damn, but she couldn't help but wish that he was suffering too.

Chapter Twenty-eight

Joe yearned for her. He couldn't sleep, food had no flavor, and nothing seemed to be any fun. He even tried to convince himself the only reason his mind invariably turned to Angel was because of the turmoil going on in her life. After all, the poor girl was alone, with no family around to take care of her.

Aware that the aftermath of fear frequently caught up with survivors days after a disaster, he hungered to be with her, to help her combat the unpleasantness. Throughout the following days and nights, he spent way too much time brooding over her aloneness. Worse—brooding over his loneliness.

She'd become an obsession. Instinctively, he sensed he should stay away from the lovely little witch. Mainly because he ached for her, craved to see and be near her—to have her. A girl, who by no stretch of the imagination could be called a one-night stand, she was a "forever" woman. Not his type at all.

During the times he'd weaken, he'd remind himself about her gambling habit. No way could he deal with an obsession like hers. It scared him silly just to think about what his brother had gone through: the collection agencies hounding him constantly, the humiliation at the checkout when they rejected his credit cards, the turmoil their children suffered, and, most of all, the perpetual lying.

Best to cut off this crazy infatuation right now, keep himself occupied and his mind on something else. And the way the world often worked; the universe granted his wish.

There was an unusually heavy workload in his medical clinic where he only worked mornings. Plus, two emergency callouts with his Search and Rescue unit.

A typical Sunday family barbecue helped pass one day. His mother sat across from his father at the end of the table closest to the kitchen and began passing bowlfuls of steaming broccoli, carrots, and potatoes, while his father carved the huge roast. The odor from the dinner wrought memories of many others just like it.

"I read in the Times Colonist that the earthquake's damage was centralized in the city, and that a lot of business owners are in financial ruins."

When she looked his way, Joe knew his mother had specifically directed the question to him. He answered, "Many people don't choose to pay for earthquake insurance and now they're suffering. It's quite a mess along Pandora, Fort and Johnston. On some of the other streets the damage is more sporadic."

"I have no doubt you were called in to help." His father passed him the gravy and he poured a good bit over his mound of potatoes and meat before answering. The smells of succulent beef cooked just the way he liked it had his stomach grumbling in joy.

"Uh-huh. Lee and I helped a businesswoman on Fort Street: Angelina Serrano. Her accounting firm took a major hit. She lost a lot of her third floor and was trapped there for hours. In the end, I had to go in and get her out."

His brother, Cody, the worst tease of them all, piped up. "Hey, I've met that broad. She's a real looker, South American if I remember correctly. She deals at the same bank where I drop off the deposits."

Stiffening, Joe nodded. "Yeah, I think she's from Chile."

Cody, ignoring the warning signs, kept picking. "Man, I'd sure like to have been a fly on the wall when you got to her. You hard-headed lug, I bet you were floored. I'm telling you guys, she's hot. I'm talking movie-star material."

"Shut up, Cody. You're just yammering because Sara's at work tonight and isn't here to control your mouth. Angelina's pretty, sure, but the poor girl suffered horribly. She's claustrophobic and ended up trapped for hours in the dark. She went through hell before I got to her."

"Oh, I bet you got to her alright."

"That's enough, Cody. And before the rest of you decide to jump in, I have to warn you that I baked some apple pies for dessert that might not be served if this conversation continues." Vera, Joe's mother, knew exactly how to control her men. Silence fell over the table as the boys swallowed their remarks and bit their tongues.

But too little too late! Now Joe was pissed. Cody's incessant teasing about any female he mentioned, goading him, marrying him off, hit a sore spot, and he knew it.

Thank God for Vera... she was one tough mother. Six sons brought up by the smart woman, who with a few well-chosen words, and a scanning scowl, returned manners back to naughty boys; she was his favorite person on the planet. Too bad she couldn't rein in their irrepressible wives as easily.

Joe's cellphone vibrated and saved him from having to put up with more of the bullshit. Excusing himself from the table, he went into the den to answer it in privacy. Hysteria in the voice on the other end alerted him. Something bad was going down.

"Joe, thank God! Please come to the house as quickly as you can. It's me, Peg Hinton. Louie, my five-year-old, started the van and backed it over a cliff. It's barely hanging there. I can't get him out. Please bring Lee and the equipment, and for God's sake, HURRY! " Her voice rose with each sentence, screaming the last word.

Peg had worked almost exclusively with Lee and Joe when she was with the team. That was before marriage, kids, and acres of garden property, surrounding a large ramshackle house, had plunged her into overload. Something had to give. Rightly, it was the volunteering for the Search and Rescue. But she missed working with the guys, and, periodically, they kept in touch.

"Calm down, girl! Stay with the kid and keep him steady. You know what to do. You hear me, Peg?"

Shakily, she answered, "Please hurry, Joe! God, please!"

The terror in her voice had the hairs on his body standing straight up, and his legs running as he called out, " Sorry, Mom, it's an emergency. Gotta go." His family was used to this over the years, and his mom already had a container of dinner ready for him to snatch on his way out. A quick kiss and a wave to the others, and he effectively changed from son and brother to a crisis professional.

He called Lee. "Where are you?"

"I'm at Angelina's helping her paint. Just her and me left. Johnnie took Coralee home. What's up?"

"Meet me at the rescue vehicle and make sure it's ready to ride. I'm at my parents, so you'll get there first. We have a problem at Peg Hinton's with her little boy, and it sounds serious. She's upset, but she's trained and will help. Call the ambulance and a backup unit to be on stand-by, just in case."

"You got it, Joe. See you there in five."

When Joe pulled up to the unit, he couldn't believe his eyes. Angelina, wearing a volunteer jacket, perched near Lee in the front seat of the truck.

Joe motioned Lee to come and talk to him. "Are you crazy, man? We have an emergency here. Why did you bring Angelina into this?" His voice radiated anger, but his impulse to protect her from any unpleasantness was the main cause.

"She wanted to help out with Peg, keep her calm and give her an arm to cling to. From the way you acted, I figured Peg's husband must be on the road."

Looking into Angelina's determined face, Joe had to agree with Lee. She could be helpful with Peg and the other kids.

Mutinous, her huge eyes dared him to send her home.

"Fine, let's go."

Chapter Twenty-nine

Miraculously, just a few minutes later, Joe, Lee and Angelina arrived at the scene to find Peg's training had kicked in. Joe realized she'd started setting up for the rescue by clearing the area. Good!

With dire threats of punishment, she'd ordered her other two kids to stay on the veranda. Her husband, Glen, a long-haul trucker, was on the road and not expected back until the next day, so the poor woman was coping alone.

"I can't believe this is happening," she moaned. Grass and dirt stained her shirt and pants, while copious tears ran unchecked down her cheeks. "When I went back to get the twins, I only left him alone for a few seconds. The little devil always fights to get into his car seat by himself. So I opened the door to let him inside and forgot I'd left the key in the ignition."

The wail which finished off her sentence had Angelina moving in, arms ready to embrace. The thankful glances sent her way by Lee and

Joe made her realize that they didn't have the time to deal with the mother's hysterics and she was needed for this precise reason.

Peg, getting control of herself, scurried alongside the men and prattled on. "Oh, God. I'm so thankful you're here. I made him promise to stay quiet, but without someone there talking to him, he could get antsy and move around." Without realizing, her hand clutched Angelina's and she dragged her along too.

Using the powerful flashlight, Joe and Lee strode to the edge of the cliff, where the crushed fence now lay in pieces, and looked over. It was a deadly, zigzag course going downward, ending in a rocky creek bed.

By what he could see in the darkness, Joe figured the total drop could be close to eighty, maybe even as much as a hundred feet of shrubs and blackberry brush, sporadically interspersed with thin young alders and cedars. The vehicle had come to a stop with its back wheels balanced precariously on a rocky outcrop. The front wheels facing them looked to be airborne.

Jesus! It was bad. The ground could give away at any moment. They had no time to lose.

Whimpering noises from nearby would have broken a heart harder than Joe's and had him taking a few seconds to reassure Louie's guilt-ridden mommy. "Be brave, Peg. He's a smart little boy and we'll get him out. I want you to stay with Angelina, and the twins. She's here to help you. Lee and I have got this covered."

Joe knew that no matter how trained a person might be, when it was a life and death situation involving their own child, they weren't reliable. They'd need to rescue Louie without Peg there next to them, getting in their way.

Thankfully, Joe and Lee worked so well together that a strategy session wasn't necessary. They separated, making their way down to the van. Joe called out to Lee to grab the front grill and put his full weight onto that area. Because his hundred and seventy-five pounds could help stabilize the vehicle, it might just give them the edge they'd need.

Joe quickly worked his way to the back window where he could barely make out the silhouette of the boy's head. The glow from his flashlight illuminated the tear-stained cheeks of a five-year-old, his huge eyes filled with terror.

The older van, engine still running, was perilously wedged on the cusp of the cliff and the slightest mistake could make the entire weight shift, allowing it to swing over.

Softly, Joe called to the boy, his voice calm. "Hi, Louie! Okay, little man, Lee and I are here to get you out. But for now, I want you to stay right where you are until I say to move. Got it?" Joe's voice was mesmerizing, reassuring, keeping the child quiet and focused.

"Okay, Joe. I won't move. I promise."

"Not even your nose or your nose hairs."

"I don't have nose hairs."

"You will when you're my age. You have to pluck them, or they get in your food." Joe checked under the car to see if there was one side more stable than the other.

"Gross! My dad doesn't have them."

"I guess I'm just lucky. Attaboy, Louie, keep still. I'm almost ready."

"I wanna get out now, Joe. I don't like it here anymore." The wavering voice let Joe know that the child was barely holding it together.

"Right, let's get you out! Do you know where the button is to open the window?"

"I'm not 'lowed to touch that button. Mommy will be mad."

"No, she won't, because I'm giving you permission. I want you to slowly move your hand and push it down. Don't let go. Open the window all the way. Great! Attaboy!"

"Can I get out now, Joe?"

"Hey, look at the front of the car. You see Lee there, holding it steady? You're fine, big boy. He won't let anything happen to you, right?"

"R-righ-right!" Crouching with his hands covering his face, Louie peeked through his fingers.

"See. Lee's like Superman. He'll keep the car from going anywhere. Everything's fine, sport. Just remember to move real slow. Now... slide over to this window where I'm waiting. Don't move too fast."

Joe, as close to the side of the vehicle as he could safely get, anticipated diving into the unstable car to grab the boy and yank him out at the first sign of trouble.

"When I reach in, let me lift you out. Understand? Don't try to help. I'll carry you. Yes?"

"Yes-s."

Joe, careful not to touch or put weight on the vehicle in any way, leaned in to grip the little boy's body.

At that precise moment, he heard a horrific crack, and the car began to shift.

Chapter Thirty

With only seconds left on the time clock, Joe knew he had only one choice. He heard the engine's noise in the background, sounding like an eerie warning. "Louie, stop crying and listen to me. I promise everything will be just fine. Stand up again."

"I don't wanna, Joe. I'm scared." Sobbing, the child's tearful reply made his heart drop.

"Hey, it's okay to be scared, son. Just means you're smart. I'm kinda scared too. But if we do this together, it won't be so bad, right?"

"I guess s-so." Louie's form once again filled the window space.

"That's my brave boy." Joe used the velvet tone he'd learned worked best with frightened individuals.

Oh, God, no! The rumbling sound of the ledge's final collapse made Joe lunge swiftly and grab at the little body, clearing the window just as Lee let out a furious yell and the car continued to plummet forward into the darkness.

***

Pandemonium broke out from the top of the hill.

The twins were cheering, and as Joe carried Louie closer to his mom's reaching arms, Peg's wet face, now wreathed in smiles, was a sight to behold.

Angelina, getting her share of hugs along with Joe and Lee, felt wonderful. She'd never again question why a person would volunteer in this way. When a rescue was successful, no other feeling in the world was as beautiful. And who knew that relief mixed with joy could be an incredible aphrodisiac, also.

She shared spontaneous embraces with everyone. But when Joe lifted her off her feet, his arms scooping her up and holding her tightly, not only did she crave his lips on hers, her heart burst open and love filled up all the empty spaces.

Chapter Thirty-one

When the two men drove away after dropping off a very quiet Angelina, they laughed, remembering the embarrassment of five-year-old Louie over his mother's behavior.

Shame-faced when they'd brought him up, Louie braced himself in Joe's arms, obviously expecting dire results for his naughtiness. Instead, Peg had swept him into her arms and covered his face with sloppy smooches full of love and forgiveness. His twin sisters soon had their turn and swamped him with even more kisses and hugs.

Being a male, even if he was still a child, Louie had glanced over at the men and sighed, bogus disgust evident in his voice. "Girls!" he'd said as he'd shaken his head.

Recounting the story again, the men howled with laughter. Sobering finally, Joe glanced over at his tired partner, whose arm leaned on the open windowsill, letting in the unique island smells of newly opened cherry blossoms from a multitude of trees decorating the highway. Western music played on the radio and the relaxed atmosphere was nice.

He glanced out the window and saw the full moon riding high, wedged between streaky, shifting clouds. Yep, he felt good. But his mood instantly soured with Lee's tentative question.

"How come you haven't checked out Angelina's place in the last few days?"

"I've been busy. Who's this Johnnie fellow you were painting with?"

"He's a great guy, an accountant who works with the girls in the office. He was out of town during the earthquake and came back early to help. We could use more hands if you're interested."

"I'm not." Joe hated the pang of jealously that resulted from his partner's explanation. Ignoring Lee's fixed stare, he questioned. "What else have you been up to? Every time I've called, you're never home."

"I've been spending a lot of time with Coralee. She's a great girl, Joe. Plus, we've all been on the lookout for that runaway, Tee."

"I still say it's strange she took off like she did. There had to have been a reason. "

"You know kids. There's no rhyme or reason to a lot of the decisions they make. Doesn't stop Angelina from caring. Coralee's worried about her."

"Worried about which one—Angelina or Tee?"

Lee laughed. "Sorry. It's Angie. Coralee says she's been acting very strange lately."

"Strange? How?"

Lee's answer came so slow, Joe had to clench his teeth, holding back his frustration. "We figure it must be her office building. Coralee says if we don't help, Angie will work like a dog to get her place up and running again, especially since she's got less than two months left to win the bet she made with her father."

Swerving, fighting to get the truck back in the proper lane, Joe cussed while Lee grabbed the dash.

"Say again? She gambled with her father?"

His voice sounded rough. Joe knew it but couldn't seem to stop. Uncomfortable with the way Lee checked him out, he toned it down, and asked once again. "Tell me?"

"I'm not sure I should. Coralee told me this in private."

"We're buddies, and you know I won't say anything to anyone else."

"Why do you care? You've not been back since the first day."

"I care. Tell me, Lee, or by God, I'll stop this truck and we'll have words."

"Sheesh! Fine. Until the earthquake, Coralee didn't understand what drove Angie so hard, making her work like a demon. She'd kept it a secret. But during the earthquake, she came clean. Seems she has to own the building and her business outright by the end of next month, or she forfeits something important to her father. That part Coralee wouldn't talk about. Just that we had to help her get back up and running as soon as possible."

"Well, hell!" What a putz!

"Not being able to pitch in is driving Coralee nuts and she's getting more ditzy every day and taking the rest of us with her. But I'm crazy for her, Joe—didn't know it would be like this."

Joe looked over at his friend. Envy and isolation ate away at him, making him feel like a shit when he should be feeling only gladness for his buddy's happiness.

Nattering on, Lee added, "Did I tell you about the operation Coralee had?"

"I know about it already. In fact, I made damn sure they followed up with more tests. I stopped in to see her the day I left the hospital and found her sleeping. I took the six readings on her pulse, and noticed other symptoms, so I had a little talk with one of the physicians."

Joe, a very astute, serious practitioner, knew the hospital staff respected his knowledge. Chinese medicine attracted a lot of western doctors. In fact, many of them signed up for courses to learn acupuncture, allowing them to give pain relief to their patients without having to write expensive, and in many cases, risky drug prescriptions. In Chinese medicine, the idea was for the body to heal itself, with help from a trained professional.

Breaking into Joe's thoughts, Lee added, "You know Coralee's crazy for me too. Can you believe it? Me! In love at last!"

Chuckling, relief coating his shame for believing the worst about Angelina, Joe said, "Just so you know. Those neon hearts flashing in your eyes, and your cocky asinine grin, are real turn-offs. Trust me, dude, it's disgustingly obvious."

"I'm so happy! I have nightmares of jinxing it up, man. I can't believe how much she's come to mean to me in such a short time."

Not really teasing, Joe insisted, "As long as your lovesickness doesn't rub off on me."

Chapter Thirty-two

Her name shattered the silence. "Angelina?" Three knocks followed.

It was late, and she was alone at the office, still unwrapping her newly arrived office furniture. Packaging, bubble-wrap, and scads of plastic surrounded her. She clutched a utility knife and was diligently cutting the cardboard covering from another office chair.

At the sound of the disembodied voice filtering through the recently installed, opaque, stained-glass window, Angelina started and peered out warily, gripping the tool harder. A mask-like, menacing face stared back at her. It was the same face she had been spending hours searching for. She dropped the utensil, rushed to unlock the door, and Tee stepped inside.

"Tee! Peewee!" Angelina exclaimed, gleefully reaching for both bodies at the same time.

Holding herself stiffly, Tee spoke as if the words had been practiced. "I know this is intense, but I have nowhere else to go." A hitch in Tee's unsteady, hoarse voice contradicted her cocky stance. "All I'm asking for is a job." She coughed once, twice, three times. "Yes or no! I'm not here to bother you." Talking seemed to make her throat worse. The bitter hacking became harsher, and it was patently difficult for her to stop.

Right then a lolling tongue in a furry face peeked out of her grimy jacket, and the wiggly body language exhibited sparks of recognition. The irrepressibly happy puppy was fighting to get out, get closer to Angelina.

***

Staring, not fully believing what her eyes were plainly witnessing, Tee shook her head and closed her mouth. This pup was the biggest scaredy dog she'd ever seen. Invariably, he spent as much time as she'd let him hide in her jacket, cowering from any human contact other than her own.

The sound of a voice he'd only heard once, and the mutt was turning traitor. Bummer!

Angelina, ignoring Tee's stiffness, swept them close.

Engulfed in a hug, surrounded by the most wonderful smell of Shalimar, and arms full of welcome, Tee let herself and the pup melt into Angelina's affection. A wonderful feeling of coming home began to sink in until she remembered to put up her usual guard.

Hauling them further into the warm, well-lit room Angelina demanded, "Where did you go? I was so worried. After you disappeared, Ray, Lee and I spent days searching for you in every place we could think of. They say Joe has been looking for you also. I suppose he felt responsible because of what you must have overheard. He didn't mean for you to leave. He was expressing cynical, unasked-for opinions, which weren't welcome. But in his defense, I suppose he was only trying to protect me." Obvious sarcasm had entered Angelina's tone. "He was sorry as soon as he realized you must've overheard him and misunderstood. We really, truly want to help you."

Angelina's anxiety came across as being sincere. Tee got it. In a flash of insight, intuitively she understood something radical. Angelina was solid, and she cared.

Stiffly, more out of habit than desire, Tee pulled out of the embrace. Hope blossoming against her will, she demanded roughly. "I need a job. No freebies, no charity—no one else involved. Just you and me. I'm a hard worker, and you won't be sorry. That I can promise. So? What do you say? Yes, or no?"

Without hesitation, Angelina agreed. "Yes, absolutely yes. But with two conditions. No—don't get your tail in a knot. They're small conditions. One, I want to call Joe. If he's available to see you right now, we'll go to him for help with your cold. If not, we go to a walk-in clinic. Your cough is worse, and it could turn into pneumonia if we don't do something about it."

Tee thought it over for a few seconds and then agreed. She felt so shitty that if anyone could help her feel more like herself again, she'd gladly accept their aid. "Okay, so what's the second one?"

"I want you guys to come and stay with me at my house. Until we can come up with a better solution, I need to know you're safe and not roaming the streets. This one is non-negotiable."

Relief poured into Tee. She closed her eyes to hide her reaction to this almost-stranger's kindness. After sensing she was under control, she peeked up into Angelina's troubled face and nodded. "For Pee-wee's sake, I accept. The mutt's pretty freaked out on the streets. Plus, he's hungry and needs a bath."

"You're calling him Peewee?"

"Seemed like a good idea. No biggie!"

Chapter Thirty-three

Sometime later, after they'd given up trying to contact Joe and instead got a prescription at the nearest clinic, both Tee and the pup were shiny-clean, medicated and fed. The exhausted canine was nestled in Angelina's cuddling arms, while Tee, swathed in flannel jammies, donated by Angelina, enjoyed a hot chocolate and a blazing fire.

Completely out of her comfort zone, Tee glanced around the room. It was a family area off the large kitchen and decorated in such a way that one instantly thought of an old Spanish villa. Gigantic Boston ferns, their fronds trailing, were perched on top of two white marble pillars and showcased the identical red and gold plush couches that angled toward the modern fireplace. A large-screen television, erected on the wall above, played music in the background. Swathed draperies in reds and gold lush fabrics subtly draped the windows in such a way that the night sky and the lit gardens outside were a mesmerizing scene to those inside.

Angelina cut into her inspection. "Tee, tell me about yourself. I'm not prying; I'm truly interested."

Tee lowered her head, her shaggy, damp locks covering her face. For the first time in her life, she felt she could open up, tell the truth, share herself. She hesitated, but the need to connect finally broke her normally rigid control. "I have a dream, you know, a kind of goal for a good life. But I guess my reality has been more of a nightmare. Like—they say how a person will hit a low point, and everything after is uphill? Well—like, I keep sinking."

"I'm so sorry, Tee. Things have been pretty bad for you. I get the feeling you're running from something or someone. Is it from your family?"

"I don't have a family."

Angelina stared and waited.

"The system, for many kids, actually does work out sometimes. But in my case the whole thing collapsed. I went from one foster joke to another. Some of the families were nice but they never lasted. My lousy attitude was the excuse they used. Most of the social workers—and I had many—were shitty. Oops, sorry! Like—rotten, to say the least."

"Hey, kiddo, it's not your fault. Life shouldn't be so hard for young people in your situation. You're the innocent minor, and the system should be able to find the right notch for every child to fit into." Angelina was furious, picturing Tee as this square peg being forced into a round hole. No wonder so many of the young people today rebelled.

Once started, Tee was on a roll. The deluge of words wouldn't be stopped. Finally, there was someone she felt an affinity with, and the intense need to talk was like an overloaded pitcher of milk flooding the sides. For the first time, her sick feeling of utter loneliness vanished, to be replaced with a vibrancy and friendship totally new to her.

"There was one social worker who was sincere," Tee admitted. "She didn't try to spoon-feed me the yada-yada routine. She was straight-up." Hands clasped, trying to think of the right words, she closed her eyes for a minute.

"Tell me about her." Her voice full of interest, Angelina prompted Tee to continue.

"Well, she seemed truly eager to be a support. She kept telling me that she wanted to make a difference. That she cared about her job and the kids. I liked her. In fact, I trusted her."

As if she knew this wasn't going to end well, Angelina seemed to hesitate but then came to a decision. "Go on. Tell me what happened."

Tee couldn't look at the woman next to her. Instead, she stared at the crystal rocks scattered amongst the flames. "I used her. To give me information she shouldn't have. But it was my life I was fighting for." She turned to Angelina and all she saw on her face was interest, no disapproval, or judgmental frowns. "I'd been after her forever to tell me about my parents, and where I came from. I'd always wanted to know, and no one would tell me. All they'd say was I had to wait till I was the appropriate age and go through the proper channels." Tee sighed, trying to gather her composure. Every time she thought about her begging and the refusals, her bitterness returned

Angelina continued to stoke the sleeping puppy. She never said anything, only waited, probably sensing there was more to come. Tee knew she was passing a line of no return, but her resistance was low, and Angelina's gentleness more than she could fight.

Not being able to stop, she added, "It was her last day working as a social worker. She was moving to another city with her husband and quitting her job because she was expecting a baby. While I was having my last appointment with her, she got called out of her office and left the computer files open. Truthfully, I've wondered if she did it on purpose. I mean, she knew I was being left there alone—right?"

"What did you do?"

"I accessed my file and found some of my personal stuff. Like, my mother was very young when she had me, and I was born here—in Victoria."

"Is that why you've come here?"

"Yeah! Everything was crappy back in... ah, I can't tell you."

"That's okay. Go on."

"Well, the idea of going into another foster home wasn't cutting it. Being the new girl in yet another school was more than I could handle. I'm glad I ran away."

"I get the feeling that you're a teeny bit rebellious, aren't you?" Angelina broke into the telling silence after the verbal outpouring. She grinned, encouraging Tee to get her joke.

Tee's found herself wearing a one-sided smile. "You could say, I'm a little bit of a bitch, but, Angelina, you have to understand. My life stank. I came here as soon as I could grab some cash and sneak away."

"You're on the run, because you took money?" Angelina clenched the puppy so hard, he awoke and his little tongue, licking her hand, had her easing off.

"Nah! I never stole a cent in my life. I earned every penny planting trees in the spring. It was lousy, backbreaking labor, but good money for a hard worker."

"You planted trees? That's difficult...and...dangerous. How did you manage to convince the employers you were old enough to work?"

"Bogus social insurance numbers, male name and clothes, and attitude. I'm a good actress."

Angelina laughed just as Tee had hoped she would. "At least, now you're a clean, medicated one. I'm sorry Joe wasn't available, but it's probably a good thing you've got the antibiotics to clear up the infection. How you've managed these last few days, I'll never know."

Tee had seen Angelina's disappointment when they'd called Joe and he hadn't answered. She stored the information away and responded to her new friend's questions.

"I went to one of those shelter places for the last few nights, but I got in mega-trouble for coughing, and I couldn't face going back tonight. Plus, I had to hide Peewee from them, or they'd have kicked us out. Tonight, I had made up my mind to find a doorway when I spotted your lights still on." What she didn't admit was that she and the pup had made many trips past the old building, constantly being drawn back there. Lucky for her and Peewee, tonight they'd finally found Angelina alone.

"I can't tell you how glad I am my shipment arrived just as I was leaving, and I decided to hang on and take a look. It's the new furniture for the offices we're going to set up on the first floor so we can start working again next week."

"I can finish unpacking the rest tomorrow, if you want? It's my fault you left everything tonight. I'm a good worker, Angelina, I promise. No one has ever complained of me not doing my fair share." This was an important feat to Tee, a cred in her world that bought instant acceptance and respect.

"We'll see how you feel tomorrow. Since I brought a load of stuff home with me, Monday is soon enough to return to the office. As I explained, my grandmother whose home this is, flew to Las Vegas to meet my parents. Which means, we'll have the place to ourselves. Rosario, the lady who's looked after my grandmother for years is back from visiting her sister in Chile and will be returning tomorrow to make us breakfast and look after the house. She's wonderfully sweet. She'll love having someone else to fuss over. Since I'm seldom home, and Grandma's often travelling, she complains of not having enough to do."

"You have a maid? Hey, I've never known anyone with a maid before."

"She's not a maid. She's a friend of my grandma's who happens to work for her. The story goes like this. Many years ago, before my parents were married, my grandmother was visiting Chile to meet my father's people and help plan their wedding. There was a dreadful commotion in the yard next door. The noise brought my mother and grandmother at a run in time to watch a drunken moron beating the maid and her small boy. Both Grandma and Mamá flew into a rage, and managed to chase away the maniac who happened to be the maid's husband. He was demanding her earnings, which she hadn't received because the house's owner had left on an extended vacation and hadn't had the decency to pay her before leaving. What attracted my grandmother was Rosario's defense of her child. She never let the animal near the boy but took each blow herself. Right then and there, Grandmother took Rosario and her little boy, Jorge, into safekeeping."

"Yess! Good for them! Oh, sorry, go on."

Chapter Thirty-four

Relief flooded into Angelina as she watched young Tee's enraptured, expressive face. Good, she cares, thought Angelina. "It was the last day of Grandma's visit, so she decided to hire Rosario, help her and her son emigrate to Canada by acting as their sponsor. She would give Rosario work, not charity, which she would have refused. In this way, she made it possible for them to escape their nightmare and have a chance at a good life. Today, Jorge, Rosario's son, is an architect, having graduated a few years back from Victoria University, and Rosario has looked after my grandmother ever since."

"Wow! What an awesome story. It'll be chill to meet her. But are you sure she won't mind me being here?"

"What do you think?"

"Right! Gotcha!"

Up to now, Angelina had been careful not to ask leading questions. She sensed handling Tee was a delicate matter and wanted to pacify her. Not to prod or irk her but establish a good rapport. The time had come, she thought, where questions would be accepted. However, it was still an approach that needed to be tactful.

"Sweetheart, trust me, I don't wish to pry, but did you by any chance find out your mom's name or her old address?"

"Just the hospital, the city where I was born, my mother's first name, and the year she was born. It was confusing trying to scan the documents and memorize everything as fast as I could. Looks like I'm my mother's daughter though—following in her footsteps, young and in trouble."

Stiffening, Angelina blanched. "You're pregnant?"

Overcome with mirth, chuckling in her husky way, Tee violently shook her head. "Uh, uh," she crowed. "No way!"

Jokingly, Angelina pushed at Tee's thin shoulders affectionately and stopped when she heard the ferocious sputters from Peewee. He'd moved to lie between them on the sofa and was now glaring first at her and then at Tee, uncertainty clearly visible. "Little beast," she ruffled him playfully, and then scooped him up for hugs and smooches.

Once she'd satisfied the little fellow that she had no intention of hurting his mistress, she glanced up to find Tee's eyes brimful.

"Oh, Niñita, come here." She reached for the teen's shaking body, hugged her close and rubbed her thin back. Poor little girl needs a good cry. And a good friend.

Chapter Thirty-five

Bright and early on Monday morning, Angelina and Tee arrived at the office and met up with Ray. The sun was teasing its way through the clouds giving warning of a warm day in the colorful, flowery paradise of downtown Victoria. All around there were signs of busy crews hired by the damaged businesses to restore their locations back to their former charm. Hard work was the order of the day for everyone. Angelina couldn't stop smiling when she acknowledged the major efforts being made, not just by her, but the whole neighborhood. She shifted her daily bundle of bribery from Tim Horton's and reached out for Ray's arm.

"Ray, you remember my friend, Tee? I've given her a job to help with the cleanup. Maybe you can keep her busy?"

"Hey," Tee smiled warily.

"Yeah, well oats are cheaper, and grass is free," Ray chanted the old ditty, obviously recognizing the girl from the other day.

Slumping into a petulant stance, the chip on her shoulder hanging out and visible to anyone with knowledge of youngsters—and Ray had that in spades—Tee seemed to react instinctively. Before any damming words slipped out, she must have caught the teasing glint in his eyes, and realized that his whole countenance was relaxed, not at all antagonistic. "Not on these streets," she answered guardedly.

"You got me there, little girl." His face broke into an irresistible grin.

Angelina saw Tee melt and breathed a sigh of relief.

Stretching his back, his round belly protruding at the waistline of his well-washed denims, Ray turned to Angelina and said, "Leave this one with me, Angelina. There's a whole lotta work here, so if she's a worker, she'll be busy. If not, you can have her in the office, cause I donna wan' her under my feet." He added teasingly, "Looks a might chintzy to me."

"Chintzy? Hey, ol' man, I'm a hard worker; just make sure you keep it coming."

Angelina interrupted. "Tee, please don't overdo it today. There'll be plenty more when you're feeling better."

During the rest of the day, Angelina watched out for her new friend, and she saw Tee working harder than there was any need to.

***

Tee was tiring faster than on any of her previous jobs. Knowing it was the infection she was battling and her body's unhealthy state that taxed her muscles, she tamped down her irritation. She had no choice but to accept the fact that it would take time to be at her best. It was still frustrating. The intense need to show everyone how worthy she was pushed her beyond her ability to keep up, and if it wasn't for her dogged stubbornness she would have collapsed in a heap and ended up bawling again like she had a few nights earlier.

She still couldn't believe that she'd broken down like that, and in front of a virtual stranger. Except, Angelina didn't seem like a stranger at all. That was the difference. But she had to remember that other people had let her down before. Best she keep her affections under control and not take any chances.

Finally, the call came for a lunch break.

When she appeared from where she'd been working on the third floor, it was in time to hear Ray singing an Italian aria, forcefully and unharmoniously.

"Too bad you're such an old man. You could be on Canadian Idol," Tee snickered, deciding to test the waters with a joke.

"Hey little girl, watcha your mouth. I'ma still hot stuff," he bantered.

"Sure, on a geriatric ward." First, she chuckled, and when she saw his phony leer, she giggled.

Looking surprised and then delighted, the old Italian softie spoke. "It's good to hear you laugh, Tee-short-for-trouble."

Then he sang even louder. His Italian was more pronounced, his love of opera apparent in his musical choice, but his tone was utterly, completely... painfully off-key.

"Aw, Ray, cut it out. I'ma dyin' here," Tee said, teasingly.

He stopped mid-note and answered her. "I'm sure your instinct for survival will kick in shortly. Come here and eat your lunch!"

"Dictator!"

"Brat! Hypothetical question here! Say I was to make the rule that workers had to show respect to their boss alla time. Whatcha gonna do about that, little girl?"

"Only thing I can do. Get ear plugs!"

Chapter Thirty-six

Some days later, Tee, who was toiling tenaciously, diligently ripping at the chunks of fallen bricks, lathe, scraps of wood and gyp rock, looked up to see Ray watching her. She had painstakingly formed the mangled mess into an organized pile, but not without painful blisters seeping on the palms of her hands, and cuss words spitting uncontrollably from her mouth. Yanking and muttering, she cursed a blue streak: "Ow, dammit, shit...!"

"Brat, you gotta eat with that mouth." Ray yelled, castigating her with his hands on his hips.

"Eat," she blasted, "I'm full up from all this sh-tuff." Kicking at the powdery whitish mounds of fine plaster and filmy dust made her feel better.

She slipped off her work gloves, lowered her facemask and perused the fresh sores on her aching hands. Then she wiped her forehead with the sleeve of her T-shirt that had seen better days, obvious by the faded dragon motif splashed across the front.

"I'm astonished at the amount of work you've accomplished up here, missy. But you gotta slow down. Dean sniveled yesterday that you don't stop. He's eighteen and having trouble keeping up with you."

"Yeah, well, he works harder than me. Probably trying to show off. He's your son after all."

Ray laughed. "He hasn't been sick recently and should be able to do a lot more than you shrimp, so stop trying to compete."

Tee watched as the old man surveyed the space. The damage on this side was intense, so destructive they'd been forced to shore up the roof and, in places, tarp the areas that had completely buckled.

Turning to leave he said, "I came to tell you there's lunch downstairs. Come, take a break, eat, and rest for a while. Angelina'll take a stick to me if you get sick again. You work too hard. It's enough now." He turned away; certain she would follow—in her own good time.

"I want to check out this last corner." Holding a couple of fingers up towards him, she reiterated, "Two more minutes." She headed towards a particular area of pandemonium where large pillars were twisted, crisscrossed, and lying over heaps of crushed furnishings. Pieces of lathe and wire mesh coated with broken slabs of gyp rock, and segments from the collapsed roof were scattered in all directions. They were sharp and dangerous, and made the pathway difficult to traipse over.

In the midst of this upheaval, a bright purple color grabbed her eye. She'd spotted it earlier half-exposed from a recessed opening in the top pillar. It was a diabolically clever hidey-hole, and the thrust from the quake had probably broken it apart. She worked her way closer, being careful where she stepped, and cautiously lifted the treasure from amidst the mess. Squatting to investigate, she determined the purple to be an old Crown Royal whiskey bag—actually there were two— probably doubled for strength. The heavy weight of the bundle spiked her fascination.

After tugging to undo the cord, the contents left her open-mouthed and bordering on hysteria. Nestled in the decaying old bag was a whole shit-load of gold coins, all in mint condition, all enclosed in special plastic covers, and all beautiful. She started to count the cache and after she hit fifty, she gave up.

Without further thought she hiked up the heavy bag in her arms like a precious baby and ran screaming down the stairs.

"Angie! Angie! Come quick! You ain't never gonna believe what I just found. It is in-frigging-credible! Oops! Sorry, Ray," she caught his look of distaste as she went screaming past.

Chapter Thirty-seven

It took them all some time to settle down after Tee's awesome discovery. Blunting the excitement, Angelina overrode everyone's proposals as to how she could make the most use of the money, including a cruise, new wardrobe, jewelry, and everyone's favorite suggestion—donating it to a newly formed charity fund thought up by Johnnie called 'Employee Wage Increases'.

Tee was all for that suggestion, but bursting their fun-bubble, Angelina stated unequivocally, "I'll have to see if the previous owners are reachable. Since the late 1800s to the 1920s are the dates on the coins, I guess any time after that would most likely be the time period I should check into. Come on you guys! You know the money belongs to these people or their predecessors."

Johnnie interrupted and qualified, "I'm almost sure anything found on your property is yours or could even belong to whoever found it. It's a finders-keepers kinda thing."

Angelina listened and then added, "Maybe you're right. But I still intend to hire a private detective firm I know here in town, and we'll at least try to return the money to the proper owners."

Meanwhile, no one had paid heed to other people drifting in and out of the open building, hanging back during the excitement. Therefore, suspicious characters went unnoticed. That is, except for Tee. She was disciplined by prior circumstances to always be watchful. And what she saw, she didn't like at all.

***

Angelina's mind drifted a few seconds while she dithered about whether or not to call Joe and tell him the news about Tee literally finding a bag of gold. He'd returned her call from days before when she'd left a message about Tee being back and sicker than ever, but he'd kept the conversation short and to the point.

"Did you take her to see a doctor?"

"Yes, of course! We tried your office first but couldn't reach you, so I took her immediately to the local clinic. They gave her a prescription. She's better now and is working here at the office with Ray's crowd."

"Don't let her overtax herself. She'll be feeling pretty weak for some time."

"Right! Telling her to slow down is—well, it's impossible. The minute our eyes are turned, she's back at it. Works harder and faster than anyone else on Ray's payroll, including his sons, and that's saying a lot."

"I'm surprised she stuck around. Where's she staying?"

"She's with me at the house; her and the little puppy, Peewee."

After Angelina admitted this, there was silence at his end of the line. She pictured him reigning in his temper.

His voice hardened. "Are you still at the house alone?"

"Not really. Rosario, our housekeeper, is back home now."

Softening his tone, Joe answered. "That's good. I just hope you know what you're doing?"

"So far, so good! Joe, she's a great kid and she needed a friend."

"Well she found the best, Angelina. Oh-oh! Gotta go! I'll call you soon."

"Ciao, Joe."

From the minute they'd hung up, a strange kind of loneliness had seeped in, invading her heart. At least, she'd suspected that the yearning, sickly feeling was loneliness. Never having felt this way before gave her nothing to measure it by.

I wish he'd get out of my head! She was sick of stumbling over him every time she let her mind wander. She needed to let it go... let him go.

Now faced with the decision as to whether she should chance him hanging up on her again, she dithered, watching her hand slowly reach for the phone.

Leaving it up to fate, she punched the button, only to hear his answering service ask her to leave a message. Instead, she hung up. Guess that's my answer.

Chapter Thirty-eight

Disgusting night noises of spitting, groaning, and hurling kept Tee fearful and awake. In the background, sirens and brakes squealing, drunken arguments and yelling evoked nauseating memories of other nights she'd hoped to forget. Regrettably, life had a way of spinning in a-hundred-and-eighty-degree twists every so often, and here she was again on the streets of hell.

She fetched a piece of folded cardboard to have something between her and the filthy ground, decorated with used needles, condom wrappers and other unspeakable soiled garbage.

Then she wrapped a discarded, dirty grey torn blanket, with ragged edges and most likely crawling creatures, around her skinny shoulders. Tugging her skater tuke down over her forehead, she covered most of her face. Lastly, she bent over her tote and draped her arms over her raised knees, wanting to give the impression to anyone checking her out there was no problem here. Patiently, she waited for the right moment.

Little by little, she shuffled herself and her gear closer to where the thieving bastard lay with his arms clutching his ragged backpack. It was frayed and held together in a few places with safety pins and duct tape. But it sheltered what she wanted and so her eyes never left it. She slumped down against the damp cement and successfully faded into the background.

To most, it was a squalid, smelly concrete underpass, but for others less fortunate, it was a sleeping place. She knew that as long as she kept her head down and didn't show her face, the thieving bastard would ignore her.

Her plan was solid. Hang in next to the loser and wait for him to take a hit. She knew he would; invariably there was no choice. He needed it more than he'd needed the last one.

This cock-eyed notion she had of capturing the lost treasure and returning it to Angelina was a sucker play, but she guessed it didn't matter. She cared diddlysquat about what happened to her. The important thing in Tee's life right now was Angelina, her first true friend. And proving to her that the young girl she'd helped was worth every bit of the energy and trust she'd invested. It was the only way she knew of saying—you were right. I'm a good person. Thank you.

Like dust mites floating in a shaft of sunlight, random thoughts drifted around in her conscience. Trying to beat back the fear and stay awake, she purposefully allowed her mind to wander.

I miss Angie and Ray. What is it about Coralee that seems so familiar? Where's Joe, and how come everyone pussyfoots around when his name comes up? Dean must have a girlfriend...

Her head started to drop, and she shook herself awake. Smarten Up! Concentrate.

Dragging her attention back to the matter at hand, Tee watched sneakily. She could see by the amount of drugs the dude injected, he was trippin' big time. He must have scored with one of the coins. It was only a matter of time before he would be in la-la land, the way he was using. Hopefully, then she could get close enough to wrest the prize out of his grasp.

Eyelids at half-mast, arms shielding her upper body, knees clenched, she schemed. First, wait till he's totally out. Next, watch to be sure everyone else nearby is too far-gone to care. Then carefully, gently, take the bag. And finally, run like freakin' hell.

Easy! No sweat!

Then why are you crying?

Chapter Thirty-nine

Joe was sick and tired of avoiding Angelina. And he was sick of Lee giving him The Look. And he was tired of hiding from his family. Worst of all, he was fed up with kicking his own ass. As hard as he tried, he couldn't get her out of his thoughts, and dammit... he had tried.

Once he'd discovered that his worst fears about her gambling were utter nonsense, there appeared to be nothing stopping them from being together. Except—of course— he wasn't interested in commitment, no matter who the chick was. Even Angelina! No way–no how!

He'd held out for over a week, with just a few phone calls between them that he'd replayed continuously in his mind. Hell, the only real news he'd received was second-hand, passed on by Lee. Seemed even nice ol' Lee was losing patience, as the last question he'd asked had gotten him a terse reply.

"Angelina's stopped asking about you. The rest of us don't bring up your name because we hate seeing her unhappy. Considering the fact you don't want to get seriously involved with any woman, I'm thinking it's best you stay away and leave her alone."

"You're saying I can't be her friend? Is that what you're telling me?" Joe picked a fight and felt foolish the minute the words left his mouth.

"What I'm telling you is to either shit or get off the pot. You can't have things both ways, man. Either you're straight up with her from the beginning and lay it on the line—friends only—and then act accordingly. Or don't come around. That's what I'm saying."

"I hear you. Hell, the whole office heard you. What is it about this girl? Everyone, including you, shields her like you're Acting Bodyguards for the First Lady."

Lee gave him a look like he'd do with an ornery child. And it pissed him off. He bristled but listened.

"You don't really know her at all, Joe. She's special. At first, I liked her because she was a victim who'd handled a nightmare with class, not like some of the others we've helped in the past. She sincerely cared more about her employees than she did about herself. Plus, Coralee is nuts about her. Now that I've spent more time with her, I find she's incredibly smart, amazingly compassionate and has a sense of wit and style, which astounds me. Meanness is absolutely foreign to her nature. Her office staff—they adore her and would do practically anything for her. People who elicit such a huge amount of affection are rare and need to be protected."

"Wait a minute, now you're saying I'm out to hurt her?"

"Not intentionally, no. What I'm saying is she isn't one of your usual girlfriends. You can't dally with her."

Joe bit down on his rising anger. "Angel's not a child, Lee. She has a mind of her own."

"Not with this kind of thing, and don't mess with me here. She's astonishingly shy with men. You probably noticed it yourself."

Joe thought back to the beautiful woman standing in front of him in her driveway, dressed in a turquoise T-shirt and jeans, holding his flowers, her eyes guarded. As per her custom, she'd welcomed him with a kiss, and shyness had radiated like waves from her trembling body.

Lee continued. "Some of the things Coralee told me about her—which are private, and I won't breach her confidence—led me to believe she hasn't dated very many men. She's way out of your league, Bro."

Joe's interest ramped up in an instant. Thinking he'd get the scoop; he moved closer and used the old charming smile.

"I'm not talking, pal." Lee shot him down.

"She's a grown woman, Lee. One who, by the way, has put me in my place a few memorable times and doesn't strike me as being weak at all."

"You're right, she isn't weak. That wasn't what I was trying to say. She's vulnerable, which is a whole different scenario."

"Okay, I promise. If I stop by the office, it'll be strictly a friendly visit. Besides, to tell the truth, I've felt like a worm ignoring everyone there. Also, I wanted to check up on young Tee and see how she's doing."

"Tee? She's the hardest working, cheekiest kid I've ever met. She's Angelina's biggest fan and has managed to charm all the rest of us."

"Has she told anyone her real name yet?"

"Nope. Angelina has made everyone promise to leave it alone, and not mess with the girl. Figures she'll tell us in her own good time."

"What does Coralee think, now that she's out of the hospital and she's met her? I guess she's not back to work yet, but I'd put money on it, she's been to the office."

"She won't stay away, can't is more like it. She's been to the office already bugging everyone to let her 'do' something. Angelina's standing firm and won't allow her to get back to work until her recuperation is up. She's only welcome to visit. It's been an uphill battle, let me tell you. When my doll sets her mind on a certain course, nothing can budge her."

"Should make for an interesting future for you two," Joe chuckled.

"Since she's set her mind on me, I'm pretty sure I won't have to worry she'll start looking anywhere else. Suits me just fine."

"I'd be keen on getting to know her better. I like what I've seen so far, and you two will make a great pair. I might come around to the office soon. Indifference doesn't suit me, Lee. Honestly, I'd like to help."

"If you say so, Joe. Ruthlessness doesn't suit you either. So, take care. It's all I ask."

Chapter Forty

"What do you mean, where're the coins?" The frozen horror on Ray's face was sufficient for Angelina to clue into the fact that he didn't have the Crown Royal bags either, and he'd been her last hope.

After the initial excitement of the find, everyone had quietened down, and it was decided they'd finish off the day's work and hold a celebration later.

Leaving the bags of coins in an unlocked file cabinet drawer in her office, Angelina had taken for it granted they would be safe. Retrospectively, she was wrong—disturbingly, shockingly wrong. The purple velvet bags had disappeared... vanished. Devastatingly worse was the fact that Tee was gone too. They'd looked but couldn't find her anywhere. And her backpack was missing also, the one she kept with her always.

At once, Ray organized a meeting with his son Dean, Angelina, and Lee, who arrived subsequently just in time to be briefed on the ironic story. Angelina's newly finished office, the only room with privacy as the door had been installed early that morning, was the most sensible place to convene.

Ray started the discussion. "I've questioned alla my guys and none saw the bags. In fact, none were even in this room today. Besides, they've all worked with me for years and I'd trust every one of them." The quiet in the room felt uncomfortable.

Cutting to the chase, Dean said, "Angelina, you can't believe Tee would take the money. She just wouldn't."

Lee interrupted. "If the amount in those bags was for real, then the coins will be worth a fortune on the streets, and we all have to admit that's familiar territory for her."

Angelina wordlessly shook her head. Dean looked towards his father respectfully and waited.

"No way," Ray interrupted, flinging his hands in the air in a typical Italian way. He challenged Lee to argue further by the cocky stance he adapted, portraying a paternal shielding role. "If she'da wanted the money, why'd she show it to us to begin with? Why didn't she just hide it and keep it? I say—no way!"

Nodding, looking from face to face, Angelina confirmed his opinion was mutual. No hesitating, no discussion, Tee's innocence and loyalty to them was as unequivocal as theirs to her. But where was she now? And where was the loot?

A rhythmic knocking had everyone turning hopeful faces to the doorway. Joe entered; his face full of smiles that soon fled after he noticed the roomful of worried expressions. He raised his eyebrows. Then with snake-like speed, he moved to squat in front of Angelina and gripped her hands.

"Why is she crying? Lee, what's going on? Ray, do you mind getting her some water? Angel— baby—what happened? Is it your family?"

Seeing him was too much for Angelina. She choked up and couldn't talk. It was his fault for being so nice to her. Adroitly, Lee filled him in on the day's happenings.

Deep inside, Angelina couldn't believe Tee had left without a word to her, or anyone else for that matter. The sassy teen had become important to them, and everyone was feeling betrayed by her lack of courtesy. A call to Rosario elicited the fact that Peewee was fast asleep in his fancy new basket. Tee would never leave without her pet. So, Angelina knew she'd be back, but in the meantime where was she?

Joe patted her hands, stood next to her chair, and restored her faith in him by his reaction. "I don't believe it! From what Lee's been sharing, the kid works like a dog and was well treated here. And for someone like Tee, that's huge."

Angelina slumped, loosening the stressed pose. Her hands, which had been grasping and pulling at each other, rested. After twisting like a wild thing in her chest, her heart calmed, while nerves she never knew existed stopped pounding at the back of her head.

To have Joe support Tee was tantamount to finding another bag of gold. Better! Because money she hadn't worked for didn't have any real meaning for her, but Joe's defense, well... that meant everything.

Having him express so clearly what everyone else thought opened a flood of speculations, discussion, and decision-making. First, they all agreed that calling in the police would only be done as a last resort.

Plans transpired and in no time three vehicles were traversing their chosen routes, focusing on finding a cocksure, spiky-haired female adolescent—street-savvy, but in probable danger.

Surprisingly, Joe maneuvered Angelina into his truck with typical male arrogance, and they were soon on their way. Even though the evening was balmy, twinges of apprehension kept Angelina scrunched

up in her seat and leaning forward. Her hands were still getting a
workout.

"Angel, I promise to drive real careful tonight. No accidents! You
can relax."

Not that dazed, she answered. "I'm no angel, Joe. Call me Angelina,
please.

"Sorry, I guess it's how I think of you."

"Yes, well, my dad used to call me his Angel during the times he
wanted me to obey. Sorry, but now it grates."

"Got it. I'll try and remember. Just know, when I call you Angel, it's
a form of affection and not a means of exploitation."

"You're right. I'm way too sensitive. To change the subject, Joe, I
can't believe how many homeless there are here in the city. I guess I
never realized what a problem we have."

"Many folks choose to stay on the streets, Angelina. They like their
lives in the open—especially in the warm months. Others, unfortunately, have no choice."

"That's what Tee said. She also told me that the first night she was
in Victoria, she slept under a culvert not far from Milestones on Wharf
Street. I remember it because she explained that she could see through
the restaurant's lighted, wraparound windows. She'd watched all the
people in the booths eating and enjoying themselves, wishing she was
one of them. I had intended on taking her to eat there as soon as my
grandmother returns."

Swinging his old truck around, maneuvering an illegal U-turn, Joe
headed in the direction of one of the city's most popular nightspots. "I
know the place. Hold on." He reached over to throw his arm in front
of her in case the acceleration caught her unawares.

Appreciating his thoughtfulness, she righted herself and continued. "She told me it made her feel so sad to see all those families having

fun, while she was surrounded by misery and zombies worn out by drugs or alcohol."

"The poor kid! I hate to imagine anyone living in those circumstances, especially a youngster like her."

"She was terrified, and desperately afraid. I remember her telling me how she'd narrowly missed getting mugged. Because she was new, some of the livelier—I think she called them—posers suspected she had money in her backpack and were determined to take it away from her. But she's a quick thinker, and talked her way out of the mess, gave over the last ten dollars she had, and was able to slink away before they decided she was lying. It's hard for me to believe she'd go back there, but since I can't think of anywhere else, it's worth a try."

Searching out her window, Angelina zoomed in on the sidewalks full of happy travelers and wandering couples. Serenity was the norm for those folks. Whereas her heart was tripping overtime, and the sickness nestled in the bottom of her stomach undulated, clambering to come up. She swallowed, taking deep breaths.

Through a haze of tears, she observed the brightly lit store windows, highlighting sale signs and selections of artfully arrayed merchandise. It all reminded her that prosperity didn't stop for anyone or anything.

Joe turned into the lane by the restaurant and parked in the lot below. He hesitated and then reached for Angelina's agitated hands. Tenderly he brought them to his lips and kissed each palm, rubbing the backs with his thumbs, caressing them smoothly.

"Sweetheart don't look like that. We'll find her if she's here, and if not, we'll keep looking."

Trusting, she placed her worried face over their clasped hands, and her long pony-tailed locks floated freely over his lap.

Chapter Forty-one

Moaning huskily, Joe laid his face on top of hers, cheek on her hair and breathed in her perfumed essence.

His heart jumped into his throat and left him stunned. Pounding, with a rhythm so unlike its norm, it beat hard and fast, leaving him under no false impression as to why. His head might have tried to make a decision regarding this woman, but his body had always known the truth.

From the minute he'd seen her in the rubble, hiding on the floor next to the desk, face full of worry and cheeks smeared with tears, he'd had only one thought... to bring back her smile.

Suddenly, an alarming crash had them raising their heads and turning to locate where the noise had erupted. Screams, louder screams, pounding feet... Then an endearingly familiar figure emerged under the streetlamp and was savagely grabbed from behind, frantic panic stamped on her features. Tee!

Bravely, the diminutive girl fought her attacker, ferociously kicking and making headway, until another disembodied figure staggered drunkenly into the fray, thinking to join the fight.

Joe rushed from the truck and headed straight for them. He dropped the oncoming drunk with one backhanded swing. Then reaching down, viciousness taking control, he swung Tee's attacker so hard he sent him flipping and sprawling a good twenty feet away. He started after him, but Tee obstinately grabbed his shirt from behind and effectively calmed him down.

"Don't sweat it. Let's just get out the hell outta here, Joe. I've got the bag, and those creeps are like—so wasted, they can barely walk, let alone fight."

Putting his arm around her shoulders, Joe lifted the proffered bundle and helped Tee toward the truck. They met up with Angelina who dropped the huge misshapen piece of wood she'd searched out and reached out for Tee.

Shock still evident in her emotionally charged voice, Tee chattered like a magpie. "Am I ever glad to see you? Those losers were pissed right off! What are you doing here anyway? How did you know where I'd be?" Her adrenaline had spiked and was obvious in her shrill voice and the gushing words she couldn't seem to control.

Joe answered her, smiling. "Get in, scamp. Calm down and catch your breath."

"Let her talk, Joe. She wants to share." Angelina smiled at him softly, her eyes full of gratitude. In the meantime, while all the horrors of the night were told, her caring arms continued to shelter a grateful Tee.

Chapter Forty-two

When they first arrived home, after her shower and a lovefest with Peewee, Tee joined Angelina and Joe in the family room. Spilling over with the need to talk and tell her story, she approached the couple sitting together and conversing about the incident.

Angelina patted the sofa. "Just so you know, Tee. We weren't the only ones looking for you. I called off the troops and told them you were safe. They all send their love."

"They searched for me?"

"Of course, silly. I made your favorite hot chocolate. Come!"

Wrapped in a warm, fuzzy lap rug, encircled by a giant of a gentle man on one side, the ministrations of a loving friend on the other, and Peewee snuggled in her lap, she organized her thoughts. Putting her cup of hot chocolate down on a nearby handy coaster, she started.

"It was that twisted snoop who took the bag." She turned to Joe and said, "The one you threw away like so much useless litter. I saw him the first time when we were all excited about the find; he'd been listening at the door. Then later, I was late coming down for coffee, and I spotted him from the stairs when you were all having your break with Ray in the small office off the foyer. The slime was coming out of Angelina's office with the bag stashed in his jacket. I ducked down and he didn't see me. I remembered him from the first night I was in the city, so I trailed him—"

"Why didn't you call out before he'd left with the money?" Joe interrupted her spiel.

"I couldn't take the chance. He was too close to the door. He'd have split before anyone would have stopped him. All I could think of was to follow him and get the money back."

Angelina made a choking sound and got their attention. "Tee, the money was never important. I was scared sick about you disappearing."

Tee felt a huge wave of love wash over her and she reached for Angelina's hand. "I couldn't let him take what belonged to you. It wasn't right. I waited until the dude passed out. Then I eased the bag out from under him and backed away. Darned if just then someone didn't come around the corner and see what I was up to! He yelled. I guess it woke the loser up, I'm not sure; I was in too big of a hurry to get the hell outta there." Shuddering, she remembered the fear ramping up her adrenaline until she could barely breathe, let alone run.

With Angie's arm surrounding her and Joe's admiration obvious, a sweet warmth started in her stomach. There was satisfaction, for sure, but something else that she'd never experienced before overrode that feeling... approval. She leaned her head a little towards Joe, and he smiled gently.

"Angie, I'm stoked you remembered what I told you about my first night in Victoria, and where I'd slept. I bet you're the first person who ever remembered anything I told them, or ever cared enough to remember. Thank you."

Leaning over, she willingly, and for the first time she could remember, offered a cuddle to another person.

Angelina melted towards her. "You're very welcome, little girl. And thank you for saving the gold. If it turns out we can't find the owners, and I get to keep it, half is yours. Without you, there wouldn't be any at all. So that's a promise."

Tee had many goals, the most important being to find her mother. But her big dream was to go back to school, and even one day to university. This windfall might enable her to make that fantasy come true.

"Sweet!" Grinning so hard her face felt stretched, she turned to Joe.

"Thanks again, Joe. You're my hero!" She stood up with his help, limped over to the doorway and blew him a cheeky kiss. Then spoiled it all with a huge yawn.

"You're welcome, sweet thing," he drawled.

"Sorry! I'm bushed. I feel like I could sleep for days."

***

After she left, Angelina and Joe sat quietly in front of the glowing fireplace. The faint smell from the enormous bouquet of carnations behind them added ambiance to the surreal moment for Angelina.

Joe broke the tranquil silence. "You had faith in her right from the beginning. How did you know she was such a good kid?"

Memories flooded and Angelina sifted through them to answer as honestly as she could. "It's strange, really. From the very first time I met her, she reminded me of someone. Now, when I look at her, I only see Tee. But I think it's why I trusted her from the first moment."

"I'll admit, it scared the livin' bejesus outta me when I saw her dashing into the light with those two doped-up idiots attacking her."

"You got there in time to help, thank goodness." Filled with admiration, she turned to look at him.

"Because you listened," he reminded her. Closing the gap between them on the sofa, he gathered her in his arms, leaned his chin on the top of her head and whispered. "Heaven's so close."

"Did you say something" Her soft eyes, darkened with need, caught his.

Nervously, he lied, "I was talking to myself. I do that sometimes."

She looked at him and liked everything she saw. Admired his expressive cat-green eyes, the dimpled smile covering his beautiful teeth and, more than anything, the lips she yearned to taste.

His large, muscled body had appeared in so many of her recent fantasies, and now, here he was—so close—just a kiss away.

Fragrance, musky and manly, drifted around them. She closed her eyes and leaned into him, blatantly urging, silently begging.

He swept her closer, breathing hard until the sound changed to a lustful moan.

Pliant, swooning, her dreams coming true, she melted into his arms. Good Lord! At last!

Tenderly holding her head in his hands, he lowered his mouth to hers. At first he used just the gentlest of touches, nipping fleetingly at each side of her mouth. Then he sucked on her bottom lip until she gasped. His tongue slowly inched inside to find hers.

Liking the taste of this man, she shyly greeted him. His foreplay created burgeoning sensations throughout her body and all of them overwhelmed. Pools of wet heat gathered and overflowed, waiting for him to enter and douse the flames. Her tender breasts ached, yet at the same time tingled. Stomach muscles quivered with rippling sensations and clenched in harmony with the fire that had been ignited.

***

Joe knew this Angel was his for the taking. With every writhing movement and rasping sigh, she blissfully led him on. Seductively, lowering all barriers, she opened herself to his greater knowledge.

If her body touched his anywhere else but his lips, he'd be a goner. She'd be like water to a dying man in the desert who understands that sweet liquid would restore his sanity and his life. Only Joe also knew Angelina deserved more than a few nights of hanky-panky, and he had always been a one-or-two-night stand kinda guy. No ties, no long romances, no commitments. That was his motto, his creed—Joe's Law. Plus, he'd promised Lee he'd leave the girl alone.

With shaking hands, a throbbing hardness between his legs and rocks in his head, he backed away and stood up so quickly, she all but fell off the couch.

"Aw, Angelina, this shouldn't happen. I gotta go." Never had a man walked away feeling sorrier for himself.

While he huddled in his truck, cursing for long-suffering moments before he could drive away, he never once gave a thought to what she was going through.

Chapter Forty-three

Arriving at Coralee's apartment a few days after her friend's release from the hospital, Angelina got hit with an interrogation. "Tell me the truth as my best friend."

"Right! The truth is I actually weigh a hundred and twenty pounds, not a hundred and fifteen. I lied."

"That's not what I meant, fatty. I want the other truth."

"Oh that! So I'm not the virgin you always believed I was. I never bothered to correct your inaccurate assumption; instead I ignored you."

"What? You had me fooled. So let me get this straight. What you're telling me is my best friend is a plump slut."

Laughter rang out as both girls broke up. It was so good to play again. Especially for Angelina, who desperately needed her spirits lifted. Finally, Coralee got herself under control and became serious.

"Honestly, Angelina, tell me if you think I should get some surgical treatments." She held her hand up before Angelina's dismay could be expressed. "I met a girl in the hospital who told me her doctor is a famous plastic surgeon and that he's fantastic. She's now sporting Hooter boobs, has lost thirty pounds to liposuction and looks fantastic. I've been reading up and I could have a breast augmentation, a face-lift, lip plumping and... still have a teeny-tiny savings account."

Angelina's first inclination was to hit her forehead, and her next was to hit Coralee's. Instead, she butted in and said, "Hopefully, there'll be enough left over for psychotherapy. Come on, Coralee. Just because your heart suffered damage, your brain cells weren't affected."

"Don't joke, Ange. This is major. For the first time in my life, I want desperately to be pretty."

"Mi amiga, in case you're even a tiny bit serious or solely searching for compliments, I will reiterate as I have on numerous occasions. You aren't pretty because you're more attractive than pretty. Your legs are the envy of every woman in the office. You're so perfectly proportioned; it's enough to make us hate you. We're all jealous of how good your clothes look on you, even with your bizarre sense of dressing. As much as I love your face, I've never been half as attracted to it as Lee seems to be. I see him gazing at it constantly like he'd devour you if he could. So if you are determined to undergo a medical procedure, I strongly suggest you choose a brain transplant."

"Ange!"

"Silencio!"

Good naturedly, and with a shamed face, Coralee said, "Okay, okay – I'll be good." Crinkling up the paper with the surgeon's information, she threw it over her head, not looking or caring where it landed. "Subject closed! I have some good news. My doctor has finally agreed to let me go back to work next week, as long as I don't overdo things."

Angelina, childlike, clapped her hands in glee. "You've made my day," she crowed. "I'll be so glad to have you back. But honestly, if you need more time, you know it would be covered. However long it takes for you to be a hundred percent ready, I'll willingly wait. Or maybe you should think of coming back for only half a day to begin with."

"Oh, I'm more than ready to work the whole day." Coralee turned serious. "You know me. I'm not a halfway kind of person. It's all or nothing. Besides, I promised I'd rest in the evenings and on the weekends. I want my life back. I can't wait for Lee to meet the real me—not Coralee, sicko and patient."

"I happen to think he's nuts about the sicko."

First Coralee made a weird face at Angelina, and then grabbed her hands. "He's been wonderful. He makes me laugh. I've never been happier in my life. I'm afraid of this much happiness, and you know, this time, I believe with everything in me, he's the one I've been waiting for. I'm scared silly because I know I've said this before, Ange, but trust me, this time I mean it from the bottom of my heart. He's the only man who's ever made me feel this way, my so-called soul mate, the yin to my yang, the Sonny to my Cher—oops, not a good comparison."

Reaching over, full off affection, Angelina patted her cheek and replied, "Querido, slow down. Look, I'm happy for you. I know it's real this time. I've never seen you this radiant before. We see quite a bit of Lee and he's got the same goofy glow. He's always happy, and acts like a man who can't believe his good fortune."

"He's perfect for me. Not the complex, hot-shot, sex idol Joe the hunk is. And he's always emotionally available for me and everything I care about. The ultimate is that he's crazy for kids. All we need now is for me to get better so we can start..."

"Hold it! Shouldn't there be a small ceremony in those plans, some-where?"

"We'll get around to it. Since we've only just met, I don't want to rush things, but trust me, it will happen."

Angelina jumped up and whirled around crazily. "I'm going to be a bridesmaid," she sang. "I'm so happy for you, Coralee."

"I'm happy for you, too, Ange. By the way, when were you going to share about Joe showing up and whisking you off in his truck, and about finding the young chick? Did I tell you that I met her a few days back when I stopped by? You were in a meeting. She's a firecracker, eh? I liked her; she looks a person straight in the eye. Attitude aside, she had some smarts. Intelligent smarts, not mouth-smarts."

"Oh, she can be smart-mouthed too," admitted Angelina. "Once you get to spend lots of time with her, you'll take to her even more. Wait till you see how hard she works. Her and Ray make a great pair; both are stubborn, funny, and incorrigible. She gets along with Johnnie, too; calls him Johnnie-be-good."

"I'm so looking forward to being back to work with you guys. I've missed it madly. Speaking of Ray, how is he?"

"He's good, and his work is unsurpassed, flawless in every tiny detail. The first floor is slated to be ready next week in time for your homecoming. Wait till you to see all the new furniture and the new top-of-the-line computers we installed the day before yesterday. We're all using the first floor on a temporary basis until the third floor is ready. It's a colossal job but evolving. I have full faith in Ray's construction genius."

"He's a pet, alright. Is he still mad at Joe?"

"Not that I know of. Why would he be mad at Joe?"

"It was something Lee mentioned."

"What did he say?"

"Oh, nothing. I must have gotten it wrong." Coralee turned away; her expression inflexible.

Experienced with that look, Angelina knew not to push. "Okay, be stubborn, don't tell me. Anyway, I'm off to take Peewee for a walk on the beach. See you Monday morning." With Chilean-style hugs and kisses dealt with, Angelina closed Coralee's door behind her. No sooner did she let go of the doorknob, she felt her smile slide to be replaced with her recent wretchedness. The question returned to haunt her. Why was Ray angry with Joe?

Chapter Forty-four

Let loose, the small golden-haired terrier look-alike, ears flopping and tongue lolling, maniacally chased the gulls gathered on the beach. Berserk with gleeful anticipation of catching his prey, he ran frantically in one direction and then the other. The annoyed birds squawked, maddened by the forced abandonment of yummy tidbits.

Strolling along behind the delusional pup, Angelina began to unwind and soak in the beauty of the scene. Gathered at her neck in a loose ponytail, she'd hoped to confine her curls, but the wind wouldn't be denied. It blew the heavy mass every which way until it annoyed her. She stopped, gathered the strands together and wove it into a braid to keep it out of her face.

Happily meandering along, she happened upon a sight that saddened her heart. On a washed-up, sun-bleached log, a woman sat with a coffee in one hand and a cellphone in the other. Deeply absorbed in her gadget, she paid no attention whatsoever to a small, dejected boy, a toy truck dangling from his fingers, his eyes focused despondently on her. His body language reflected boredom and loneliness. Angelina wondered how the silly woman could bring him to a child's wonderland and then ignore him.

Shaking her head, she continued on her way. She paid little attention to others who strolled along, enjoying the perfect, warm afternoon. The lone males were of no interest to her, and the couples made her feel solitary.

***

When Joe came up behind the tiny, preoccupied woman, he knew at once it was Angelina, and that God had it in for him. He clenched his sweaty hands and gritted his teeth. Go figure that he'd run into her. Hell, missing her was the very reason he'd come to walk the beach.

Buried in his head, she'd penetrated deep, and no matter how he'd lectured himself, she wouldn't be shaken. He'd woken up from dreams filled with her beguiling smile, her soft skin—even her smell. Haunted by the what-might-have-beens, he'd hoped the strong wind and aggressive exercise would purge her from him so he could be free.

Just then, Joe spotted two ogling fellows whose heads swiveled to check out her retreating figure, and he knew his glowering at them was way out of line.

She's mine!

As soon as those words hit him, jealousy flared and burned his gut like a vicious case of acid reflux. He gritted his teeth and stuck his hands deep in his pockets. Leave her be, Joe. Don't mess with fire.

Repeatedly, with conviction, he'd warned himself to stay away. She wasn't a good-time girl to score with and dump when the party was over. He knew wife-material when he saw it. What pained him was how perfectly she would have fit in with his family. They would love her. But she wasn't for him and he had to respect that fact.

Grumpily, he turned to go back to his truck. He hadn't noticed Peewee gamboling in the sand until he saw a huge German shepherd streak past him in the small puppy's direction. The larger canine had obviously taken a dislike to sharing his domain with the usurper and intended to teach the little mutt a lesson. With his scruff standing stiff, growls intended as a precursor to the attack, Joe knew poor little Peewee was in for trouble.

He might have been able to sneak away from the woman who hadn't seen him yet, but the yapping puppy knew Joe and was running frantically to get to him, his furry face alight with the joy of greeting.

Suddenly, Peewee realized the danger from the approaching ferocious aggressor. Trying to put on the brakes only caused him to skid and then flip ass-over-teakettle and be a perfect target. Without another thought, Joe sprinted and scooped up the pup a few seconds before the maniac could do any damage. An elbow in the lunger's chest put an end to that nonsense, and so did the harsh yell he used to scare him off. The excited, tongue-lolling mess he cuddled close quivered in his arms and let loose little cries of fear. In the time it took to soothe the frisky pooch with gentle pats and hugs, while allowing the facewash the agitated pup bestowed on him, Angelina had approached.

Her sexy, accented voice calling his name created a predictable reaction. His guts tightened, adrenaline kicked in and his mouth lost all the moisture. He looked at her and melted. While his eyes devoured her prettiness, gladness overrode resolution. From the back she was perfection, but from the front, the woman radiated with pleasure, and that, he couldn't resist.

***

Angelina couldn't believe her luck. As if her yearning had created the flesh and blood man, she sent up a thank-you to those unseen spirits who were on her side. She looked to see how he felt about the chance meeting and her heart dropped. How could this man be so unaffected, and she be so infatuated—so utterly, deliriously, euphorically, stupidly infatuated?

"Hi, Angel." He lowered the puppy to the ground and waited for her to approach.

Amazingly, she felt none of her usual annoyance at someone using that term, and not a bit of her habitual shyness. On tiptoes, she reached out her hand and leaned over to kiss his cheek in polite salutation.

He intertwined his fingers with hers and lowered his cheek. Then he pointed at the puppy again chasing the birds along the shoreline. "He had a close call from that German Shepherd."

"I saw what happened. Thank goodness you were there and could help him. Even though dogs are allowed to roam the beach untethered till the end of the month, I should have kept him on his leash. He's such a little fellow..."

Just then a gust of wind captured her hair and unwound strands that flew everywhere, some covering her face.

As Joe captured a handful and caressed the shining mass, holding it back to protect her face, the world stopped dead. In a vacuum of delight, she stared into his eyes which were now fully engaged with hers. Neither moved. No one spoke. She melted at the adoration plainly written on his features.

Emotion, too heavy for her to handle, forced her into his waiting arms and they hugged. No words were spoken. They didn't need to say anything; the moment of perfection seemed to soothe both wounded spirits.

Finally, Peewee's frenzied barking had to be acknowledged. Angelina turned her back to Joe, and felt his arms hug around her waist and snuggle her to his body. They both watched to see what had disturbed the agitated pup this time.

Incredibly, hundreds of seagulls—a spectacular sight—lifted on the air currents, floated simultaneously and then soared every which way. They were a vision of spiritual joy on shifting airflows. The uniquely sounding screech, multiplied by the number of birds, rang like a cacophony from an orchestra not expected to ever make it to a Broadway concert hall.

A fleeting but distinctly fishy odor attacked her senses and added further to the reality of them being on the seashore…. together. Taking her hand delicately in his, Joe guided her through the driftwood spewed randomly over the weed-choked bank to reach the walkway. They settled themselves comfortably on one of the many benches, resting close together.

"I wondered if I'd see you again," she said without forethought. Once she heard her words, she bit her lip and stuttered, trying to take them back. "I-I'm not scolding you. It's just that you left so suddenly the other night."

"I did. I'm sorry. I know there's been a lot of work to do, and I wanted to help you—"

She interrupted before he could continue. "I don't need a worker or a boss, Joe. Just a friend. I like to handle things myself, and not rely on anyone else anyway." Shush, Angie, and stop being so stubborn!

"And I can't help being an interfering male and wanting to assist a lady in need. My mother brought me up to be a gentleman and to be useful. But let's not go there now. Today is too perfect. Let's just enjoy the view."

The ocean was beautiful. Its surface, like a sparkling mirror of icy blue crystals, rippled from strong gusts of wind. And the clouds hovering above reflected on the water, darkening it in some places and lightening it in others.

As they sat quietly, Angelina realized she was tongue-tied and prayed he'd start a conversation. After a short uncomfortable silence, he asked, "What made you decide to live in Victoria?"

"Actually, I was born here. Since then, every year, we came to visit my grandmother. I grew to love Victoria. As I became older, I found it harder to leave. Worse, I hated to return to the sheltered existence my father and brothers forced on me. I was suffocating there. Here, I was allowed many freedoms, and as I grew older, those became more and more important to me. Finally, I had to make a choice. Either remain in Chile and be the daughter my father wanted or prove to him I could be the woman I wanted."

When she fell silent, he said. "Tell me more."

"Well, mi papá owns a large accounting business back home, where I've always dreamed one day I'd work. Of course, my vision was that I would assume my rightful place alongside him and my two brothers, and eventually be accepted as a partner. I'd earned the appropriate credentials so there should have been no problem."

"What happened?"

"Let's just say this wasn't in my father's plans. He's an old-fashioned Chilean who has other goals for his only daughter. Over the past two years, I've been trying to prove to him that I'm as good as my brothers and can work just as hard. If all goes well, in less than a month, I'll own my firm outright, and he'll have his proof."

"I am impressed. I guess your brothers must be very proud of you."

"Are you kidding? They're positive I've gotten advice from some man, and only Lady Luck has kept me from going under. All my life, they've tried to take care of my problems. They're like two old women, and as much as I love them, they drive me batty." Sensing she'd said enough, Angelina changed the subject. "What about you, Joe? Were you born here?" Angelina could not believe she had gone on and on about herself. Strangely, she felt surprisingly comfortable with this Joe.

"Yes, I'm the baby of the family. I have five older brothers, all married and all scattered around the city."

"Your poor mother."

"Poor mother? Be serious! The woman is blessed," he teased.

"Is she still in therapy?" Angelina teased back.

He laughed uproariously. "No, they released her last year on probation."

Giggling, and loving this side of him, Angelina continued to probe. "Are your brothers following suit with large families?"

"They're all working on it. So far, I have seven nieces and nephews, and two more in the chute."

"Why haven't you followed the rest and surrendered to wedded bliss?"

"Me? Not gonna happen! No wife, no kids—and no plans to change." His spiel erupted and sounded well-rehearsed.

Feeling heat in her cheeks, Angelina babbled. "I love kids. One day I would like to have a family, but I guess first I need to hook me a dutiful husband." Not knowing how these words would inflame him, she grinned, wanting him to join in the joke.

Joe stiffened and leaned forward to grasp his hands together between his knees. Then he looked at her, his eyes flashing. "You mean, trap some poor sap so crazy in love, he won't be able to say no to you. You'll lead him around with the proverbial ring in his nose, and the sucker will be so infatuated, he'll let you, even love you for doing it. He'll give up his space, his freedom, his pride, his balls, and what's worse, he won't even care. I saw it happen with my brothers. Now they're manipulated and controlled. It's pitiable, and what really burns my behind is that they pretend to be happy."

Just then a very tired, bedraggled, soaking-wet pup skidded to a stop, shook himself and sprayed both of the before flopping down beside Angelina's feet, happy and exhausted. Glad for the chance to change the uncomfortable subject, she dug in her pocket for her keys and stood.

Joe rose at the same time and before she knew it, he'd reached for her hands. His good mood having returned, he swung her arms back and forth and asked, "Do you want to head over to my mom and dad's with me for a family barbecue? If I don't appear on Sundays, my mom leaves threats on my voicemail, and text messages me with insults all week."

Surprised delight filled Angelina and it must have showed on her face. His smile widened and a twinkle shone from his eyes. Suddenly shy, she lowered her head, released his hold, and bent to brush some sand from Peewee. "I'd love to, but I must check in with Tee. She was sleeping when I left, but she'll probably want company by now. I stopped to visit with Coralee earlier, so I've been gone most of the day."

Joe stooped to help her hold the wiggling pup still. His voice changed, becoming gentle. "Have you called anyone in Social Services, or the Missing Children's Registry about Tee yet?"

Affronted and knowing she shouldn't be, Angelina bit out. "No and I'm not going to. She's safe with me. I'm giving her time to come to terms with what her choices are, and what she wants to do. School is our biggest priority, and so far, she's receptive."

"For her to enroll in any school she needs her papers; you know that."

"Of course, I know. I'm biding my time until my grandmother gets back, and we'll figure out something together. Right now, I thank my lucky stars I found her in the first place. What if she hadn't appeared that day?"

"Then you wouldn't have this worry. You can't live by what-ifs."

"Worry? You mean I wouldn't have had the joy of knowing her. I consider Tee a bonus in my life, not something to regret. And I use 'what-if's' as a way to remember how lucky I am." His piercing gaze stopped her from continuing.

He nodded; his eyes now hooded. "Just so you understand, I'm on your side. If there's anything I can do to help, let me know. In fact, I was thinking we should ask her to come with us to the barbecue. There'll be lots of people there and great food. You think she'd like to tag along?"

Angelina's surprise covered her face so even a blind man wouldn't have missed it. This perplexing guy continued to shock her silly. "I'll call and ask her, and thank you for the invitation."

Chapter Forty-five

As soon as Joe pulled into the driveway, Angelina saw that his parents lived in a wonderful, huge, two-storied rambling home. On three sides, the wrap-around verandas were festooned with daffodils, tulips and other spring blooms. The front of the house, beautifully maintained with manicured lawns, fish-laden pools, and small bridges, thrilled the onlooker. On this exceptionally warm day, the flowering gardens were delightful, and set off the green-trimmed, white house perfectly.

"Joe, is it okay for me to wander in the gardens for a few minutes? It's really cool."

"Sure, Tee. We'll be with the rest of the family. Join us when you're ready."

A group of young adults and children were milling around the roomy, enclosed backyard that sported a collection of comfy garden chairs and loungers. There was an opulent stainless-steel barbecue prominently displayed to the side of a rambling cedar deck where the men had congregated. Nearby, large steel and glass tables were set, ready for the food.

First, Joe introduced Angelina to his mother, and then left her in the care of the Davidson women while he went to fetch cold drinks.

"I'm happy to meet you, Angelina." Vera Davidson introduced the other five women sitting nearby. Automatically, Angelina slipped into her customary greeting mode and bent to shake each woman's hand as she bestowed gentle kisses on their cheeks. This ploy seemed to break the ice and they all beamed at her in return. "Joe phoned to say he'd invited two friends and we were to behave ourselves, not ask too many questions and to make you feel at home," Vera said.

Angelina laughed, shaking her head slightly. "How chivalrous your son is."

The others giggled with her, some nodding and others scoffing. "Joe is all about Joe. Don't mistake us, he's a sweetheart. But he has some very strange ideas about women."

All ears, she listened politely and watched as Vera Davidson's scowl put an end to the others' gossip. Just then Tee approached.

The girl had dressed with special care for the afternoon. Her hair, which she normally tucked into a cap, was highlighted with lines of red sprayed-on color, and shaped with gel. It looked provocative, modern—a bit overdone? Maybe a little! But nonetheless, to Angelina, she appeared endearingly cute. Multi-colored plastic doodads adorned her artful hairstyle, and she had inserted earrings which were designed in such a way so as to give one the impression she had five holes in each ear. Her nose ring, fake also, the prevailing fashion today, drew one's eye and most likely encouraged ridicule from old fuddy-duddies.

The jeans she wore—her usual uniform—looked washed out, holes place strategically and wrinkled lines around the thighs, but regulation for today's youth. Her blouse, the first Angelina had ever seen her wear, was white, lacy, and a distinct change from her normal T-shirt style.

After introducing the shy youngster to the other women, Angelina said, "I never thought to ask if you use sunscreen. I have some in my bag if you need any?"

Tee grinned and pointed to the large straw object next to Angelina's chair. "You have the whole drugstore in your bag. Thanks, I'm cool."

Some of the kids, watching this byplay, must have decided Tee was also cool, and they declared open season on her. Angelina figured her funky looks appealed to the little hellions, and they wanted her attention.

Before they could drag her away, Carmen, one of Joe's sister-in-laws broke in, "If these monsters bug you too much, Tee, just wave or flash me a sign and I'll rescue you." She laughed as she made this speech, but no one could mistake her seriousness.

"No problem. I like kids," Tee answered, apparently telling the truth.

Just then a little guy about three or so, wearing baggy jeans decorated by a small chain hanging from the pocket to the waist, and an oversized red hoodie with an emblem SK8, written like graffiti in black and blazoned across the front, pushed his way into the group looking for his mom. His dark brown hair was slicked upwards in a spiked fashion, but a stubborn cowlick, creating a curl to the left side of his forehead, distorted the total effect. Stunningly familiar endearing green eyes, prominent in this family of handsome men, shone from his angelic plump face.

He went right up to his Uncle Joe, who'd appeared carrying two drinks, and stared hard into his face. Then he reached to grasp his hand and pulled so that Joe was forced to pass the glass of wine to Angelina and a coke to Tee and kneel. He encircled the child with his strong arms and hugged him. The boy leaned back, pulling away, and stared belligerently at his uncle.

"I misted you, Uncle Joe. You dinn't come to see me and I misted you so bad my misser got sore." Having said his piece, he hugged his open-mouthed, stunned uncle, and then moved away.

Stopping by Tee, he gave her his eagle-eyed once-over.

"Hey, little dude, what's your name?" she asked.

"Danny. Uts yours?"

"Tee," she said. Then she hunkered down to his height. "Want me to push you on the swing?" She pointed to the play set in the corner of the garden, where all the children's activities and riding toys were.

He studied her, his head held at an angle. She stared right back until suddenly, her eyes began to bug out and go cross-eyed.

Chortling, instant buddies, accepting her with an adorable smile and by lifting his arms, he astounded the family who watched this byplay. Mouths hung agape, and every face wore identical stunned reactions.

As soon as the little boy and teenager moved out of range, everyone started talking at once, especially Carmen, the boy's mom. Looking at Angelina, she shook her head wonderingly.

"Danny is so shy; it's been near-to impossible to take him to a daycare or playschool. And getting a babysitter? Well – forget it! Even with the family, and we're talking people he's known all his life, he's very picky about who he wants to be near. He went straight to your Tee and even asked to be picked up. It's amazing! I'm speechless."

Joe, catching Angelina's eye, asked a silent question with a raised eyebrow. Her answering smile and nod let him assume that she was happy and comfortable. He then joked with his favorite sister-in-law, knowing he'd be booed and chased off. "Speechless, Carmen? Ah—I don't think so!"

Watching him amble toward his father and brothers, Angelina owned up to the fact that he had the sexiest way of moving she'd ever noticed in any man. If eyes could eat, she'd just consumed a full-course meal.

"Are you and Joe an item?" The woman sitting to her left, introduced to her as Sara, Cody's wife, interrupted her musings.

Feeling as if there was more to the question than ordinary interest, Angelina scrutinized the girl before answering. She thought for a moment and decided the serious expression on the other woman's face was an indication that she wasn't being nosy, but she cared about Joe and was extending a friendly hand.

"An item? Oh no! We're just friends. New friends actually! I've only known Joe since the earthquake. I was one of the victims he rescued, well sort of." Her secretive grin caught Sara's eye.

"He loves working for the Search and Rescue. Some weeks they call him every night."

Wondering how Sara knew details about Joe's daily life made Angelina hesitant to say too much. She knew Joe tended to be closed about his personal affairs. She'd picked up the vibe from the man himself, and then Lee's descriptions from time to time had made her aware of this trait.

She glanced over to see his brothers open up their group and include him in with jostling camaraderie. Her softened gaze was unconscious and revealing.

Laughter reluctantly returned her attention back to the women's group, and she caught Carmen's teasing grin. She grinned back and shrugged her shoulders.

"He's something, ay?" Carmen leaned over and whispered behind her hand. "Us girls tease him that he's pure eye candy."

"He is that, but I bet he hates you saying it. I haven't known him for very long, but what I do know is that there's much more to him than how he looks. So far, he's taken on an earthquake to rescue me, helped Tee when she needed a strong arm and he's fast becoming a wonderful friend."

"Don't get me wrong. You don't need to stick up for him with me. We all think he's pure gold. Everyone here cares about him. It's just that we'd like to see him settle down. He's a wild one. All the Davidson boys were, but he's the last one single, and he's even more skittish than the others. You'll have your work cut out putting a bridle on that wild stallion."

With a wink Angelina answered in droll tones. "Did I happen to mention that I won many ribbons for bareback riding when I was a girl in Chile?"

Infectious laughter between the two had the rest of the ladies wanting to know what was so funny, but the subject was diplomatically changed.

Angelina's eyes searched again and found Joe easily. He was by far the tallest of the brothers, and in her opinion the best looking. But at the moment, he wasn't the happiest. In fact, he looked down right grumpy.

***

"Where's Dad?" Joe asked, looking around the yard, noticing his father's absence.

"Getting the steaks so we can start the cooking," his oldest brother, Lon, answered. Then he looked over to where Angelina was sipping a glass of wine, visiting happily with the wives.

"Hey, bro, your girl is gorgeous and... hot! Let's see how long you stay unattached with her on your horizon. Soon, my man, you too will be blindsided, handcuffed, married and loving it. My advice to you, little brother, is to get very used to the terms 'honey-do' and 'Yes, dear.'"

Chapter Forty-six

Later that same night, lying in her luxurious bed, Angelina could almost pinpoint the minute when Joe had changed. After approaching his brothers, he'd become distant, flippant, and terse, scowling at everyone. Like a shapeshifter with the ability to switch to animal form, Joe possessed the power to alter from being enthralled to man not interested. What could have happened to transform him from suitor to stranger in a matter of a few minutes?

She was relieved they'd used her car to drive to his parents' place, as it had been the perfect way to leave him behind after she'd grabbed Tee and escaped soon after dinner. A smart girl, Tee, had said very little on the way home, except to mention how much fun she'd had with the brats, and what an awesome family the Davidsons were.

Invitations to come back any time had resonated out as they'd taken their leave. Phone numbers had been exchanged between Angelina and Joe's female relatives. Lunches, get-togethers, and shopping trips had all been discussed and left open with promises that they would happen soon. Even Tee was inundated with offers, and freely gave her number to all the moms with babysitting on their minds.

They were warm and wonderful, all except for the person who mattered most: Joe. While they were leaving, Angelina had seen his mother giving him the evil eye, and he'd sheepishly walked them to the car. But he'd been distant and unlike the person she'd arrived with. Angry and hurt, as far as she was concerned, this gringo had flipped on her for the last time. She lay there remembering their last exchange.

"Are you sure your brother doesn't mind driving you to get your truck? I could drop you off? It really isn't out of our way." Angelina made the suggestion, politeness being second nature to her.

"No, it's fine. Lon and Carmen live close, and it'll give me extra time to spend with little Danny."

"To relieve his sore misser?"

"Something like that," he smiled ruefully.

Lying against her plumped-up pillows, she remembered his last grin, but she most of all remembered the wretchedness apparent in his knockout-green eyes. As inexperienced as she was, she knew he had some nasty demons to deal with. Wrestling with the tangled blankets yet again, the questions reverberated.

What had happened to the great guy at the beach? Had she done something wrong?

And more importantly, what had his brothers said to make him change so drastically?

And... why the hell was she crying over him... again?

Chapter Forty-seven

"Weren't you terrified to stay with those losers under the bridge? What were you thinking?" Dean demanded of Tee, while they sat together, eating ham sandwiches during their lunch break the next day.

Shrugging, she answered. "It wasn't the first time I've spent the night at that place. The little bit of money I'd brought with me had been stolen. So... I teamed up there with some of the others broke and homeless like me. At the very least, I'd figured the cops wouldn't pick me up." Thinking about losing her money reminded Tee of the stomach-sinking horror she'd felt once she'd realized it was gone. She also remembered the bitch who'd befriended her and was only after what she could get.

Dean interrupted her pondering "Why were you running from the cops? You can tell me. I promise I won't turn you in."

Even grinning, he looked solemn, and she heard the ring of truth in his tone. Instantly, a budding warmth wormed its way into the pit of uncaring she'd built for self-protection. "I...I just ran away from the freakin' system. Everywhere they placed me got worse. You know? It was creeps with their over-indulged weird kids, then sleazeballs I had to hide from, and scum who thought they were better than me. One day, I was with my social worker who meant to farm me out yet again, and she left me alone with my files. I found out I was born here in Victoria. I saw my mother's name—well, only her first name. But then and there, I decided to come and find her if I could. She didn't want me when she was fifteen, but maybe things have changed for her. You never know, and I don't really care. Nothing could be worse than my life up to now." She shuddered and looked away so he couldn't see the scared little girl she kept hidden.

Dean tried to catch her eye, but she refused to let him. She didn't want his pity. With her body stiff, she pulled away.

Full of sincerity, his low voice stopped her moving. "I know if I tell you the truth, say how sorry I am that life has been this hard for you, you'll get all ornery and take off. So, I'll just say that I really want to help. Have you started searching yet?"

Hesitating, she answered him. "Don't know how. But I'm saving all my wages. I figure I could use the same agency Angelina hired to find the owner of the gold."

"Good idea. Look, I have to ask. What if your mother doesn't want you to find her?"

Anger sprung from deep inside. Her voice shook with emotion, and she stared him down. "If she doesn't want me, I don't want her! It's as simple as that. I've lived all my life with people who don't want me and I'm never going to again. Ever!"

Dean put his warm hand on her arm and caressed the skin lightly. "We want you. All of us! I heard Coralee say that if Angelina's grandma had a problem with you living there, she would take you home with her."

"Coralee said that? She's chill, dude! She took me shopping a few days ago after work, and we had a blast. Like, she helped me pick out some rad tops, and even sneaked a crazy-nice white blouse into my bag when I wasn't looking. I'd put it back cause it was harsh—you know—expensive, but she'd gone and paid for it and then gave it to me as a present."

"She's a cool lady."

"Yeah!" Not wanting to come across as too needy, Tee bit her tongue and kept her response short.

Dean continued, "There's more. When Pops questioned Angelina about you, she told him not to worry because you would always have a home with her. She has total faith in her grandmother falling under your spell and working out some kind of a miracle with her posh friends to get you enrolled in a school as soon as they can."

Emotions rioting, Tee swiveled away and got to her feet. "We'd better get back to work, or you dad'll fire our butts."

"Hey, before we go, I want you to know something. If you ever—and I mean ever—need a friend, I'm here. The same goes for my dad. He's your biggest fan. If my mom was still alive, I firmly believe he'd have put in to adopt you by now. It's all we hear about at home. You shoulda be working as hard as Tee, yada, yada; she'sa smart, she'sa strong, she'sa funny, blah, blah. It's a good thing I like you."

Never having had anyone say such a thing to her before, Tee just gave him a friendly push and then rushed off to hide in the washroom until the tears stopped and the swelling around her eyes diminished.

***

The next week was hectic. Accumulated overtime hours were beginning to take their toll on everyone's nerves, not just Tee's. Ordinarily, the atmosphere in the office was relaxed and jovial. The co-workers had a functional rhythm of working together, tolerant and comfortable with each other.

But then, Tee knew that Angelina had been the heart, the brains, even the spirit, bolstering everyone else. Her attention to details and her indefatigable drive had carried them along, happy to follow her lead.

Until lately! Now she was no longer their gutsy, funny boss. Instead, she looked haunted and sad. Many times they caught her staring off into a world of her own imagination until something like a phone ringing would bring her back to earth, and she'd be in a frenzy to get back to her files. Most of them had no idea why she behaved this way, but Tee did. She blamed Joe.

Chapter Forty-eight

Head down, Angelina gave thanks for her wonderful crew who had all pitched in to make sure they were running at full speed this week. Her massive pile of files had saved her from letting her thoughts roam to where they traveled too often, to a man who one minute she wanted to kiss, and the next kick in the ass.

Stop it! Do what you love best—work. Angelina figured she still had time to win her wager, but now more than ever, she needed to concentrate on her priorities. Suddenly, Chile had begun to seem like a haven to her, an escape from recent painful experiences.

Today, completely surrounded by damaged, dirty ledgers piled on every available surface, she immersed herself in her job, living in her own little world. Except for the actual day of the earthquake, their computer files were up to date. All the spreadsheets and the accounts for every one of their customers were organized and balanced.

As an added blessing, she'd purchased top-of-the-line, extra strong, steel-paneled filing cabinets, expensive, but proving to be worth every penny. Since their walls were replaceable, the repairmen had been able to knock through them to get the books out. Though somewhat messy, ninety-nine percent of the files were legible and usable. The ones that had taken a beating were those laid out on the desks the day the quake struck.

Her customers would be thrilled at just how little damage she had sustained. After the episode, she had meticulously spent hours calling each and every one of them explaining about her security systems and assuring them once she had reopened, their individual files would be swiftly updated and kept current. Their support and well-wishes had been overwhelming and had given her the impetus to work all the harder.

Just then a well-tailored man knocked on the office's open door. "Are you Angelina Serrano, owner of Serrano's?"

"Yes, I am. How can I help you?"

"I'm Phil Cowden, attorney for Nathan Black, one of your clients."

"He's one of my best clients and a very nice man." Confused but businesslike, Angelina stood to shake his hand. Quickly lifting the folders from the chair closest to her desk, she made a gesture for Mr. Cowden to sit, which he ignored.

Nerves pounding, roused by the serious look on the man's face, she said, "What can I do for you, Mr. Cowden?"

Rather than following her prompt to sit, the uncomfortable-looking man searched in his briefcase and soon handed her an envelope. "If you have any questions concerning this situation, please contact my office." Seconds later he was gone, leaving behind confusion and dread. Nerve-wracking premonitions made her hesitate, until curiosity compelled her to read the letter.

Undisputedly, the damning sheet of legal mishmash put paid to all her dreams. She'd failed! Crazed laughter hit first, and then came unleashed fury. A notebook, innocently lying on her desk, was the first victim of her lack of control and was soon followed by the pen she'd been squeezing. Finding no release to her built-up frustration, she pounded the desk and a slew of Spanish blasphemy followed.

Ya basta! She'd had enough. Life had been kicking her in the ass for long enough. No more!

Grabbing her purse, she shoved the letter into the side pocket, stuck her cellphone next to it and hightailed it to the front door. Coralee and Lee sneaking a clinch in the hallway pulled apart. "Angie, what's happened?"

Angelina looked neither right nor left but headed straight for the exit. "Nothing I can't handle."

She stormed outside, only to skid to a standstill when she noticed Joe leaning against a Search and Rescue truck, looking better than any man had a right to look when all she wanted to do was write him off for being MIA.

He straightened and approached warily. "What's wrong, Angel-ah-lina?"

This man was getting to her. "Nothing! I just have to go and see a man about a lawsuit."

"Excuse me?" He blanched. "What's happened?" He stood in her path and wouldn't let her go around him.

"What do you care? You're hiding out here, so we won't meet. Think I don't know?"

He had the nerve to look somewhat sheepish but belligerent at the same time. "You're wrong! I didn't want to bother you, and Lee just had to take a minute to confirm plans with Coralee."

"Bah!" Her hand slashed in front of his face. Then her eyes dug holes into his dubious excuse, and he looked away. It was only because she had something else on her mind that she took pity on him. "One of my customers sent his lawyer with a letter to accuse Serrano's of embezzling funds from their accounts. I'm on my way to tell him what I think of him for sending his lawyer to do his dirty work. He couldn't even face me himself. Bastardo!"

"He's crazy! What kind of proof did the guy give you? His allegations must have come with some kind of justification. Have they started some sort of investigation?"

Staggered by his questions, Angelina's brain reassembled from furious self-pity to participation. "You're right. Those are valid questions, and I know just the person to ask." Angelina turned away from Joe, and at a fast pace, she started down the block.

"Hold it. Where are you going?"

"I'm going to tackle Mr. Black in person and get some answers to those very queries. No-one calls me a thief and gets away with it. Not without a fight."

Joe continued to walk beside her, while at the same time he sent a text message. "I'll just let Lee know to wait for me."

Stunned, Angelina stopped. "Now why the heck would you do that?"

"Because I'm coming with you. Considering the mood you're in, things might get out of hand. And there's no way I'm letting you deal with this situation without back-up. Lead on."

Her heartbeats had accelerated the minute she'd seen him. But nothing equaled the pleasure his words brought. However, stubbornness kicked in and she wouldn't give him the satisfaction of seeing her gladness. "Do what you want, I don't care."

She stalked into a building two corners away, prowled past the receptionist, who jumped up and then made her way to the office that had Sam Black written on the door. A young man stood slowly; his brow raised in a question. "It's okay, Stella. I'll handle this." He waited until she closed the door behind her and then looked at Angelina and Joe. "Can I help you? I'm Sam Black."

The yummy man, handsome as sin, standing with his hand extended, could have posed for GQ, or starred as a hero in an action movie. Angelina forced saliva into her dry mouth and croaked, "Sam Black? Then you must be Nathan Black's son."

"Yes, Nathan's my father. How can I help you?"

"You can tell me why the hell he sent his lawyer to serve me with this ridiculous allegation." She threw the letter at him and crossed her arms.

"I'm sorry to have to be the one to tell you, Miss Serrano, but we're accusing you because there's $80,000 missing from our accounts. And the only drain there can possibly be is through your company."

Angelina's pulse quickened and she felt faint. "It can't be. Our people are as honest as the day is long. They would never steal from anyone. There must be a mistake and I intend to find it. We'll be going over every one of your accounts; the details of every transaction. Your daily ledgers, journal entries and your month ends. I'll even hire an independent auditor. Señor, you'd best start working on an apology—a real one."

A sardonic smile lifted one side of Sam Black's face. He looked first at Joe and then to Angelina. "I don't think so, Miss Serrano, and that—I'll admit—is regretful."

Angelina noticed Joe's frown at the flirtatious way Sam Black bowed and then guided her to the door. Maybe Joe stood taller, and had a lot more muscle, but any man as good-looking as Sam should be licensed.

Chapter Forty-nine

Tee tried to sneak out of sight when she saw Ray bearing down on her. Unfortunately, he caught up.

"Hold it, munchkin. The clock says five-thirty—quitting time. You're still getting over that rotten cold and it's my butt on the line if you have a relapse."

"Aw, Ray! Dude, you must have eyes in the back of your head. I'm waiting for Angie anyway, so I'll just finish up this last bit. Don't sweat it, okay? Lighten up! I'm fine now."

"I'll be tellin' you when you're fine, cookie. That wasn't a request. It's an order. You get your tail outta here. There's no more work to be done until Monday—Capisce? Anymore of your lip, and I swear I'll spill the beans to Angelina about how you're not taking care of yourself."

"Fine, you sneaky ol' man. I'm finished." With that Tee threw her hands into the air, in a gesture similar to one he would have used himself and strutted with exaggeration to the main office.

Seeing hyperactivity in the office at a time when normally everyone would be shutting down for the day had her questioning Coralee. "What's up?"

So far, Coralee had treated Tee with kindness and a distant kind of acceptance. She hadn't demonstrated suspicion outwardly, but Tee had the feeling it was always there, underneath. She knew she was being watched, closely.

Coralee nodded her head towards the chair closest to her desk. "Come over here," she said. "And keep this to yourself."

Something was wrong. Tee knew it, in the same way she knew it was bad.

Coralee looked deeply into her eyes and Tee held her gaze. Stare trouble down! That lesson had been well-learned over her short but unhappy life.

"Angelina's been accused of stealing money from one of her clients. A sleazebag lawyer came today with a letter, serving notice that she has a week to return eighty thousand dollars, or they'll file a suit against her."

Tee bolted to her feet. "No way!" Righteous anger simmered. Having a dislike of being touched or touching, careful to never instigate it, Tee reached out unthinkingly to Coralee and grabbed her by the hand. "There's no damn way Angelina is a thief."

Tee saw a warm smile light up the other woman's face. Holding Tee's hand in both of hers, she squeezed gently.

"Don't fret, sweetie, we have the proof to set things right. It'll take time and oodles of work, but we can prove Serrano's is scrupulously honest."

"What can I do to help?"

Coralee nodded as if to say—I knew we could depend on you. Tee unexpectedly felt a shifting of emotion inside her chest.

"How about you heading down the street for some pizza and soft drinks?" Coralee reached for her purse, but Tee stopped her going there.

"I've got it covered." She couldn't help her proud tone and blushed.

"Thanks, kid. This is going to be a long night. We'd better feed the troops to keep their brains active. Thank God tomorrow is Saturday. We can stop working on our other accounts and concentrate strictly on this one."

"Just so you know, I'm sticking in here with you guys tonight. Find me something to do that'll help her." With her message stated loud and clear, Tee stomped out of the office, scowling at the world.

Chapter Fifty

For the first time in days, Tee had no lingering symptoms of her recent cold and was feeling healthier than she had in a long, long time. Wrapped in nothing but a large bath towel, believing herself alone in the house, she'd decided to go to the kitchen and fetch a cup of hot chocolate.

"I'm aware the youth of today have changed significantly from when I was young, but I must say it's a bit risky wandering around in your birthday suit with only a towel for protection, don't you think?"

Tee shrieked. Reeling, cowering, she totally crumbled, unheard of behavior from a gutsy girl whose defenses were always on high alert. For some reason, in Angelina's home, she had lowered her guard, feeling safe, warm—blissfully happy.

All thanks to Angelina and Rosario, two wardens who were freaky about her taking her medicine, getting enough sleep, not to mention the quantities of wholesome food they'd plied her with. Secretly, she loved the attention and felt normal for the first time in her life, or at least as close to normal as she could possibly imagine normal was.

At Angelina's request—okay, orders—Tee had promised to spend her Saturday morning sleeping in, maybe coloring her hair and taking time for herself. She had a full intention of going into the office to help the others, but to keep Angelina cool; her plan was to show up later.

Rewrapping her rebellious towel and slowly turning, she masked her fear with her trademark cheekiness.

"Hey? Give a girl a heart attack?"

"Pardon me? What about the stroke I'm contemplating? Little girl, I do appreciate your young healthy attributes, but if you please, could you adjust your cover." The towel had slipped again at the mention of the old lady possibly croaking. Frantically, Tee tightened the cloth over her smallish breasts and tucked it under.

"There now! I am Evie Butcher, Angelina's grandmother. This is my home and I assume you're Tee, ah... short for trouble, my granddaughter's guest. Would you be so kind as to join me in the sunroom? When you're respectfully clothed, that is."

"Yeah, okay." Speechless and mortified to be caught in such an awkward predicament, Tee was at a loss for words. Not a normal comfort zone for her.

As if she had expected no less, Grandma Evie nodded and headed briskly into the kitchen, and Tee rushed to her room to get ready. Nervous, and disliking the feeling, she made sure her teeth were sparkling and her hair was sufficiently tamed. Then she donned a T-shirt that was one of her newest.

What if the old lady doesn't like me? Doing an inspection, she looked in the mirror, scanning herself like a stranger would. Seeing nothing out of the ordinary that would mark her as being a misfit, an unwanted child or a someone close to losing it, she shoved her hands in her pockets and headed down to meet her fate. Be nice, don't freakin' get your shit in a knot... try and make her like you.

A tray dressed with fancy dishes, a hefty platter of cinnamon buns, butter, flowered blue napkins and strawberries coated with thick cream was waiting along with the old lady when Tee, fake cockiness restored, bounced into the room.

She stopped in the doorway to survey the scene. Angelina's grandmother had fluffy white curls haloing her lined face and piercing blue eyes that stared at Tee with a warning. I might look like a lovable, little old lady, but beware...

"Are you going to stand there with your mouth open, child, or will you join me?"

Tee, flustered, moved forward at the beckoning from the matriarch waiting for her.

"How did you know me?"

"Who could mistake Angelina's description? She hit the mark, right down to the flower tattoos and the – um – delightful ring through your nose. Your hair was further proof. I must say I don't believe I've ever seen that particular shade before. Somewhere between plum and magenta, I should think."

Bristling and unable to stop herself, Tee slipped into character. "Are you dissin' me?" she asked. It was hard to tell since the twinkling eyes and the softness in Grandma Evie's voice made the old lady hard to read.

"The only "dissin " I'm doing is dishing up your brunch. Come here, please, help yourself." In a queenly fashion, Evie waved her hands over the coffee table where the tasteful banquet was displayed.

Gladly digging in with gusto, Tee's groan of ecstasy from her first bite of cinnamon bun changed the atmosphere.

"You like my cinnamon buns?"

"You made these?" Talking with her mouth full didn't seem to faze the other woman, and Tee was glad she'd ignored her slip in manners. "How come you're here? Angelina figured you were staying in Vegas with her parents."

"I made up a fictitious story about a forgotten dentist appointment and came home early."

"You mean you lied."

Grandma Evie bristled. "I never tell lies." When she saw Tee's raised eyebrow, her eyes lowered. "Well... only in an emergency," the old lady admitted, winking at an intrigued Tee.

"And this was an emergency?" questioned Tee, sticking to the subject like a baby sucking his thumb.

"When we talked to Angelina after the earthquake, her voice reassured me that the crisis was over. She wasn't in any danger and there was no need for us to be with her. In fact, she implied we'd be somewhat of a hindrance because she had so much to do. Let me tell you, it was difficult to talk her father out of rushing here to deal with her problems. Both her mother and I had to use all our wiles on the man. Knowing how independent and protective Angelina is about controlling her own business, we worked hard to calm him. We suspected it would take time for the repairs, and since we had a full itinerary lined up, there was no hurry to return."

Tee's admitted. "It was true—at the beginning." Protecting Angelina came easy.

"Except for the fact she had downplayed the severity of the damage. I saw it for myself when I had the taxi drive me past the office building this morning on the way home from the airport," Grandma Evie said rather sternly. "Again, my granddaughter's voice was normal, even happy when she described the remodeling, and also the success of Coralee's operation. Other than certain nuances, which I took for affection in her voice when she explained about you, the gold and your service to her, she continued to sound happy and upbeat. Mind you, I have to admit there was always a strange inflection when she mentioned Dr. Davidson, who, by the way, I'm anxious to meet; she still came across as our independent, in-control girl. Then yesterday, her voice rang false. I sensed fear, worry and even disillusionment, so here I am. Do you have a story you need to share with me, Tee?"

"It's nothing but pure bullshit, is what it is," Tee said, ranting, forgetting herself in her righteous indignation. As soon as the swear word reverberated around the room, she stiffened and her eyes swiveled to her companion. How could you forget, you idiot?

Ignoring Tee's tension, Grandma Evie reached over to pat her hands. "Tell me, child. I want to help my Angelina, and I can't unless I know what's happening here."

Feeling her shoulders loosen, Tee ignored the panic attack and answered, "Some moron who Angelina's company does the books for is trying to charge her with fraud or stealing, cooking his books— something like that. It's bullsh—crap. Angie wouldn't even keep the gold coins we found buried in her own building. Said they likely belonged to the previous owners. In fact, she hired a private investigator to find the people so she could return them. Seriously, she's no more a thief than I am."

"Tee," Grandma interrupted her, "you are welcome to stay in my home for as long as you wish. Angelina needs friends like you. And so do I."

Tee felt another shift happening deep inside. She allowed this woman to join Angelina in the space she occupied and wondered that her heart didn't burst from so much tenderness. Worried that tears weren't far away, she croaked the words, "Thank you," and the other woman reached for her.

With her rough fingers firmly wedged between both of Grandma Evie's soft palms, the elder said firmly, "I think it's time I made an appearance."

"Good thinking, Mrs. Butcher. I was going to head downtown myself as soon as I finished getting ready."

"Little girl, you will refer to me as Grandma or Grandma Evie, whichever you prefer. Mrs. Butcher is used only by strangers and people I don't particularly care for."

"Sweet! I've never called anyone Grandma before so... ah, yeah, I'd like to." Tee knew the grin on her face was probably pathetic, but she didn't care. Grandma!

Chapter Fifty-one

Later in the day, Johnnie stopped Coralee at the bottom of the stairs and pulled her into the small alcove underneath.

"I'm going to shoot that bloody Joe," he spat out. "Unless Ray gets to him first."

"Did I happen to mention I have an old shotgun I'd be happy to donate? I'll even clean it and buy the bullets. We can e-mail each other from our jail cells to keep in touch," she answered, half-joking.

"Christ! I liked the guy. Thought they looked good together. Who'd have thought he'd end up being a player."

"He had me fooled too. I'm so goofy-in-love with Lee, I missed what was happening right under my own snoopy nose. At first, they seemed to tippy-toe around each other, and then it looked like they were beginning to hit it off, but something's happened. Her anger at the Blacks' treachery hides it somewhat, but it's like she's in a trance—walking, talking, working, but the essence of Angelina is buried under blankets of sadness or something. I can't explain it, but it's breaking my heart to see her like this. Okay, I'm in. Let's run the creep over with your SUV."

Just then Lee sauntered by and spotted the two gossipy slackers. "What's up?"

Coralee turned on him, Johnnie at her back. "We'll tell you what's up. Your hustling, jackass friend is breaking our best friend's heart, the spineless shit."

"Hey! Back off!" His rare vehemence shocked them both. "You don't really know the guy, but he's a mess too. He told me today Angelina was stalking him."

Before they could refute his statement, he held his hand up to continue, "Made no sense to me, so I point blank asked him what the hell he was talking about. He said she's buried herself so deep in his head, the cost of seeing a shrink to eradicate her was going to devastate his budget this year."

Agog, both Coralee and Johnnie listened, smiles slowly starting to form. Coralee spoke for them both. "You're saying he's got the hots for her. That he's smitten. That it's not only Angelina?"

"Oh yeah! He's a goner," sniggered Lee.

"Well! Bloody hell! Why doesn't he tell her and put us all out of our misery?" Johnnie piped up.

"Because he hasn't admitted it to himself yet," Lee answered.

Ever the cynic, Coralee interrupted. "He's rejecting his own feelings—and her. The guy's a conceited bum who probably figures she'll pine away waiting for him to come around." Fuming on behalf of her pal, Coralee glared at both men.

"No." Lee broke in again. "He's not like that. Joe's an honorable guy. He wouldn't hurt anyone on purpose. I guess he's scared silly he'll end up like his brothers, and consequently he's always shied away from getting too involved with a certain kind of girl."

Johnnie asked, "So what's wrong with his brothers?"

"They're all married."

"Oh... gotcha!" said Johnnie, nodding his head up and down, instantly zeroing in on the problem.

Eyes shooting daggers back and forth to both men, arms folded aggressively, Coralee sputtered, "And so?"

Johnnie put his arm around her shoulders and, for the first time in days, looked his old cheerful self.

"Hang in there, babe. All is not lost. Most guys go through some sort of trauma when the idea of getting hitched looms on the horizon. It's lame, pitiful, even shallow, but reality nonetheless."

Lee kicked in. "He's fighting with himself to stay away from her, and he's losing not only her, but his spirit. He's a miserable, sorry-assed copy of who he used to be and, let me tell you, I miss him just as much as you guys miss Angelina."

"We're going to have to get involved before this thing goes too far," Coralee schemed out loud. "I'll get back to you guys as soon as I have a workable, doable plan. Okay?"

***

"Check," were the two replies clearly heard by the eavesdropper at the top of the stairs, who'd been perched there, listening since the beginning of their conversation.

She thought, so this is what a jumpstarted motor feels like. Filled with anticipation and hope—incredible antidotes to heartbreak—she hopped up, lifted her leg and cocked her knee over the banister. Down she flew...

Right into Ray who hadn't yet left for the day.

No explanation was necessary. When he saw the stars in her eyes and the unholy grin on her face, he chuckled.

"Shes-a back!"

Chapter Fifty-two

A visit from the private investigator, Adam Small, was the next diversion in Angelina's suddenly re-established happy life. The man had stopped by to give her an update about her treasure.

"It seems all the previous owner's family has died out. In fact, his wife passed away a year after selling the building to you. Her estate was ironically left to a local charity. Now, I do believe by law, you are the owner of the bag of gold coins because it was part of the property when you purchased it. Check the facts with a lawyer if you're still confused, but if I were you... well, never mind. Do what you have to do."

Angelina listened to the P.I. and decided she would take his advice. Some days earlier, she'd made a phone call to her company lawyer and had been given the same recommendation.

"The young girl, Tee, who first found the gold and again recovered the bag after it was stolen, will be given half. The rest will be donated to a charity here in Victoria. Since I didn't earn the money myself, I don't feel any right to it," Angelina stated unequivocally.

Admiration appeared on Adam's face and made her blush. "I don't know if I could be as generous in your place."

"It's not generosity, its civic conscience. The addict who tried to steal the bag of coins was a teenager. Something has to be done to get these young runaways and substance abusers off the streets and into rehab. And I know just the guy who works like a dog towards that goal. He'll give me a hand finding the right organization that'll use the money in a functional way that'll help a lot of kids. What better use could the money have?"

"I have to admit your plan sounds pretty special. If there's anything I can do, let me know."

"Actually, there is one thing I wanted to discuss. Remember me mentioning Tee? The girl who saved the bag of coins? She has a job for you. Do you have time?"

"Absolutely, all the time she needs."

Angelina lifted the phone and made an inter-office call.

A short while later, Tee arrived, furiously brushing down her working clothes. "Sorry to be so dirty. If you want to wait for a few minutes, I can clean up a bit?" She looked questioningly at Angelina.

"No need, Tee. I want you to meet Mr. Small. He's from the agency we hired to help us find the previous owners of the gold coins. And, he has some good news. It seems I bought the building from an old woman who had no living family. Looks like we get to keep the gold. Even though I don't know the exact amount yet, as I promised, half is yours."

"You're serious?"

"Oh yeah!"

"There is a God!" Prayer-like, Tee clasped her hands in front of her face.

"When we talked about the chance of you coming into half the money, you explained your circumstances. You said you'd been saving your wages in order to hire an investigator to find your birth mother. You can afford it now."

Having a hard time forming words, Tee stuttered. "I – I only have her first name, and my date of birth. I know I was born in Victoria, at the Royal Jubilee Hospital, but that's it."

From the breathless way she spoke, Angelina was aware of how important those details were to Tee.

"What's her name? And your date of birth?" Adam began to fill in a form taken from his briefcase.

"Her first name is Brenda, and I was born on August 7, 1999. That's all the information I have. I don't know if she tried to find me, or if she wants to be found by me. I've lived in Toronto all my life and grew up in various foster homes—too many of them. They didn't like me enough to keep me. Can't for the life of me figure out why?" She grinned, then shrugged her muscled arms and shifted to her customary I've-got-attitude stance.

"It's not a lot to go on, but I'll give it my best shot. I'll need you to fill in this registration document giving me permission to carry out this work on your behalf. It'll also need to be signed by your guardian since you're underage."

Cutting in and giving Tee the look that said—shush—Angelina asked, "Where do I sign?"

Adam Small had barely closed the door when Tee shot across the room to Angelina, choking her with an emotionally aggressive hug.

"Angelina, thank you! Thank you!" Dancing around the room with typical teenage abandon, Tee, for once, acted like a normal adolescent. Angelina loved the pure youthful spirit of the girl, instead of her usual contrived don't-mess-with-me persona.

"Tee, what surname did you write on the document he gave you to fill in? I noticed you were careful not to let me see the name, but I really think it's best to let me know, don't you?"

"You're going to be pissed at me, but I just couldn't put my own name down. I never, ever want to be that person again. I love being Tee. And I hate the other me. So, I borrowed Grandma's last name, Butcher. Do you think she'll be very mad at me?"

"To tell you the truth, I think she'll get a kick out of it. It's best you tell her though; in case the investigator calls you at home."

"I will, I promise," Tee said, calming down. A shy look appeared on her face. She ducked her head self-consciously. "All my life I've wanted to belong to someone. Maybe now, I'll have the chance."

"Even if the outcome of this search isn't what you've dreamed of, baby, always know I care about you and you'll have a home with me for as long as you want. That's a promise."

"Thank you, Angelina." Tee was touched and showed it by the shine in her eyes and the huge smile she couldn't seem to douse. Because it was an expression not normally seen on her troubled countenance, it added a delightful charm that one didn't normally think of when Tee came to mind.

"And... if nothing comes of this endeavor, you and I are going to sit down and put all our cards on the table. Then we'll go to whatever agency we have to and see about some legal stuff."

"You'd do that for me? Why, Angie? Why me?"

Angelina recognized the hovering emotion Tee tried to hide, but the continuous waves of affection were more than the youngster could control. Her feelings were powerful and her tearful reaction unexpected.

Angelina moved in close and put her arm around Tee's shoulders. "At first it was because you reminded me of someone. Obviously, a person I cared about, because you were important to me from the first time we met. But then I got to know you for yourself and now you're just Tee. I need to be sure that you're safe and happy. It's about you now."

For a few seconds, Tee lowered her head to rest it on Angelina's shoulder. Then she straightened, mopping her eyes with her fist. "Now look what you've done. I'm so happy here, I'm not sure anymore if I want my dream to come true. I love living with you and Grandma Evie. But I have to try, Angelina. I actually have a real chance with this money behind me. And, if it turns out my mother doesn't want me in her life, then she's the one losing out."

Clasping the youngster's face between her hands, Angelina held her tenderly and looked straight at her. "Tee, if she doesn't want you, I do, my friend. Both Grandma and I do."

"God, Angelina. You've been so good to me." Tee choked up and her voice cracked. "You make me feel awesome. Most days I think I know exactly what I want, and then I look around me and see all my new friends, and I'm back to wondering again. My head's all goofed up. You see, all my life I've thought of nothing else but finding her. It's all I've cared about. I've felt a link or connection to who I think of as my mom, and it's kept me from ever settling for anything else. But at this moment, it scares the hell outta me. What if I've started something here I can't stop and it turns out badly?"

Angelina was astounded at the teen's abilities to alternate between bottomless lows and mercurial highs and then back again. Only the lows were places no-one Tee's age should ever have to go, and Angelina promised herself that if she had anything to do with it, the young girl wouldn't have to suffer them again.

"We'll take it one step at a time. First, let's see what Adam comes up with. Okay?"

"Okay!"

Chapter Fifty-three

A week later, the telephone's shrilling made Angelina jump, yanking her from deep concentration. "Miss Serrano, this is Sam Black. My father would like to make an appointment with you. As you might expect, we received your financial report from the auditors, and would appreciate a chance to discuss the results and make our apologies in person."

Singing a little song in her mind, Angelina kept her voice free of the giddiness. "When would be good for you, Mr. Black?"

"Please, after all we've been through, I hope you'll call me Sam. My father is anxious to see you as soon as possible. We would be happy to come at your convenience."

"After lunch today, say two pm? I'm sorry, but my morning is full." She couldn't help feeling righteous for keeping them waiting and relieved that it was the truth.

"Two o'clock will be fine. We'll look forward to meeting with you then."

Angelina leapt from her black leather swivel chair and charged into the outer office.

Loudly she crowed, "I just made an appointment with Nathan Black and his son Sam for two o'clock this afternoon. They want to apologize in person. We did it, you guys. In a little over a week, we reconstructed and presented the books to the auditors, and proved our innocence. Gracias Dios!" she gulped and promptly burst into tears.

Instantly surrounded, she struggled to control herself. It wasn't until Coralee said, "Stop it or you'll have us all bawling and you and I both know, Johnnie's pathetic when he's emotional," that her tears changed to laughter.

***

Coralee knocked at Angelina's door precisely at two pm to admit Sam and Nathan Black. Her childish grimace behind them when leaving the room forced Angelina to bite her cheeks rather than laugh.

Standing, shaking hands, and politely inviting the two men to take a seat gave Angelina time to let the nerves inside her settle and relax.

It was noticeably foreign to Mr. Black's nature to be in a situation where he was forced to apologize, but he was a gentleman of the old school. With steely resolve, and a professional code of ethics that demanded he lower his pride, he spoke, enunciating every word harshly. "Miss Serrano, I believe you've met my son, Sam, who has agreed to join our company. He was out of the country for years and only recently returned."

Angelina was still trying to decide if the man could possibly be genuine. No male had the right to look this good – not without plastic surgery. She stifled a smile at her silliness and remembered the impression she'd gathered from their first meeting. Nothing had changed. From the top of his fashionably styled blond hair to his expensive leather shoes this man could sweep any woman off her feet and make her happy to fall. Of medium height, with every inch put to first-class use, and using his sexy eyes like a pro, he smiled in a slow intimate way as he held out his hand. "You said I'd be the one apologizing at our next meeting and I'm happy to admit you were right."

"Mr. Black..." He raised his eyebrow, his stunning brown eyes and slightly insolent attitude telling her that wasn't acceptable. Shrugging, she changed her mind and said, "Sam, thank you for saying that."

"Angelina, my firm has given all our business to Serrano's for almost two years, since you first started up, and your performance has excelled any other firm we'd used previously. Your standards have been of the highest caliber, and it has been a pleasure doing business with you." The older man, visibly upset, looked much more aged than the last time she had seen him, maybe a month or so before the earthquake.

"Muchas gracias," she said, interrupting. "May I offer you gentlemen a coffee or a cold drink?" Maybe a beverage would help to relax poor Mr. Black senior.

"No, thank you," both answered in unison.

"Angelina, the bottom line is that someone in my own organization, thinking your books would have been destroyed by the earthquake, took this opportunity to misappropriate the funds. You have been fully exonerated, and the fact that you were ever implicated is intolerable to me. Especially since I have had the honor to work as your father's lawyer here in Canada for many years and was asked by him to help guide you when you first came to Victoria. My relationship with him will suffer from this situation I have no doubt, and for that I am truly sorry."

"I don't see why he has to know. I have said nothing about our problem to anyone other than my staff and a few very close friends."

"I don't deserve your thoughtfulness, child, but I gladly accept it."

"I won't tell if you don't." Angelina reached over to pat the old man's quivering hands. "Por favor, can you explain to me what happened?"

"My personal assistant, who held a responsible position and was therefore able to manipulate the outcome, made the allegations. It was also this person who arranged for the lawyers to draft you the scurrilous letter and victimize you. The ingrate has since been fired and is no longer with our company. My faith was such that full access to the bank accounts and adequate power enabled the unconscionable thief to carry on right under my very nose."

Having said this, the older man slumped back in his chair as if an unbearable weight had slackened the stiffness in his spine. He looked devastated, destroyed, a quivering mess.

Angelina, with a heart softened by pity for the suffering man, was on her knees next to him in an instant. She scooped up his shaking hands and rubbed them warmly. In a gently chiding voice, she cajoled, "Nathan, please do not be so concerned. I've always maintained daily back-ups and kept them in the safe at home in case of emergencies. It's how I was able to restore your files so quickly and accurately. All is well now. Your books are in order and up to date, my company is in the clear and we are still amigos, si?"

Next to her, Sam, also on one knee, put his arm consolingly around the older man's bowed shoulders and coaxed, "Please, Dad. Angelina has accepted our apologies and mercifully is still our accountant. All is well. Let me take you home now."

Mr. Black senior nodded his head and angled a gaze at Angelina, his eyes blotchy with red veins throughout. He lifted a hand marred with age spots and wrinkles to pat her cheek like one would a child. "Why couldn't I have had a daughter like you?" He sighed heavily and got up to leave. Standing, leaning strongly on his son, he went to the doorway and turned.

"Thank you, my dear. Sam will be in charge of our company from now on. Therefore, if you need to speak with someone, he'll be glad to look after you."

"That'll be fine. Please go straight home now and rest. Don't fret another minute over this unfortunate mistake."

"Thank you, Angelina," Sam added. "Would you by any chance be free for dinner tonight? It would be my pleasure to escort you for a lavish meal at a very exclusive restaurant," he grinned, "as my father's guest of course."

Seeing a fleeting smile hovering over Nathan's countenance while awaiting her reply, Angelina agreed purely to bring cheer to the despondent older man. It did—immensely.

After they left, Angelina took a few minutes to chastise herself for wishing the invitation had come from someone other than Sam. A handsome devil of a flirt who couldn't see the treasure he kept rejecting. But it was past time to stop thinking of Joe as the only fish in a sea of sharks. She needed to start respecting her own worth.

Oh, Joe!

Chapter Fifty-four

At the end of the day, when Angelina left a mite early because of her date, Coralee had both Lee and Johnnie in the corner working on nefarious plans to get Joe back in the picture.

"What's this Sam guy like?" Lee asked.

"He's obviously experienced, a lover who would know how to treat a woman. I can spot one of those hustlers a mile off." Coralee giggled when she saw jealousy flash over Lee's face. "Down, tiger, I never did like his type. Too smooth! Any man who looks better than me isn't one I want to compete with."

Johnnie listened and nodded at Coralee's sentiments. "I just had an idea. Lee, maybe you should invite Joe out for dinner tonight? You say he's been down in the dumps lately, so a good friend would want to cheer him up."

Coralee squealed, "You brilliant busybody, I love it!"

Lee looked from one to the other. "What?"

"It's simple. John-boy and I will tail the couple as they leave Angelina's house and call you to tell you where you will be taking Joe."

"Aw, Cora honey, I don't know? It feels kind of sneaky."

"So? And your problem is?"

"I'm in as long as I get to drive the surveillance vehicle." Johnnie smirked at the long-faced guy sitting next to him.

"One day, he'll thank you," Coralee pushed.

"You think? When he's in the slammer, serving fifteen for murdering his once-upon-a-time best friend? I'm telling' you, Coralee, I don't feel good about this."

"Let's put it this way. Do you really want to have kids?"

Jumping up, Lee raised his arms beseechingly. "So why should that bum get off scot-free?" He looked from Johnnie to Coralee. "Right?"

"Damn right!"

Chapter Fifty-five

That evening, Tee, Grandma Evie and even Rosario were skulking around the living room, waiting to catch a glimpse of the expected escort. Tee wasn't sure how she felt about this date: edgy, confused, frustrations niggling. It should be Joe, she thought, still a fan. Not sure why, since he'd made Angie sad. But somehow, Tee understood that he was all mixed up and just as unhappy.

Earlier, Grandma Evie had worked hard, trying to get Tee to accept a substitute for Joe, solely because of the misery her girl was suffering on account of his indecisiveness. "If this Adonis can put the sparkle back into my little girl, then he's welcome."

"Yeah! But you didn't see him. He's too pretty. And he ain't Joe."

"He isn't Joe."

"Like that's what I've been trying to tell you."

Upon Sam's arrival, after all the introductions were made, Peewee took it upon himself to voice his own opinion. He growled first, decided it wasn't a strong-enough protest, and tried biting the intruder's pant leg. Not impressed but nevertheless a gentleman, Sam picked up the incorrigible little devil and handed him over to Tee. She quickly squeezed him to her protectively, secretly in agreement with his antisocial performance.

Sexy, but in a demure way, best described Angelina. Her face exuded a modest amount of makeup, while her black hair had been gathered into a bundle, piled on the top of her head, and pinned there with two rhinestone barrettes. Under the lights, the ebony shine highlighted the sculpted curls and drew the eye.

Her sultry body, dressed in the two-piece, little black number, prominently displayed her fabulous breasts and her erotically shaped backside. Naughty rhinestone-studded spiked heels seductively displayed her slim legs. And the short skirt finalized the lethal combination.

"You look fantabulous!" Sam's eyes glittered his approval. From what Tee could see, he all but drooled down the front of his stuffed shirt.

Shaking her head, eyes crossed until Grandma caught her and gave her the uh-huh look, Tee made up her mind. What a moron!

Grandma Evie moved into his space, and with a steely-eyed stare, she forced his attention her way. "You will take care of my granddaughter and treat her appropriately. She's been very busy of late and is deserving of this night out. But, on the other hand, she's overworked herself to the point of exhaustion, and would be well-advised for an early night."

Looking shocked at the tone of the older woman, Angelina swept her into a hug and spoke soothingly, "I won't be late, Abuelita. But don't wait up." After she shared hugs with Tee and Rosario and a pat for Peewee, she and Sam left behind three displeased females and one short-toothed, disgusted puppy.

Speaking for them all, Tee said despairingly, "He's too smooth and too full of himself. And... he's not Joe!"

"My sentiments exactly," said Grandma Evie, wrapping her arm around the teenager. "Let's go and have a big mug of hot chocolate and a double hit of marshmallows to cheer us up."

"Goodie! I'm your girl."

"Awesome!"

***

As she sat across from Sam in one of Victoria's exclusive dining rooms, Angelina admitted she was enjoying the indulgence. The restaurant, swanky and very expensive, had dark paneling, huge green plants to give patrons some privacy and a large, mirrored bar as the main focus. The décor screamed exclusivity, with no expense spared for customer service. Right from the many windows overlooking the Marina, to the snowy linens showing off the gourmet food and modern squared white plates decorated by a master chef, Angelina felt pampered.

Sam ordered a bottle of expensive wine with a suave pretentiousness that left her cold. After all, she came from a land where ordering wine was a daily occurrence. Aside from that, Sam proved to be a courteous and talkative charmer.

Angelina's biggest defense against her lifetime of shyness was to ask a lot of questions and put the spotlight on the other person. Except for the hours she'd spent with Joe at the beach, her normal course was to sit back, listen and hide. Only her fantasy lover, with eyes the color of lush green velvet, had rendered her weak with enough lust and hope that she'd opened up to him.

"How is your father?" Angelina asked during his first lull. "I was worried about him when you left the office today. He looked terribly defeated somehow."

"I believe he's broken-hearted more than anything. He didn't tell you himself because he was too ashamed, but the person who created this whole disaster, stealing from the company and lying to him, was my young half-sister, Bree."

"Oh, no! I am very, very sorry. No wonder he looked so devastated. Disillusionment is hard to bear, but when your own child is responsible, it must be simply unbearable."

"A couple of years after my mother died, my father re-married and Bree was born. Both he and his new wife were ecstatic. By then, I was in my pre-teens, lived most of the year in a private school and was pretty much self-sufficient. Being their only child, they doted on her—to her detriment."

"How sad!"

"It is sad. I must admit that I've always found her to be pampered and willfully selfish. We've never gotten along, and now with this betrayal, we never will."

"I'm so glad you've come home to help Nathan through this terrible time."

"Yes, I've promised him I would look after the business until he's ready to return. What makes matters worse, he's alone again. My stepmother passed away last year."

"Oh no!" Angelina felt blessed when she thought of how her own life held no comparison.

"My father believes that Bree lost control with her gambling and bad behavior about that time. Before then, she was Momma's little girl, and had more restraint."

"The poor girl needs help."

"You mean, the spoiled brat. One of the conditions of us not calling in the police was that she had to agree to visits with a counselor who my father has been in touch with. As disillusioned as he is, he told me that no matter what she's done, she'll always be his daughter, and he'll always try and help her. I only hope it isn't too little too late."

"I don't believe it's ever too late when it's a person you love who's in need."

"I wouldn't put my money on it. However, he's adamant and wouldn't listen to reason."

"Your father mentioned earlier you had returned from overseas?"

"Yes, I was in London, working for a large law firm. It was an interesting job, one I enjoyed. When they offered me a full partnership, it was about the same time that a family friend called about Father's failing health. After this fiasco, I'm glad I turned them down and came home instead. What about you? Have you always lived in Victoria?"

"No, I was born here, but raised in Chile. I moved back not quite three years ago to live with my grandmother, and eventually I opened my own business."

"I'm very glad you're here. Sorry it was under such unpleasant circumstances that we met." Ruefully he shook his head. "But I'm exceedingly grateful we did."

His penetrating gaze tried to capture her darting eyes, but discomfort left her flinching and not able to sustain his probing. His hands reached for hers to still their fretful fidgeting.

"I can't believe how lucky I am," he said. "Meeting you seems like Fate is working in my favor. I hope we can spend many hours together, learning more about each other."

Lulled by the charismatic character and good looks of the guy, Angelina smiled and was charmed.

***

That wasn't the case for Joe, who, at that moment, entered the restaurant with Lee. He stayed long enough to see the cozy couple holding hands in the seductive, low-lit atmosphere of the opulent venue. Long enough to feel the gut-wrenching rush of adrenaline that made a man want to kick ass. Long enough to clench his teeth, his hands, his temper, wheel around and storm out. "You want to eat there, buddy, you'll eat alone. I don't like this joint."

Lee responded, "I couldn't agree more."

Joe stopped his head-long rush and pointed his finger at Lee. "Not one word." His tone grated, raspy and full of malice. None was directed toward Lee who stood nodding, his eyes full of contrition and his overly large ears reddening in commiseration.

Chapter Fifty-six

Knowing one is an ass takes a certain amount of self-examination but changing your ass-like ways took skills Joe didn't want to use or acknowledge. Honesty, clear thinking and of course principles were a few of them. He knew Angelina had to come first. She wasn't a slutty girl with loose morals, a one or two-night smorgasbord of lust. She was a classy woman, and not to be tampered with, not by anybody

In his brain he knew he had no right to her, and he should be happy that she'd found someone to treat her properly. But his body had other ideas. He ached for her something terrible, and as much as he'd tried, he couldn't turn it off.

Tied up in knots of sexual visions and fantasies, which in turn had him spending hours each day constantly shifting his groin, trying to find a more comfortable position, he fought to keep his distance. If he came anywhere near the Angel, he knew, without a doubt, he'd be unable to control his hunger.

Except, every time he thought of their day on the beach, the times she'd treated him like he walked on water, her eyes lighting up when she'd thought he didn't see, he wanted to be with her more and more.

His life was in ruins, and not sleeping was adding to his turmoil. He had to do something soon or go crazy.

Even his favorite niece, Diana, innocently conspired against him. At last Sunday's family gathering she'd climbed onto his lap, snuggled in his tentative arms, and said, "Uncle Joe, how come you don't have no little kids for me to play with? You like kids, don't you?"

"Of course, sweet thing. I like you so much I think I'll eat you." Nibbling at the four-year-old's tummy provoked peals of laughter, and that had everyone smiling. Diana grabbed his face between her tiny hands and switched on her serious expression. "Uncle Joe, if you like kids, why don't you get some? Don't you like mommies? Cause you need a mommy to have childrens, you know?"

Out of the mouth of a babe came the words of a wise woman. Words no one else in his family would dare to speak, and on a subject no one else would broach. Miraculously, there was a ten-second silence while smothered grins and comically embarrassed grimaces produced nervous laughter.

The other kids, not sensing the tension, ran through the room breaking the spell. The little inquisitor, having a very short attention span, forgot the question upon seeing the fun the others were having. She launched herself into the melee and left her poor Uncle Joe shattered.

A reprieve, he thought, nervously. That was before his imagination betrayed him and formed an image of a tiny, fairy-like creature with her mama's long black curls and his family's impressive green eyes.

Later, at the door before leaving the house, Joe hugged his father. "Dad, thanks for dinner. It was great as usual."

"Son don't thank me. This is your home. It might not be the house you live in, but it is and always will be your home."

"Man, don't you get tired of having us kids around every weekend? I would think you and Mom must crave downtime from all this hullabaloo of families, children and all our problems and worries."

"Every once in a while, we feel the need to get away, and so we do. More often than not, we thank the good Lord for our blessings: all six of you and your additions... and your noise." The patriarch chuckled, his hair almost as dark as Joe's, his build similar and his greyish-green eyes twinkling.

Joe had always thought that his family had a unique way of getting along with each other and it stemmed back to his parents and their love for their kids. At times, he'd felt like the odd man out, but then had decided it was because he was the youngest and the only one still single.

His dad interrupted his thoughts with more insightfulness. "That's what's so special about families, son. We're always there for you and in all ways. If you need someone to talk with, your mother and I are both available. In fact, we can see you're dealing with a load right now. If we can help—just ask."

His father's final words plagued his thoughts all the way back to his apartment and through the night. Were his bachelor opinions wacky? Did he need to talk with someone, get his mind unfixated on this negativity about relationships and marriage?

Realistically, he accepted that his disenchantment was a cross to bear. His ornery beliefs, that most women were bottom feeders, stopped him from having the same happy smile on his face that he'd seen on others. Take Lee, for example. The guy was loopy all the time, glowing, whistling—ridiculously smug.

Joe thought about his own past. Was he so negative because his first go-around at the marriage game with Sara had turned sour? Nah! What had upset him more was that after she'd married his brother, his sore heart had healed so fast, he'd lost faith in his ability to even recognize the real thing.

Hours of castigation led him to make a decision. He knew only one reliable source, one person who had the forbearance to put up with his dithering obtuseness, and who would be straight with him, no touchy-feely answers. He dragged his sorry butt out of bed, put on the coffee, and called his mother to make a date.

"Hey, gorgeous, feel like letting your favorite son take you for lunch?"

"Who's speaking please?"

"Not funny! Don't be a pain, Mom. I need to talk."

"Hey, babe, I'll make you a deal. You talk and I'll listen, and then it'll be my turn to talk but only if you promise to listen with an open mind?"

"You're on. So who pays?" He teased her, as was their usual way.

"You ask, you pay."

"Okay, then. The Sticky Wicket at noon. Don't be late. Wear a pink rose so I'll recognize you." He hung up chuckling, feeling lighter than he had in weeks.

Chapter Fifty-seven

Vera, Joe's mom, swung around to hug her husband who had been listening in on the conversation. They were working together setting the kitchen to rights after the night before when the whole family had been present.

The morning was their special time of the day. They'd have a leisurely breakfast and read their weekly magazines and newspapers over numerous cups of coffee while spending time in their favorite room of the house. Since he did most of the cooking and she the baking and salads, it was a comfy place for them both.

"I think your little speech in the hallway last night did the trick. He wants to talk," said Vera.

"I'm guessing our little Diana got him thinking also. The gods must be watching. It was perfect timing and the best thing she could have said."

"I've never been called a god before, but sometimes Grammas can put ideas into little minds, and voilá...!" Vera laughed uproariously at her husband's flummoxed look.

***

Joe, poking at his lasagna, had been nattering on about absolutely nothing.

"Joe, could you stop with all this big-word malarkey and get to the point of why you asked me here?"

"I think I'm in LOVE," he yelled, frustration echoing loud and clear. As soon as he heard the words, acceptance slammed into him like a wrecker's ball demolishing an old building.

"Somebody call 911. We have an emergency." Vera's eyes twinkled and he saw her actually bite her lip.

"Take me seriously, Mom. I'm in trouble here."

"Joe, love isn't a disease you can heal with a pill or an infection that antibiotics will miraculously clear way. It's a miracle. A privilege and a blessing only the most fortunate of us experience. To find someone to love, and, hopefully, who loves you too, should bring you joy."

"Then why am I so miserable?"

"Because you're a wuss who doesn't have the sense Mother Nature gave a bird or a bee. Joe, what if you'd met the only woman you ever wanted, only to find out she was already married, or sick with a horrible disease, or someone who doesn't like men? Then you'd have the right to feel sad."

He shook his head despondently. "How could it happen? I don't want that whole love and marriage thing."

"Joe, to love one another is the way men and women are supposed to feel. Do you remember what I've always told you about living your life? The lessons are the cracks and bumps in the road, but how you pass over them and rebuild them is the learning. Son, Angelina's a beautiful, warm, and lovely girl, and if you wait too long someone else might just appear and snatch her right out from under your pinched-up nose."

"How did you know it was Angelina?"

"You're kidding, right?"

Grudgingly, he shrugged, then added, "That's why I'm here. She was out with some stud the other night and thinking about it makes me crazy. How can I be so selfish? Not wanting to commit to her myself, but unable to bear the thought of her being with someone else? I'm a self-centered scumbag, Mom, a scared—"

Cutting in, Vera said, "I know just who can help you straighten out your thinking. I'm calling a crisis meeting tonight with your brothers. Don't shake your head like that, I'm setting it up right now and all you need to do is tell me what pub you want to meet them at. It'll be the boys' night out."

Joe smirked. "The question is, how many can get permission from their little women?"

"Don't be an ass, Joe. They'll be there. As long as you don't chicken out, I have a feeling tonight will be your reckoning, son, and it's way overdue. I also want you to keep in mind, the only one of my sons who isn't tremendously, glowingly, ridiculously happy at this moment is you."

Chapter Fifty-eight

It was a good thing using taxis were on the menu tonight, along with a huge platter of red-hot buffalo wings, tacos dripping in salsa with mounds of beef mixed into melted cheese and large platters of fries and gravy.

The most important items served were the pitchers of beer in weird jugs. Designed to accommodate the liquid on one side and the ice on the other, ensuring cold beer for as long as the ice lasted, the containers were emptied quickly and replenished just as fast. Drops of condensation glistened on the outside of the glass and ran in little rivulets, pooling on the table.

The blissful waitress kept her eye on the group of handsome men, and straight away spotted any need for refills. Wiping the collected moisture off the table gave her a perfect excuse for getting as close to her male customers as she possibly could.

"Joe," said the oldest brother, Lon, opening the discussion, "where did you get the cockamamie idea that we're all unhappy? Trust me, buddy, you couldn't be more wrong."

Glancing from face to face, Joe saw all his brothers wearing identical silly grins and nodding in unison. Platitudes would have rung false. Spontaneous truth didn't.

"You guys are happy! I can't figure it out. I've always thought married life was a prison and you guys were the prisoners."

"That makes our wives the jailers. You can't have a very good impression of the girls we've married," said Dave, the second oldest brother after Lon. "In fact, Pat's been trying to tell me you have no respect for her, but I put her off all the time. I keep telling her she's wrong about you."

Andrew, his middle brother, married to Joe's least liked sister-in-law, Mary, piped up and added, "All the wives want a better relationship with you, but you're so sour all the time, they've decided to back off and give up. I don't blame them, as the last time you were at our house, Mary was furious at your attitude and the way you treated her friend."

"With a name like Mary you'd think she'd be a soft-hearted, devout creature, but that sure as hell isn't so. I'm sorry, Andrew, but Mary scares the hell outta me." Joe made a comical expression.

"Granted, she's a bit of a ball-breaker, incorrigible. Okay...at times harsh, but a more loving softie you'll ever meet when we're alone with the world closed out. Until I came along, her life was wretched, so I've made allowances. She's changing, Joe. Once the baby's here, she'll realize she's safe in our family, and things will be even better."

"Granted, she seems different when she's with the folks, but when I get stuck alone with her, it's like she's another person altogether. And you, Charlie, your Teri has made life hell for you with her gambling problem. How do you handle it the way you do? I've never once seen you lose it."

Charlie's jade-green eyes, identical to Joe's, changed from listening to furious in the space of a few moments. He was the family's philosopher, the gentle soul of the group, but even he had his limits. Now, borderline hostile, he snarled, "I'd level anyone else who had the audacity to discuss my wife like you've just done. But, little brother, I'm holding back, because Mom asked me to, and because you, my lad, are one mixed up chump. Teri's so-called problem stopped the minute she realized that nothing she could do would turn me off. I love her, and as soon as she felt secure with me, she didn't need the addiction. Counselors helped also, and now that the twins are here, she's been happier than ever. I'm telling you this so you understand, Joe, no-one's perfect. We all have to work through things."

Fortuitously aware he'd overstepped the line, Joe defused the moment with a dorky grin. "I'm sorry, man. For a while I thought Angelina had a similar problem, and it was enough to send me running in the opposite direction. Luckily, I found out it wasn't so. But I've always wanted to tell you that if there was anything I could do to help, some treatments I know about that might prove useful, don't hesitate to have Teri come to see me."

Grudgingly, Charlie answered. "Don't suppose I could afford you, bro."

"Hey, man, there's a special family discount. No charge!"

The jocularity from when they'd first arrived at the pub was revived, and another round was called for.

Lon spoke up again. "So... is it finally getting through that thick scull of yours that we're all happily married men? Is there anything else about our lives bothering you?"

Deciding to go all out, Joe asked another question that had bothered him. "Okay! What about you, Lon? You and Carmen are always having spats."

"Spats?" Lon looked shocked at first and then he grinned. "It's teasing, Joe. Aren't you listening? We hardly ever fight seriously, and we never go to bed mad at one another. Mostly, we get along great, and spend a lot of time laughing together. Sure, we have our moments like everyone does, but think how boring life would be if we agreed all the time? Quick assumptions and conjectures don't always add up to the truth, Joe. You have to pay attention to people."

"I'm beginning to see that. I'm a self-centered idiot," was all he could answer.

As the beer continued to flow, so did the camaraderie. Each brother told stories of the loving relationships they shared with their spouses, how they'd met, fell in love and the dreams they had for the future. For the first time since he could remember, Joe felt thoroughly a part of the group, and not an outsider. He even told his own saga about how Angelina had been there to save his backside not once, not twice, but three times.

He took a lot of ribbing from the boys, and it felt so damn good.

Chapter Fifty-nine

"My prime rib was phenomenal," Lee announced, as Coralee reached for his proffered hand to help her from the truck.

"The smoked salmon penne was to die for," she argued, mostly for the sake of getting his goat. Catching sight of Johnnie and Angelina as they approached, she coaxed them into the on-going battle escalating between her and Lee since they'd left the restaurant. "Johnnie, tell this big lug the salmon penne is the house specialty and was superb."

"The penne was superb," Johnnie said, playing along. "In fact, I'm so full, I probably won't be able to move, let alone dance tonight," he teased.

"Hey! You love to dance, John-boy. No way you could sit and watch the crowd without getting up and showing off." Angelina hadn't caught the twinkle in his eye.

"I don't know, honey. But that penne was filling." He faced Coralee with a grin.

"Like hell you say. You'll dance, boyo. You promised," Coralee scoffed.

Then she caught Johnnie's wink and thought again what an enjoyable fellow he was. It broke her heart that the only woman he'd ever loved had left him a widower.

Following a week of Ange's morose face, Coralee had determined she'd had about had all she could handle of misery and heartache. Each day that there was no word from Joe, Angelina's vibrant glow had diminished a little more, until by the week's end, she was back to being the dejected creature they all hoped had disappeared for good. She'd even refused invitations from Sam Black. But as far as everyone was concerned, that was a good thing.

So, Coralee and Johnnie came up with the idea for this night of fun. Anything was worth the effort to get Angelina out of her slump, and to have her smiling again.

Coralee, pulling out the big guns to talk Angelina into coming with them, shared her delicious secret and it turned the tide in their favor. The fact that Lee had proposed the night before had made celebrating mandatory. They were going to buy the engagement ring the next day and didn't want to say anything to anyone else until then, but Coralee couldn't keep it from Angie a moment longer.

"Coralee, I'm so very happy for you. How wonderful! Your eyes have sparkled all day and now I know why."

"Lee wanted me to promise not to say anything until we got the ring, but I wouldn't. How could I keep this from you? I knew damn well it would be impossible."

"I'm glad. Of course, we have to go and have a good time. I promise not to let on that you told me." Angie hugged her and Coralee sensed her friend fighting to get her emotions under control before she let her go.

"Could I ask for two huge favors?"

"Granted."

"You didn't let me tell you what they were?" Coralee had laughed.

"Doesn't matter. Whatever you want, it's yours."

"Okay but don't blame me when you see the maid of honor dress I've picked out for you to wear."

Angie had blanched. "Uh... maybe I spoke too fast."

"Ha! Gotcha. Will you stand up with me?"

Another hug and this time Angie clutched hard. "Yes, of course. I'd be honored. And what's the second favor?"

"Could we hold the ceremony in your grandmother's gardens? I love her roses and it would be so special for me to have my wedding there."

"Absolutely! It's a brilliant idea."

***

The happy group, merrily squabbling and bickering all the way into the nightclub, passed under the neon-lighted sign and crowded into the vestibule.

As they passed, all waved at the pretty blonde behind the register who was serving tonight at the long wooden bar. Reflected from the mirrored wall behind, hundreds of stemware glasses hung in overhead racks and fancy bottles, colored by an array of fine liquors, were displayed for the patrons.

Bar stools were scattered. Empty ones were pushed under the overhang, and the full ones supported the customers while they visited or slouched, drinking alone. Others, more recently vacated, blocked the path to comfortable booths on the far side near the dance floor.

Music flowed from speakers on a pre-set stage where instruments were organized, sitting ready, waiting for a band to perform.

The overwhelming smell of beer filtered throughout and reinforced that they were in a pub. The low lighting, tinkling of glasses and laughter from the happy crowd produced a feel-good atmosphere.

Still laughing and carrying on, the four zigzagged between tables full of customers. A screamy laugh caught their attention and had all four heads swinging to the right just in time to see Joe with a blonde bombshell straddled across his knees. Her short skirt was hiked way up, showing long naked legs with spiked, high-heeled shoes swinging. Her arms were around his neck, and she was nuzzling under his left ear. His demeanor was of a man meekly enjoying himself.

Their gasps caught his attention. Startled, he looked up. Then he looked guilty.

***

Anguished control set in to enable Angelina to move, nod—even smile. Heart pumping, adrenaline surging, rage flooding her system, she shook her head once and the pride of her Spanish ancestors emanated in her haughty gestures. No one, unless you knew her extremely well, could tell her heart had just been smashed into tiny slivers of pain. Or that her mind was addled. Or that her body shook while her stomach churned and lurched, wanting to expel the excellent penne she'd recently consumed.

Johnnie did know her extremely well, though. He put his arm around her, and nodding to Joe, he guided her to a far booth with Cora and Lee positioning behind, flanking their friend, protectiveness uppermost in their minds.

Chapter Sixty

To resuscitate the situation was beyond Joe. First of all, the blonde wouldn't leave him alone. His attempt to throw her off his lap had failed. She clung like a barnacle on a boat's hull. It was his fault, since he had encouraged her out of loneliness, and a miserable attitude of self-pity. Earlier, he'd finally broken down and called Angelina, just to be told she was out—no doubt with the fancy man he'd seen her with a few days before.

Party Girl draped over his knee, trying hard to rekindle his attention, bit his neck and found his ticklish spot. Unknown to her, he'd already lost interest as soon as she got ripped after the one drink he'd bought her. He'd swear later, she'd used something else when she'd disappeared to the Ladies' Room. How could an average, ordinary girl turn stupid from one moment to the next without some help from another source? One he felt sure wasn't legal.

That was another reason why he'd had such little respect for the girls he'd known until Angelina came along. Too many times, seemingly ordinary girls had turned into party animals when on a date.

Thankfully, his catch-up with his brothers had re-set his values and left him with a lot of thinking to do. He just wished he'd come to the conclusion sooner that he needed his little South American Angel in his life, no matter what it took. Why'd he have to wait until tonight?

Anger propelled his resolve and his attempts to disengage finally registered with the vampire miss. Huffy from the rejection, she left him to troll the bar for another possible target who would appreciate her partying philosophy.

Joe stared at the empty table decorated with one solitary beer. What was it that his brother Dave had said the other night? It was about his wife, a poignant remark, which had stayed in Joe's memory. All of a sudden, he remembered.

"She cured the loneliness I felt even in a roomful of people. From the first time I was in her company, I became one-half of a whole. Now we are Dave and Pat, a couple. It's an uplifting lifestyle, I always belong and am involved, secure... cherished. I'd never go back to being simply 'me.' Apart, I was half a man, and with her, I'm a husband, a father—complete. I'm happier than I've ever been before."

At the time, Joe was skeptical about his adored big brother's ramblings. Now he got it. Hit between the eyes with a sledgehammer of understanding, he grasped the wisdom, the unveiled truth. Sure, idiot, when it's too late. Remorse hit him hard. Contemptuously, he cussed his cocky attitude, his stupidity. Now faced with this precarious situation, his chances to woo Angelina Serrano were virtually over.

No matter that he was a simpleton whose childish views of life's real values were skewed; she had the right to hate him. And from the broken look on her face, she did. Mercy was probably impossible.

But worth a try?

Damn right! She was worth anything and everything. If it took pleading, begging, crawling on his knees, he would do it gladly.

Turning to make his way to her booth, he looked up in time to see a display on the dance floor that had him gnashing his teeth. Clenching his fists, he sauntered to the wall and leaned against the brick divider where trailing ivy wound its way around the column. With his arms folded in front of his chest, he crossed one leg over the other, attitude screaming out from every muscled body part.

Catching Lee's eye, his force of will deadly, he beckoned his partner to come to him.

***

"Where do you think you're going?" Having been privy to the byplay, Coralee grabbed Lee's arm.

Gently removing her clutching fingers, Lee patted her hand and replied, "Something's wrong. I want to see if he's okay."

"See if he's okay? You big-hearted, softheaded dolt! What about Angelina?"

"Coralee, back off now. It'll only take a minute. Then you can use your sharp tongue to strip my skin off if you have to."

"Me?" Innocent eyes glared their anger at his retreating back. "Honey, you have no idea." Sarcasm dripped from the tongue under discussion. She turned back to the couple on the dance floor, where Johnnie was performing a miracle.

His laidback, mild-mannered personality took nothing away from his pleasing looks. Not a big man like Joe, but in his own way as magnetic, Johnnie was a ladies' man who turned female heads regularly.

Dressed all in fashionable black with slacks that fit his lithe body, he caught his share of wistful looks. Topped by an open-necked, short-sleeved, black silky shirt, which emphasized his muscular tanned arms, the enticing man looked real good. His head of thick, wavy, longish brown locks might have been his best feature, if it wasn't for the slumberous, haunted chestnut eyes, albeit lined with smile-crinkles. He was a lady-killer who didn't care. A challenge to every red-blooded woman within range! And wow, could that guy move!

Coralee and Angelina loved this man with negligible flaws, loved to comfort him with his burden of painful memories, and loved his idiosyncrasies and goofy humor. He was their friend, Johnnie, but they were always cognizant of his pleasing appearance. It was the basis for many teasing comments. To them, he was their John-boy, their supporter, their co-worker, and their best friend. So, when Angelina, hurting, angry and jealous, turned instinctively for help, he came through like a trooper.

In an instant, the man changed from friend to actor, from co-worker to admirer, from Johnnie to lover, and he did it very, very convincingly.

***

Instantly, Joe knew Lee was aware of the jealousy he couldn't control. He wheeled around, flashing a last glare at the two on the dance floor, and Lee followed Joe to his table exactly as Joe had expected he would. Habits were hard to break.

Once there, Joe all but collapsed. His cockiness disappeared like the bravado of a vicious attacking dog being tackled by one bigger and meaner. His head lowered—misery apparent—and rested in his big hands.

In desperation, he begged, "Help me, Lee. The blonde was merely a hustler working the room. I wasn't interested. God, man! You know she meant nothing. Hell, I don't even know her name."

"Shit, dude, that doesn't matter. She was slung over you like moss on a shady rock. My friend, as accustomed as I am to seeing you fend off the ladies, this time you weren't. You looked like a man enjoying the attention. Joe, you were giggling like a lovesick twit."

"The bitch tickled me. I'm ticklish as hell. So shoot me! Aw, dammit! You're right! I'm screwed." Dejected, he dropped his head onto the table. In a cracked, painfully rasping voice he lashed out at his own stupidity.

"I'm a dumb, foolish bastard."

Chapter Sixty-One

Joe didn't see the interested face of the woman standing behind him. Lee had waved her and Johnnie over, and she came because she hadn't known Joe was seated behind the dividing wall. That was, until she heard his voice. Lee's insistent beckoning, with his finger at his lips, had her tiptoeing closer. Joe, unaware of anything going on around him, was busy spilling his guts.

"Lee, man, I'm so pissed at myself. The blonde meant nothing. A jagged rock to Angelina's pure gold. I bought her a drink because she seemed as lonely as I felt. I've been flailing around with my head screwed on backward since I saw Angelina the other night at the restaurant with that smarmy bastard. I was going nuts imagining her with him. I even called her tonight, to find out she was on a date. Now she's with Johnnie. For God's sake, I trusted him. Lee, she belongs to me, and I belong to her. I know it now." In a voice filled with regret and pain, he spat out savagely, "She's mine!"

"Yours?" A voice screeched over him, driving his head up and out of his hands. His shocked eyes widened, while his lips opened to form a round hole of surprise and trepidation. "I belong to no man, my friend, especially not to an empty-headed, ticklish fool of a dithering idiot who's too blind to see the pure gold in front of him because his head is full of rocks."

That she put telling emphasis on the words gold and rocks convinced him she'd overheard his declaration. "You are mine," he grated, standing, and towering over her. "Not that namby-pamby suit I saw you with the other night." Then his finger pointed to Johnnie lounging close now, protectiveness his agenda. "You sure as hell aren't in love with this Don Juan. He's not the other half of you. I am. We belong together, Angelina," he declared, his voice lowered beseechingly.

"There is no 'we', you blockhead." She pointed at herself and said, "There's me, Angelina Serrano, blind fool." She swung her finger and jabbed it swiftly, painfully into his chest. "And then there's you, Joe Davidson, philanderer." He winced. "There has never been a we."

A harangue of Spanish followed that only a fluent speaker could have interpreted. But it didn't take a translator to know what she was saying. Idiot, stupid, imbecile were a few of the descriptive phrases similar in both languages.

The woman was a glorious sight to behold in her righteous hissy-fit. Black curls, gathered high, whipped freely back and forth, and dropped over her naked shoulders. The thinness of the satin straps on her lacy red dress, that fit her tiny physique like a glove, made one wonder if they could take the stress her flailing arms were giving them.

'Bastardo' was the last word she hissed before she slapped her fists down on either side of her thighs. She stomped back to her table, grabbed her silver bag and coat, and stormed past the revelers, who were rapt, watching her performance. Even the band, realizing they weren't the focus of attention, had discreetly lowered their sound. Angelina in full rage was something to see.

She'd have made it right out the door, but for the blonde who Joe had discarded earlier.

"Don't leave yet honey. My brother is about to rip that guy apart. I called him to come and beat his lights out for treating me the way he did. No one gets away with a brush-off like that jerk gave me." Wavering and falling over, her slurred words stopped Angelina in mid-stride.

Angelina turned in time to see a tough character waylay Joe who had started to follow her. He blocked his path and wouldn't let Joe go around him. Angelina edged closer and heard Joe, his voice sounding mean. "Hey, man, get out of my way."

"My sister says you gave her a hard time tonight?"

"Your sister's mad because I didn't give her a hard time tonight." Joe, who only had one thing on his mind, got caught unaware. From one minute to the next, he went from standing with attitude, to prone with an angry enemy straddling him.

Angelina grabbed a tray and headed into the battle. Just as she went to smack the attacker's head, she looked down at Joe, who shamelessly grinned up at her.

Throwing the weapon down on the nearest table, she yelled at his attacker, "Hit him for me too." Then she stomped out the door.

Joe had a fight on his hands. They were equal in size, but he had a mission and no time to waste. He finished off his attacker by slamming him on both sides of his head. While the whimperer's ears rang, he lifted him off and pushed him into an empty booth.

Looking around, he spotted Angelina's group. Mesmerized, they'd waited to see the outcome. He went over and asked, "Angelina?"

"Phew," said Johnnie understatedly. "I've never seen her so mad."

"She's furious," Coralee agreed smirking.

"That's my girl!" Joe grinned, foolishly. "She must care a little, or she wouldn't have gotten that angry. Right?"

"Right!" agreed three voices, while prompting hands pushed Joe towards the door.

Son-of-a-gun! Too late! He arrived in time to see her taxi pull away from the curb.

Three voices peeled off instructions behind him.

"Grandma and Tee are in Tofino for the weekend. She'll be alone at the house. Go!" Coralee pushed at him, sounding like an excited child who could foresee a treat.

"The all-night market near her place sells great big bouquets. Might be a good idea to go bearing gifts, dude." Lee added his two cents.

"You hurt her again, Joe, and I'll have to hurt you. Understand?" Johnnie wasn't smiling.

Joe stopped dead, turned, and grinned at Coralee, nodded at Lee, and put his hand out to shake with Johnnie, saying with genuine fervor, "I understand."

Chapter Sixty-two

After Joe's polite knocking got him nowhere, he gave up being the nice guy and literally banged on the door. Angelina wouldn't let him in. She was still seething. The cheeky swine could rot out there all night as far as she was concerned.

Then her phone rang. She answered, unprepared for it to be him—his voice. She didn't hang up fast enough. Once she heard his pleading, she wanted the idiot so badly it was torture keeping her anger fuelled. Every female in the world would empathize with a woman in love while her man pleaded with her to let him come close. Who could blame her for opening the door?

He bolted through and came to a shuddering stop when he saw her. She'd changed into her long sheer white cotton housecoat and a nightie that drifted as she walked. Look closely at what you're giving up, gringo!

She'd been told that she looked the picture of virginal loveliness when her grandmother had first seen her in those nightclothes. That image suited Angelina tonight. She'd checked in the mirror, turning this way and that. It seemed when she didn't wear a bra, her breasts bulged against the lace-and-ribbon concoction of prettiness at the neckline. Good!

Breaking out of his trance, Joe thrust a huge gathering of sweet-smelling lilies, at least a dozen long-stemmed red roses, scads of pink carnations, colorful mums and a heap of yellow-centered white daisies, all engulfed by masses of baby's breath toward her. There were so many flowers she had trouble holding them all in her arms.

"I hate you," she choked, glaring at him.

"You should," he answered her with such tenderness she could hardly swallow.

Don't let him to do this to you again!

She was a mess of suppressed emotions, while he stood there looking calm and cool, almost detached.

She turned and went to the kitchen to put the flowers into the sink and filled the tub halfway full of water. She wanted him to wait and suffer like she had waited for what had seemed like an eternity. She glanced up to the window and saw his reflection. Slouched in a way that drew her eyes to his groin, she hoped a reaction to her lack of clothing had ravaged his discipline.

Yes! His eyes didn't lie and neither did his body. Up to now, his words had been the enemy.

For a few seconds, she stopped, watched him, and wondered. Did his anxiety mean he wasn't confident of her response?

Was he as edgy inside as he now seemed to appear on the outside?

Did the man know how many muscles rippled in his chest as he shifted his body?

With her heart racing, she led him to the living room and stopped in front of the blazing fire. He came up behind her. With him standing so close, yet not touching, he aroused luscious tingles, starting at the nape of her neck. They shot straight to her feminine hearth, scorching it with flames equal to those in the fireplace.

As his voice whispered into her flowing hair, her knees weakened. She felt the movement from his seductive breath stirring the long strands, teasing her flesh, evoking whimpers. Her eyelids closed involuntarily, and tremors attacked her body. Like an animal sensing danger, she stilled... quivering.

His voice assumed a vibrating hoarseness that happened in times of stress or tenderness. It skimmed over her senses while he whispered enticingly, "Baby, I want to touch you. I'm starving for you, Angel. I need my hands on you soon, or so help me God, I'll go insane. You've bewitched my days and invaded my nights with fantasies so beautiful, I want to bring them to life with you—only you."

Mi Dios! Her wanton body started to sway invitingly, while her muscles weakened with throbbing desire. His ravenous need to have his hands on her skin built a mindless ache within her. But she remained silent, listening, his whispers mesmerizing. Touch me, for God's sake! Touch me now, was the overwhelming prayer clambering through her smoldering, addled mind.

***

But he didn't. He waited for some sign from her. Heart-wrenching adrenaline seeped from his chest and infected his knees, leaving him as weak as a small boy, a scared little child. Why won't she look at me? Is this too little, too late? His pulse, rapidly beating, almost choked him while his anxiety mounted.

Finally, after what seemed like forever, she fell back a step, closer to his surging, flowing heat. It was like she lost strength as the tension swelled unbearably, increasingly—intolerably.

He groaned, beckoning her to come closer. "I want to put my hands on every part of your incredibly lovely, sexy body. Then I want my lips to follow. To kiss you, touch you, press my body into yours, love you and have your precious spirit joining with mine until there is no me, no you, no time, no place, just us. That's what I want, Angel. You have to tell me now. Is it what you want?"

Her body stiffened. But she didn't look at him.

"For pity's sake, turn around. Show me! Give me some sign that you feel the same way." He all but sobbed the last word. "Please...!"

Excruciating seconds passed before she turned. Her slumberous, luminous, turquoise eyes crept upward revealing her soul, love and pride blazing proudly for him to see.

She flung herself into his waiting, desperate arms and he reacted quickly. Wrapping himself around her, he groaned, "Oh, God. Thank you." The words seemed wrenched from his lips, his tortured voice evidence of the traumatic moment.

Hugging her was heaven, and so he just kept hugging and rocking back and forth as if to spread balm on his injured, frightened spirit.

Chapter Sixty-three

His body's shuddering troubled Angelina's conscience. Wanting to sooth, she reached up and kissed everywhere she could. Tiny love kisses like a parent might give to a frightened child.

"Ssh," she whispered, at the same time tantalizing him with the involuntary rubbing of her body, back and forth, closer, and harder.

Catching on, enjoying her treatment, his lips followed the same dance as hers, softly kissing her on her forehead, her eyes, then on to her neck, changing direction to slide over her lips and then her throat.

Their breath became labored, the sounds themselves stimulating.

"Enough," she groaned. Grabbing his face, she scalded his lips with the same desires that were flooding her body. Tasting saltiness made her heart swell even fuller. He was big—yes! Strong—very! But he was also unabashedly vulnerable, exposed in his love. Her own tenderness grew miraculously and overflowed.

It was her turn to give him the same vulnerability, her gift.

"Mi amor," she said brokenly, "I'll die if you don't make me yours soon, your lover and your woman." It was obvious that her husky, accented voice affected him.

Lifting her into his arms, he laid her gently on the snowy Alpaca rug in front of the blazing fireplace and began to make her every dream come true. Hunger invaded, overcoming gentler emotions. At first, his mouth took hers in a heated kiss so emotionally charged that the large body covering hers shuddered. Then he rocked against her, his swollen need apparent.

Little by little, his shaking hands unbuttoned the tiny pearls decorating her provocative nightgown. All the while, his hungry lips unbuttoned the last coherent thought in her functioning mind. Now released, the faint essence of Shalimar floated around them. His lips moved aside the lacy edges, and with his teeth and tongue he licked and bit his way over her throbbing, plump breasts. His hands came up and made love to the beauties, then kneaded and stroked as he lowered her filmy nightwear to her waist.

Shaking with desire, she arched repeatedly trying to get closer to him. Her whimpers spurred him on and he quickly shed his shirt and lowered his nakedness over hers. Breast to breast, they rubbed back and forth, the friction igniting more flames lower down. Her hands caressed his smooth, tapered back, holding him in place. But he never stopped moving and whispering.

"Angel, you're so beautiful—so warm and soft. I love how you feel. Beautiful girl. Mine."

She answered in her own tongue. Passionately whispered, her Spanish, so very sensual, sounded like X-rated music.

Driven, he kissed her again, this time deeply as if he couldn't get enough. His tongue in her mouth licking and sucking was driving her insane. When she lost her ability to breathe, she twisted her head encouraging him to move down to her throat, where he made love from side to side, back and forth. Swollen, her breasts ached, and she wanted his lips there so badly she moaned her demand.

As if her need called to him, he found her nipples once again and lathed them with his tongue and then drew them into his mouth to love them until she cried out.

Working his way down her shuddering body, her nightgown still wrapped around her lower half prompted him to slow for as long as it took him to strip her completely. Leaning back on his knees, his eyes searing with passion, he took the time to adore her. With her hair fanned out adorning her naked body, she proudly posed for her lover.

Unskilled, unsure of her moves, and entirely unwilling to let that stand in her way, she lifted her naked arms and smiled her welcome.

And... he didn't waste any time to satisfy her demand and satiate her every cell with ecstasy.

Her provocative moans and erotic writhing were his undoing. He searched for her swollen lips with his hungry mouth and her drenched slick femininity with his swollen manhood.

With every scorching hot, surging plunge of his body, the flames in the fire leapt simultaneously in rhythm, burning the wood until soft glowing embers were all that remained.

***

Between the first and the second round of lovemaking, they stopped like all lovers to have the talk every woman wanted, and most men hated with a passion.

They were cuddled together still in front of the fire. His back was against the sofa while he held her in front of him snuggled in his arms.

Being inherently shy, Angelina had donned her nightie and respecting her naivety, Joe had slipped into his jeans.

"When did you first know you cared about me?" She was still scared to use the L-word because her memory, albeit a little rattled, was still reliable. Not once did she actually hear him say the word every woman needed to hear for total reassurance.

"From the first moment I saw you."

"The first moment?"

"You terrified me, and I knew."

She giggled. "I did not terrify you."

"Oh yes, you did. I understood right from the first time I saw you that you were a woman I couldn't mess around with. You were wife material."

Twisting around to look at his face, she saw the fond grin plastered over his expression, and the tender look in his overly bright green gaze. "Really?"

"Yep! I wanted you right from the beginning, and it drove me crazy not being able to have you."

"We both know that isn't true." Giving him her trust, she admitted. "We both know...I was infatuated."

Suffused in a glow of tenderness, he lowered his face and nestled his cheek against hers. "Not true. You loved me," he said softly.

With a sobbing breath, she kissed him, turning into his arms. "I did... do. So much." Sweet kisses quickly altered, until she pushed him away and held him there. "Muy bien, Gringo. Now it's your turn."

His chuckle made her eyes narrow, and he quickly got the hint. "Angel, I'll love you till the day I die and then into eternity. Are you happy n—?"

Her crushing lips cut off his words. Pulling away, she moaned. "Querido, how many times must I show you that I'm no Angel?"

"How about for the rest of our lives?"

Chapter Sixty-four

The morning is so lovely, thought Angelina, still wrapped in a sexually satisfied glow from the weekend she'd just spent with Joe. She saw beauty in a scene that every other day would be just the norm. Sitting with her feet perched on a pulled-out bottom desk drawer, her hands wrapped behind her head, she gazed out her window and beamed.

They'd talked about their future, and while kissing her into a state of passionate frenzy, he'd pressed to marry him soon. Explaining that Lee had beaten him to the proposal and Coralee had set their date in two weeks, she promised they could tie the knot a few weeks later. Dreaming of white satin gowns, decorating her grandmother's house and the various flower gardens where she'd promised Coralee they could hold the ceremony, she drifted.

Normally, Monday mornings tended to be her day to get an early start on a week full of projects. It was the day she eagerly anticipated during the weekend when her active mind traveled to all the tasks left unfinished the week before.

This Monday was different. Today, her mind scrolled through images of her and Joe and the time they'd spent together over the last thirty-six intensely romantic hours. Work was a four-letter word and not too important in the scheme of Angelina's fantasies. Unfortunately, though, life did have a way of moving on.

When Adam Small, the investigator, popped in and asked to have a private meeting with Tee, everyone in the office looked concerned. That is except for Angelina. Neither Johnnie nor Coralee had been informed of what Tee was doing with her portion of the funds she'd received from finding the gold. It was a secret between Angelina, Grandma and Tee— at Tee's specific request.

Apprehensive, shyly noncommittal, in case she had a mother who still didn't want her, Tee requested the situation be kept under wraps. She'd explained this to Angelina and Grandma. Henceforth, a private meeting was arranged in Angelina's office for her to hear the outcome of the investigation.

Angelina stood at the door with her hand on the knob, reluctant to leave the trembling teen alone to face the results. She'd heard the catch in Tee's voice and saw the pulse throbbing in her throat, and the sight brought tears to her eyes. She's so beautiful in her youth and yearning. "Tee, I understand you want to do this on your own, but you know I'm here if you need me, right?"

"Sure, Angelina, but I'm a big girl. I can handle it." Tee stiffened her shoulders and then patted Angelina's fidgeting hands.

Poor little grown-up baby! Careening emotions raged in Angelina's vulnerable soul. "Come here, brat." Angelina's tender South American heart insisted on the embrace. For her, the moment demanded a loving gesture. When she left the room—worry followed her. The hard part was trying to hide it from other probing eyes.

Sometime later, the investigator opened the door of the office and stepped out, closing it behind him. All eyes turned to him, and they waited. He said nothing as he made his hesitant way to Coralee's desk, and checked her happy-face nameplate, which was sitting at the edge by her coffee mug. He leaned over, whispered a few words, straightened and turned to walk back from where he'd come. He waved a thumbs-up signal toward Angelina. Then he disappeared in her office once again. Okay! Now what? She disentangled her cold hands and flexed their nerveless fingers.

Head angled in a questioning way, hands held out like she was receiving an offering, Coralee stopped next to Angelina, who stood by the filing cabinets.

Shaking her head negatively, Angelina pointed her towards the closed doorway as if to say; don't ask me, I have no idea. Profoundly confused but obviously willing to help Tee, Coralee shrugged and disappeared.

"What's going on, Angelina?" Johnnie stopped in front of her, worry etched on his features.

"I have no idea," she said, shaking her head back and forth, baffled. "All I know is that Tee had a few things she needed to settle, and Adam promised to help her."

"I wonder why Coralee was called in?"

Lifting her water bottle in the air, Angelina frowned before taking a sip. "Beats me, Johnnie. I wished I knew. Gotta admit, though, that I'm worried." Tightness in her throat made it difficult to swallow, and the water she drank never did settle the nauseating tingling in her fluttery stomach.

***

Tee, shaken to her core, didn't have the guts to face the impending interview alone. Using the necessity of factual information, and Adam's research knowledge as her bargaining chip, she coerced the private investigator to stay in the room while she revealed the outcome of his search.

He must have seen through her persuasion and the begging quality of her request. "I'll stay, Tee. And help you through the interview. I like spunk, and you're one heck of a spunky kid. In fact, I'm touched that you respect me and want my support."

"Thank you, Mr. Small. I'm still so twisted over what you told me that I don't think I could get through this alone."

"No problem. Just remember... You're innocent in this situation. As is your mother. She was tricked by a despicable woman. If we can put things right today, then I'll walk away feeling better than I have in a long, long time."

Tee nodded and continued to chew her nail, gnawing, and tearing, wishing the nightmare of the next few minutes over and behind her.

"It's going to be fine," he told her. "Quit worrying."

"Easy for you to say! What if she doesn't want anything to do with a brand-new dysfunctional family member?" Without her being aware, her finger slowly rose to her mouth again, offering solace.

Chapter Sixty-five

At the moment when the tension peaked unbearably, the door opened. Coralee popped her head in. Her gamin features broke into a welcome smile when she spotted Tee.

"Hey, kiddo, what's up?" She nodded questioningly at the man in the badly tailored, wrinkled brown suit who stood at her entrance. He was the same investigator Angelina had hired weeks before. She looked him over closely and saw a slim, muscled individual with a crooked, loosened tie, a head of messy hair badly in need of scissors and picked up on the fact that he was standing too close to the girl for her liking.

She bristled with attitude until she interpreted the straight, proud look in his level stare. She felt herself relax but knew there was something in the air which filled her once more with trepidation. She closed the door and, instinctively protective, sidled over to Tee. Supportively, she gently pushed Tee's fingers away from her ravaging teeth, laid her hand on the girl's shoulder and rubbed unconsciously.

When Adam Small witnessed this shielding maneuver, he smiled.

Masking her confusion, Coralee faced him and repeated, "What's up?"

Tee gestured toward the man, waving her hand weakly and announced, "Coralee, meet Adam Small. He's a private investigator with the same firm that Angelina used to trace the owners of the gold. I hired him to help me trace my family." At this point, her voice cracked, and shakiness forced her to stop and swallow. Seconds later, she pointed at Coralee and choked out, "Adam, this is Coralee Becker... my fr-friend." There was a noticeable faltering as she used the word friend, and it made Coralee glance at the girl as she automatically held her hand towards the investigator.

His grip held until her eyes narrowed. His calculating glance stripped away her politeness and delved past her barriers. Then he let her go and she saw him relax.

Silence enfolded them and intensified as Tee gazed beseechingly at Adam. Her hand lifted and then dropped.

Taking pity on the youngster, Adam cleared his throat and pulled out the second visitor's chair for Coralee next to Tee's and waited for her to be seated. He propped himself on the desk in front and shuffled his papers.

"Miss Becker, my client Tee gave me very few facts to start a search with. She knew from information in her possession that she was born in the Royal Jubilee Hospital sixteen years ago on the fifteenth of last month. From what I could find out through the hospital records, her mother was a female called Brenda Corley"

What? Coralee's gasp sounded loud and harsh. Instinctively, she flinched in recoil at the sound of the name. Her heartbeat ramped up viciously to where she had trouble breathing, thinking—believing.

From the corner of her eye, she saw Tee, watching her reaction and then popping her nail back into her mouth to continue gnawing.

Ignoring her shock, Adam continued. His voice took on a clipped tone like that of a schoolteacher reviewing a lesson of dry historical facts.

"I traced the evidence to where this baby was taken from her mother, kept in an incubator for weeks, and then placed with an adoptive family. She was with them until two years of age. At that time, the couple were killed in a freak motor vehicle accident while leaving the baby home alone. I talked to some of the neighbors who are still living in the old apartment building. They told me the death of the parents might have been a blessing in disguise. Turns out, the police had to be called on a number of occasions because of numerous complaints of disturbance, and towards the end, child neglect." He glanced up to see Coralee with her head cupped in her shaking hands, disbelief written all over her face.

He continued. "None of the immediate family members were willing to take the baby, and so she was placed with Child Welfare. Over the next several years, the child circulated through our imperfect, over-worked system until she ran away six months ago. Because of her age, a desultory trace was put on her, but being one of thousands of kids in her predicament, she was filed and forgotten."

Coralee felt him studying her, but she couldn't move. The pain from his report had rendered her frozen in disbelief and horror.

After a few moments, he continued. "Since Brenda turned out to be just a child herself, only two months shy of sixteen, I followed the trail to her only relative, Agnes Corlee, her mother. And I use the term lightly. This woman didn't have a motherly bone in her body. How could she, since the witch made a tidy bundle selling her granddaughter?"

"No! Good God! Stop!" Coralee broke at this point. It's not possible! Her head, feeling wobbly and unattached, swiveled to Tee and she saw pain deeply etched into the girl's pale features.

"I am Brenda Corley but I'm not your mother," she moaned. "Though God knows how much I wished it were true." Coralee, who'd stopped crying years before, broke and the agonizing release of her control was shattering. She hugged her arms around her stomach trying to stop the pain from seeping out the pores in her skin. "It's not possible. My baby was born that day... true. But she died. My baby died. I never got to hold her or tell her how much I loved her. She was all alone. To my dying day, I'll be sorry for that." Suddenly her chair fell back with a startling crash as she shot up and hobbled towards the door feeling like a sick, old lady.

Sam's next words stopped her. "Your baby didn't die, Brenda." Kindness floated through his words. "She lived! Your mother lied to you. She lied to you and sold your child. The nurses were ordered not to talk to you about the baby. They were told that you'd suffered enough grief from having to give her up. And if they spoke about her, it would only torture you. They followed your mother's orders. Not because they were trying to hide anything from you, but because they all respected your wish to give her a good home, and they understood you needed time to accept your choice. The adoptive parents were wealthy, you see; wealthy and stood to inherit a trust fund on the birth, or adoption, of their first baby. According to her sister, your adoptive mother didn't want the pain of childbirth and so it was necessary for them to buy a child. And that baby was Tee!"

No one in the room moved. Coralee's hand clasped the brass doorknob; her shoulder leaned against the white paint with her head resting on her arm. Sick to her stomach, her mind churned pathetically.

Reels of memories unwound. Being in the hospital unreachable, uncommunicative, sobbing her heart out. The little nurse, who was new on the ward, trying to comfort her, "Don't be going on this way, me lovie," soothed the Irish lass. "It's for the best, you'll see. Your baby will be in a wonderful place. God helps us to accept these choices in his own way, and he'll help you if you let him. Make this experience into a life lesson and learn from it. Grow strong. Decide that today is the first day of the rest of your life and make each one count."

Lord, but those words had lifted her and given her something to cling to at one of the darkest moments of her life. Using the advice, not at first but ultimately, she'd dedicated her future to her dead child. She'd gotten herself together and tried to move on. Wherever she went, the steadfast glow in her heart, which was the love for her daughter, went with her. When she weakened, she drew strength from that light and she never, ever felt alone.

Adam had stopped talking, likely to give her time to accept his staggering revelation. Since she hadn't moved, he continued.

"How your mother could live with herself neither I, nor the nurses I talked to who still remembered you, could fathom. They described your grief as being unconceivable, especially a small Irish nurse. She told me about a young girl who, many years ago, suffered the demons of hell for giving away her baby. She remembered you as being inconsolable for days before she was able to reach you. It seems that during your baby's delivery you had pneumonia and were terribly sick. By the time you'd regained consciousness, she said that the baby was gone and everyone believed it was a miracle you'd pulled through."

"But I had to. I had to live for my baby." Coralee fell to her knees, crumpling like a frozen cloth brought into the warmth. She turned as two people rushed toward her. Her eyes closed, because the scorching anger and murderous hatred she felt was too evil to share. Her hands came up like shields, warding off another blow. It stopped them as much as the only word she could get out.

"Why?" She wailed from behind her shaking fingers. "Christ, why?"

"Money," Adam softly uttered. "Your mother walked away with a bundle, left you broken and used the money to destroy the rest of her short, useless life."

A whimper was the only answer she had, that and a sob. Both Adam and Tee helped her to her feet and supported her frailness while leading her to a small leather sofa Angelina had placed by her favorite stained-glass window. Sliding a sheaf of papers into his briefcase, Adam stopped at the door before leaving them alone together. His last words were spoken softly. "I'm so sorry."

Chapter Sixty-six

During the six months that she was aware of her pregnancy, Coralee had loved her child immeasurably, powerfully—overwhelmingly. Nurturing her little one—those were the only memories she'd cherished from her early life. Loneliness had faded while her baby grew inside her. She had the precious unborn child to talk to, sing to, read to, and make future plans for.

While she waited to meet her baby, she'd lived in a fog of happiness, working as a cook at a diner, saving her money by hanging with her mom, who, as usual, was never around and floating through life in a bubble of joyful anticipation.

After the birth, when she'd eventually regained consciousness, her mother revealed that the baby had passed on. She also told her no one especially cared. The nurses and doctors were busy with other patients, and no one wanted to listen to the tears of a delinquent crying over her deceased, illegitimate brat... pure manipulation to keep her quiet. Her mother led her to believe that it had been the pneumonia which she'd passed on to the baby that had killed her. Therefore, it was her own fault the baby had died.

Following her mother's rotten advice, Coralee had refused to talk about the child. She just prayed that the pneumonia would kill her also, only it didn't. She'd pulled through.

It had taken a few years for her to give a damn, straighten out and make something of her future. But every single day, first thing in the morning and last thing at night, she said a prayer in honor of her little girl and repeated a promise that they would find each other again, wherever predestined souls met.

Suddenly, a stifled sob broke into her reminiscences and brought her back to earth. She spotted Tee still pacing, back and forth, her nails chomped to bleeding stumps, tears streaming. Instantly, her trancelike state shattered. Happiness, like a huge aftershock from an earthquake, shook her very foundations. This beautiful young lady with the pink hair, fake tattoos, tight working jeans and chip on her shoulder was her baby, her very own child.

Tee finally spewed. "I'm not here to sabotage your life, Coralee." Words blurted out, unstoppable. Emotionally distraught, she prowled back and forth. "I exonerate you right now from any responsibility for me." As she stalked and plotted, her voice rose. With each turn at the end of the enclosed space, her volume increased until, with horror, she seemed to realize that she was actually yelling. Speaking her final words more softly, she said, "I can take care of myself. I always have."

"Not anymore, my girl." Coralee came back at her, firmness obvious in her tone.

Despair, the foremost emotion in Coralee's heart whenever her lost child came into her thoughts, faded completely, and allowed joy to replace her pain. It was so overwhelming, that dizziness and elation fought a battle. The end result was pure bliss never before experienced.

Desolation and shame, which she had nourished all her life, melted like butter in a sizzling frying pan.

"Don't spaz on me 'cause I hired an investigator to help me find my real mom," Tee demanded, white-faced. "I had no idea what he would find in his investigation." Unintended accusations rang in her voice.

Coralee stood, wobbly, her arms extended, hands trembling. Voice caught in emotion, unworkable.

With her arms crossed, Tee stared out the window. "So? You're denying me? You can, you know. I don't really care. It's no biggie. Aw, shit! Never mind. I'm outta here," She stomped to the door and stopped with her back still turned, her hand on the knob. She didn't see Coralee's flash of panic and the hand reaching out. "It's just that I've always had this crazy notion that if I could only find you... you'd care."

Voice broken; Coralee had to work hard so that her words would make sense. "Baby girl, I've loved you every moment since I knew you existed. Every single... solitary... eternal... second." Her voice rose as the words started slowly, then sped up.

Tee stood with her hand still wrapped around the door handle, holding on, listening to the soft, love-filled voice of the woman who spoke.

"The happiest time in my life was when we were one and I carried you with me, inside me—safe and warm. When my mother told me you'd passed on, something in me died also. I've prayed every day for your soul's journey. Prayed you were a happy little angel. I can't tell you how many times I cried my heart out, because the bitch took off after she'd informed me you were gone, and she never told me where you were buried. I had nothing left of you except the emptiness and memories."

Tee's shoulders were shaking, her back still turned.

"Please come back and sit here with me again, Tee," Coralee called softly to the frozen girl.

Tee turned and swayed over to the sofa where Coralee waited. Her regular strut was now more like a delaying shuffle. With her head lowered into a bizarre symbolic, self-effacing slump—so unnatural for her confident self, she approached.

"Tell me about you, Tee. I want—no—need to know everything."

Sliding down on the cushion, Tee admitted. "After those first weir-does, no one ever adopted me. I wasn't a very happy kid. Not much liked, never mind loved. But somehow, it didn't matter. I always, always sensed deep inside—not true—I absolutely knew that once I had been loved. Hugely! It had to have been you because there was no one else."

"You felt the link too?" Coralee squeezed Tee's hands, which were now locked between hers.

"Yeah! It was weird. You were so deeply embedded in my psyche that I couldn't shake you. Your essence was like a blanket of loving. You protected me. Sounds freaky I know, but it's the God's honest truth. I had to find you. It's all I thought about, cared about." Her voice broke with emotion held in too long. She sobbed heartbrokenly, loudly like only Tee could. Gruff, hoarse cries emanating from her lost soul. Cries that were embedded for years and, up until now, stubbornly held in. Vital, cleansing sobs craving release.

Tee wrenched herself off the sofa and twisted away to cover her shameful display.

Coralee, galvanized, leapt to her side, and had the broken girl in her arms like a flash, kissing her hair, her cheeks and patting her back as she mumbled brokenly, "I do love you, have always loved you. I sang to you and talked to you for hours while you were nestled safely in my tummy." She smiled, reminiscing. "I was so scared I would hurt you, so

I read every book I could get my hands on at the library about being a good mother. I even read them to you." Giddily chuckling, she rocked her daughter back and forth, back and forth, in a motherly rhythm she'd previously recoiled from. Happy tears ran down her face, into her mouth and over her chin, but they were ignored. Both woman and girl luxuriated in their nurturing togetherness.

"What about my father?" Tee asked.

Coralee made eye contact while she shared what she considered to be vital information. Her hands gently brushed the girl's cheeks. "Your daddy was a mixed-up street kid just like me. He was sweetness dressed in baggy pants, long hair, and a constant need for a cigarette. No job, sixteen and drifting, and no help at all in my predicament. I loved him and was heartbroken to later learn he'd been killed in a car crash."

"I'll never get to meet him. I had hoped to find him as well. There were so many things I dreamt of asking the both of you. Like, what was the name you picked for me?"

"Sweetheart, your name was to be Teresa Ellie. I named you after a little girl I had as a playmate when I was small. I loved her. She was the closest thing to a sister I ever had and the gentlest spirit I ever met, always smiling and happy. I wanted that for you, so I gave you her name."

"They didn't keep the name for me. They called me Connie. I hated it because I learned it was the same name as the woman who first adopted me. When I tried to read your files at the Social Services office, all I could see of the name you had given me was T.E. and so I decided then and there it would do until I found out the rest."

"Heavens, Tee, I hate that you had such an unhappy life. For your sake, I wish it wasn't so. For my sake, I thank God you came to find me. I will never, ever let you go again; do you hear me? You're stuck with me now, kiddo."

"What about Lee? I thought you guys were getting married? You've been flashing your diamonds around here all morning."

"Don't you like him, honey? You always seemed to get along so well." Coralee's panic showed in her voice while her damp eyes grew rounder.

"Hey, Mom, don't freak out. I like him already. He's cool." Squeezed suddenly by the arms surrounding her, Tee yelled. "Ow, not so hard!" They both laughed out loud, tears forgotten.

Coralee ordered, "Say it again! Say 'Mom.' I love it! Come on, say it." Dancing her daughter around the room in a crazy loony-tunes way, she rambled on in joyous abandon.

"Okay, already. Mom!"

"My daughter!"

"Mother mine!"

"My beautiful baby girl!"

"My old lady!"

"Cheeky brat! Now you're grounded!"

Chapter Sixty-seven

The day was full of sunshine, sweet flowery smells, and happy hearts. Grandma Evie's gardens were the perfect backdrop for the milling groups chattering, laughing, and visiting.

Angelina decided to leave Coralee and Tee alone in her room so they could share some special moments together before the ceremony. Ever since they'd come out of her office the day Adam Small had revealed their relationship, a closeness had sprung up between the two that was beautiful to watch. The whole office had celebrated upon hearing the wonderful news. She wouldn't lay bets on who was happier, Tee, Coralee or Lee. Gliding up the hallway, Angelina, careful not to step on her gown's flounces, stumbled when her father all of a sudden appeared in front of her.

"Hola, Papá! Were you coming to see me?"

"Si, mi hija. Since we flew in for the wedding this morning, I've been trying to get a moment alone with you."

"Is there something wrong?" Angelina didn't like the serious look on his face. Anxiety overcame happiness and sent shivers down her backbone.

"No, no, my Angel. Everything's fine. It's just that tu mamá informed me that you weren't planning to come back to Chile and work with your brothers and me in the business. It made me feel sad."

"Well, I lost the bet, didn't I? Therefore, according to our rules, you honestly couldn't offer me a position." This was the moment she'd worked so hard for, to be vindicated, to earn the right to be proud of her accomplishments. She should be devastated for failing.

Surprisingly, after searching inside her heart, Angelina had come to the conclusion a while back that winning didn't really matter anymore. She knew she'd accomplished what she'd set out to do but had kept it a secret. No one but Joe understood. She'd earned the wherewithal to pay off her outstanding debt. But she hadn't done it.

As for as her letting her father find her a husband, that wasn't going to happen either. After all, she'd found her own, hadn't she?

A shifty look appeared on his face. He wouldn't look her in the eye. What was going on?

Taking her in his arms, her father hugged her close and whispered, "You did win the bet, querida. We both know that to be true. I think you chose not to accept the prize because you don't want to leave a certain handsome young doctor, si?"

Pulling away so she could look him in the eye, she saw his certainty. "How can you know that Papá? What makes you so sure?"

He ducked his head slightly, first one way and then the other. "I have a lot of friends here in Canada. Let's just say that I regretted having forced you into this act as soon as you'd flung the challenge at your stubborn old papá. These last two years have been hellish, not

having my little girl around. Now, I see that my foolishness has cost
me my daughter. For that, I am sorry, my Angel."

"Oh, Papá! Me too. I missed you and the family terribly. But I've
made a life here now, and you're right about me and Joe. We love each
other. Soon, there'll be another wedding to attend."

She saw the pain her words induced, sorrow he couldn't hide, and
she hugged him again. "I'll travel home often, I promise."

He squeezed her to him and sighed long and loud. "Si! That would
make tu mamá very happy."

***

When the music filtered through the laughter, everyone quickly made
their way to the rows of white-covered chairs that led to a beautiful
altar, completely swathed in pink and white flowers. White satin bows
decorated each of the first chairs in the rows, and the red carpet,
winding along the aisle, lay waiting for the bride and her ladies.

Tee had never felt so excited. Her signal to begin the procession had
just been heard. Dressed in light pink flounces–though at first, she'd
argued violently and was eventually won over by Coralee's bribes—she
had a very important part to play.

In front, Angelina looking fetching in her replica, but brighter pink
gown, started toward the waiting minister.

Tee reached out to Coralee, who was fiddling with her veil. "Mom,
this is it. No turning back. You really want to marry Lee Nivens, for
better, forever?

Laughing gaily, Coralee grabbed Tee's hands and repeated, "Do you
want to marry him with me—for better, forever?"

"Oh yeah! He's my driving instructor, he'll be the reason I pass math this year and... of all of us, he's the best cook."

"Then lead on, my girl." Coralee grinned and twined her arm with her daughter's. Half a dozen steps later, they appeared on the plush carpet.

Stunning, in a traditional white satin and lace confection, Coralee produced gasps of wonder, smiles and even a few tears from the guests.

***

During the wait for his bride, and with Joe by his side, Lee whispered, "Watch how it's done, my man. It'll be your turn next."

Lee, in a black tuxedo, had cleaned up extremely well. Thanks to Tee's bugging, he'd let his hair grow, had it styled differently, and his ears seemed diminished in size.

Using one of Tee's favorite slang expressions, Joe decided he was stoked seeing his best friend so happy. "Got it! But remember you're taking on not one but two females, my friend."

Lee shoved against Joe's shoulder and nodded toward Grandma Evie and Rosario, who were surrounded by Angelina's father, mother and two large good-looking brothers. "True, but my girls are orphans."

Joe blanched and his smile wobbled.

Lee laughed until he saw his beautiful girls and all else faded.

~*~*~*~

If you enjoyed reading this book, I hope you might like to continue with another of Mimi Barbour's fabulous stories.

The Surrogate's Secret is just the kind of story you might love. It's about surrogate mother, Sheri O'Connor, who loves her adorable twins. Since the donor parents - her close friends were killed before their birth -

she's gladly taking on the responsibility to raise them herself. When their handsome Chilean Uncle, Miguel Rivera, arrives with no warning, expecting to take them back to his country, she unravels and coldly informs him that isn't going to happen. After all, they were her eggs used in the In Vitro process.

Her argument holds no importance for him. The one-track man only cares about his dying mother seeing her grandkids and so he blackmails Sheri into a marriage of convenience. Then he whisks her and the babies off to a strange, foreign country.

Find all of Mimi's Books and links to venues here on her website Link: https://mimibarbour.com/books

See Chapter One and Two below.

The Surrogate's Secret

The Surrogate's Secret
By Mimi Barbour

NYT & USAT bestselling author

D escription:

Surrogate mother, Sheri O'Connor, loves her adorable twins. Since the donor parents were killed before their birth, she's gladly taken on the responsibility to raise them herself. When their Chilean Uncle, Miguel Rivera, arrives with no warning, expecting to take them back to his country, she unravels and coldly informs him that isn't going to happen. After all, they were her eggs used in the In Vitro process. Consequently, her claim supersedes anyone else's. Never in a million years does she dream that the South American heartstopper wants her babies so much that he will force her to marry him by threatening to withhold the money she needs for an operation for her tiny son.

Miguel knows women aren't to be trusted. Didn't his devious fiancé give him up for dead and marry someone else while he spent months being held hostage in the jungles of Columbia? If his mother hadn't brought a team to save him and end up getting shot during the rescue, he wouldn't be alive. Therefore, if the only thing that can help his Mamacita from succumbing to her wounds is to adopt his dead brother's surrogate children, then he will do anything to see that happen. Even marry the ditzy blonde whose saving grace, beside her gorgeous body and beautiful face, is her absolute devotion to her babies.

Chapter One – The Surrogate's Secret

Sheri O'Connor stood in the doorway of her twins' bedroom and watched the two peacefully sleeping. A huge swell of love filled her soul while tears of thankfulness flooded her eyes. No one could love their babies more.

Seeing that she was a surrogate mom, it wasn't supposed to have ended this way. The precious little ones were to have been her gift to a woman she loved like a sister and the man who adored her. Sadly, things change.

Exhausted, Sheri tiptoed forward to cover the two angels huddled close together in the same crib. She kissed her fingers then touched them to their silky hair. They had taken a while to settle this afternoon. It must be the heat. With the back of her hand, Sheri swiped at her dampened forehead. In Washington, DC, when it was hot, it scorched.

A doorbell broke the silence and made her wince, then grin. Oh no! Not Charly again. Her neighbor was a worrywart about her and the children. Her help had gotten Sheri through the bad times and now they were very close, but she had promised to stay away so Sheri could catch up on some much-needed sleep.

Again, the doorbell pealed; this time followed by an impatient knock. Moving quickly to the front entrance, Sheri wrenched the door open.

The tanned, good-looking man leaning against the doorjamb wasn't Charly. This mysterious male reached well over six feet and looked to be pure trouble. His head, held at a cocky angle, and especially his cold gray eyes affected Sheri. Maybe tiredness made her unusually grumpy, but she wanted her bed and this man looked like he had a mission.

Her bare feet, naked legs, and rounded belly still recovering from recently giving birth received a laser-like scan. From his scowl, he either didn't like her clothes or her looks. She noticed his full lips curl slightly as his eyes skimmed her mess of hair, which had escaped the confines of her clip and now hung in total disarray over her bare shoulders.

Not one to dress fancy at home, Sheri nonetheless wished she'd chosen something other than the low-cut, thin cotton blouse with the frills that directed one's eye to the protruding breasts below. The favored blouse never worn outside the apartment for that exact reason was her sheerest and therefore the coolest one she owned. Sheri straightened her shoulders, refusing to be intimidated.

"Can I help you?" Her voice sounded huskier than normal. Tiredness did that to her.

He eased upright and asked. "Are you Sheri O'Connor, Mary-Anne Rivera's friend and her surrogate mother?" His voice vibrated with fake courtesy, a strong accent and a mesmerizing quality that might fool a fool.

Sheri was no fool.

"Yes." The name of her deceased friend, spoken by a stranger, pierced her, forcing her to brace herself. Stepping back, she folded her arms across her stomach, this time to conceal her shaky reaction. She cocked her head, copying his style.

"Miss O'Connor, may we go inside and talk? You look ready to collapse, and I wouldn't want to upset the mother of my brother's baby. Come." He clasped her arm with one hand and beckoned behind her with the other. An emotion, very like pain, registered in his expression. It beguiled her for several seconds, until big city rules of safety kicked finally in.

She wrenched her arm away from his grasp and stood her ground. "Your brother's baby? What's your name, and why are you here?"

Chapter Two

Apprehension attacked Sheri. Before he spoke, she clasped her hands to stop them from trembling

"My name is Miguel Rivera. I am Felipe's brother." Taking advantage of her momentary speechlessness, the man moved forward into her space, forcing her to back up, and then grabbing his small bag, he closed the door behind them. Before she could react, his elegantly shaped fingers reached into the expensive, brown leather jacket, to the inside pocket, and he pulled out his wallet. He showed her his identification, aiming it close for her scrutiny. His ID security license from the federal government surprised her.

"Trust me. I'm here to help you. May I call you Sheri?" When he spoke in the low tone and turned his head slightly, for the first time, she spotted a similarity in his facial structure to Mary-Anne's husband. Contrary to Felipe, who'd always been fastidiously groomed, this man appeared thin, bordering on gaunt, making her wonder if he'd been sick recently. His black hair reached his shoulders with the flowing waves pushed to the back of his head, as if he'd finger forced them away from his face. A scruffy beard hinted that he'd come straight from the airport, as did the overnight case settled on the floor by his feet.

Upon closer inspection, she realized she should have known right away that he was a relative of Felipe's. Not only were their slanted eyes the same smoky-gray, and covered by thick, perfectly shaped eyebrows, but her careful scrutiny revealed their general appearance and strong features were similar also. The way he wore his expensive clothes should have been another indication, although Felipe favored suits whereas his brother's style looked to be more casual.

"Yes of course." Inwardly she scolded herself and then stopped after a few seconds. She couldn't be blamed for not recognizing Miguel as Felipe's relative. Even though she'd known Felipe had a brother, one he talked of quite often and had obviously adored, she'd never met him before, and his cold emotionless demeanor separated the two brothers by a wide chasm. Felipe had defined South American charm and graciousness. He'd smiled more than any other man she'd ever known, whereas this man—he intimidated.

Resentment pushed past her control. "Good of you to appear now, four months after your brother and Mary-Anne were killed." Where had he been when she'd sent the news of their death in a car accident? Or when the shock had started her labor pains, and she'd had to face the birth of his brother's babies alone?

"You're right to be annoyed. I should have been here, Sheri. And I would have if at all possible."

Sheri recognized his acute frustration and stopped her recriminations. Don't be so judgmental. He's here now. Give the man a chance to explain.

Why did her instinctive fairness always have to override the very few occasions when nastiness kicked in? Because she was a pushover, that's why. The guy did look exhausted, and ill, and the visible misery trapped deep in his eyes coaxed her sympathy. Okay, she'd listen. If he doesn't have a good excuse, she decided, then I'll boot his spiffy ass outta here.

"Come with me where it's a bit cooler," she said, her voice softened considerably. She led him to an airless crowded living room where a wobbly ceiling fan twirled, hummed, and intermittently groaned.

Tucked in the corner of the small space nestled a playpen and other baby paraphernalia. A quilted baby seat sat on the floor and on every piece of mismatched furniture, some sort of evidence that babies lived in the apartment could be seen.

She motioned for him to sit on her sofa while she folded into the thrift-store, ivory-colored rocker. Light filtered through the white sheers and intensified the pale green walls. The room sparkled from her ministrations of the night before when, sleepless and brimming with an overabundance of energy, she'd cleaned. Now she felt glad she hadn't just vegged out and watched one of her pre-recorded TV shows.

Sheri's days and nights seemed to be reversed due to all the feedings she had to manage, and many times her way to deal with the latest heat wave was either to read, work, or watch some brain-dulling program. Her low-budget place looked its grungy best, but she had to admit that today extreme weariness ended up being the ultimate price.

"Can I get you a glass of iced tea?" She motioned towards her dewy glass full of ice and golden-brown liquid set on the small coffee table.

"No. Thank you. I've come as quickly as I could to see—"

Unconsciously her hand lifted, palm towards him. "My friend and your brother were killed over four months ago." She emphasized the words brother and months.

Miguel's large frame seemed to shrink right in front of her eyes. Both hands lifted to his hair as he threaded his fingers through the wild mass. Finally, he looked up. "Yes, you are right. My mother and I were out of the country. We didn't know anything about Felipe until yesterday morning when we returned to Santiago. I'm sorrier than I can ever put into words, but our absence was unavoidable." He hesitated and added words that softened her heart. "And unforgivable. We will have to deal with our guilt. I understand you did everything possible to find us. I regret you could not, and that you were forced to carry on with the funeral arrangements alone—especially when you had your own grief to deal with, and a small baby to look after."

"Not one small baby. Two. A boy called Rafael and a girl, Carrie-Anne."

"Two? How wonderful!" He smiled for the first time since he'd arrived. Sheri, shocked by the difference white teeth and curved lips made, felt the ice further melt around her attitude. Now the resemblance to Felipe became undeniable.

Not a person to hold grudges, and hating to be at odds with anyone, Sheri smiled as well. Because she couldn't shake off feelings of depression once the babies were born, the doctor explained to her that many mothers underwent slight personality changes after delivery. No one could blame her for having the occasional meltdown. Especially since, she'd given birth to surrogate twins and buried their parents within the same week.

After their return from the hospital, she'd struggled to stay positive and keep things going. Without the help of her neighbor Charly, she didn't know how she could have managed.

A cleared throat recaptured her attention, and she raised anguished eyes. "Sorry. For a moment you looked so like your brother that it brought back memories."

"Memories of Felipe?"

"Yes, and Mary-Anne. She and I met in kindergarten and were closer than sisters. We grew up next door to each other and shared all our secrets. She wanted nothing more than to stay home and be a wife and mother and I wanted to travel the world." She sighed and smiled. "Funny thing the way life throws out unexpected hurdles. Mary-Anne left our small town in Canada to move to New York to pursue her job, while I remained to look after my father."

He returned her smile and surprisingly, her heavy spirits seemed less weighty. "But you live here in DC now?"

"Yes. After my father passed away, I had nothing left to keep me home."

"No husbands or boyfriends to hold you there?"

Angry disgust replaced the soft look on her face, and his reactive frown made her aware that he'd seen her change. In a clipped voice, she cut him off from the subject. "I left no one behind who mattered."

"I see." He nodded; his attention riveted.

"Mary-Anne begged me to come and live here so we could be near to each other. Once I arrived, she found me this apartment and I settled in."

"She was an editor, wasn't she? Worked for one of the big publishing companies in New York?"

"Yes, but after she met and married Felipe, they sanctioned her moving here to Washington so she could be near him. It was either move her or lose her. They gave her their blessings and a company laptop. I guess they had no choice. She would have quit because she loved him more than anything." Emotion welled and filled her with sadness. In a husky tone, she added, "The only strain in their relationship was her overwhelming need to give Felipe children. Ironic isn't it?

He owned half of an In Vitro clinic, spent his days helping others get pregnant, and then finds his own wife can't conceive."

"Therefore, she hired you to help them—"

Did he sneer?

She cut him off. "No. I offered my services, and they both gratefully accepted my gift of love."

Seeming to realize that he'd overstepped, he backed off and added. "So he mentioned when he called home to tell us the happy news."

He'd put Sheri's hackles up, and she felt the bitchiness return. She stood, hinting his time had run out. Then looking down she added, "Mary-Anne's requests were clear about her remains, and because I knew nothing of Felipe's wishes, I treated him the same. I buried some of his ashes with his wife, but I also saved some to send to his beloved Chile as soon as I could contact your family. I hope that meets with your approval?" Sheri stared at Miguel. She noticed his hands tremble as he rubbed at the beard darkening the lower part of his face. The little sign of weakness in such a strong man affected her more than anything else had in a long time. She moved over and sat on the sofa near him, then reached out involuntarily to touch his shoulder.

A grim expression replaced the fleeting vulnerability. "That was very considerate of you. My mother will be pleased to have some part of him placed where she can visit often." He kept his eyes lowered.

"It's what Mary-Anne would have wanted," Sheri said. "She loved him so very much and felt extreme affection for you and your mother when they visited Chile on their honeymoon."

"And we thank you," Miguel said gently. "Now, I've come with a proposition." He spoke the words in a low voice, which caught her attention. In seconds, his face altered, a steely look replaced the sadness.

She shivered with apprehension and eased away from him.

"Whatever amount my brother offered to pay you for having a baby for him and Mary-Anne, I will double. No, change that. I'll pay you whatever you want. As the uncle, I claim the right to adopt the babies, and take them home with me to Chile, to live with their grandmother."

~*~*~*~

*** *If you'd like to continue with this story, click here to for Mimi's website where you'll find all of books with links to various venues. https://mimibarbour.com/books*

Afterword:

Thank you so much for reading *I'm No Angel.*

This was actually the very first book I ever wrote, and I made every mistake a new writer does at the beginning. I hid it for years before making enough drastic edits so it could finally be released. But I did loved writing the story, and I hope you enjoyed reading it too. If so, I would ask you for a favor. Wherever you purchased this collection, please take a few minutes and leave an honest review. Authors enjoy hearing how readers like their stories, and hopefully, others will see your words and choose to buy the book because of your sentiments.

My website at http://mimibarbour.com now has all my books listed with links to the various publishers to make it easy for you to return to where you bought the book and to find my other work.

While you're there, I'd really appreciate it if you would sign up for my newsletter so I can keep in touch. http://bit.ly/MimiBNewsletter. I only send out newsletters approximately once a month. It's usually full of sales and freebies along with my personal news. (You have my word that your address will never be shared.)

Hugs,
Mimi

About the author, Mimi Barbour

MIMI BARBOUR: New York Times & USA Today Best-selling, award-winning romance author has written nine series, many single-tiles, and participates in a huge number of box collections.

She lives on the beautiful East coast of Vancouver Island and writes her books with tongue-in-cheek and a mad glint in her eye. The fans all agree that it's the fascinating characters she creates which makes her writing so entertaining and brings them back for more of her magic.

"The favorite part of my job is meeting the characters from each new book. Designing them the way I want and having them act however I think they should. It's thrilling, especially when most of my make-believe folks are people I would love to interact with in reality."

Contact me:

My website: http://www.mimibarbour.com/
Or on Facebook: Mimi Barbour Fanpage
Please sign up for my fun Newsletter: http://bit.ly/mimibarbourne
wsletter

or

Write to me anytime. I love to hear from my readers.xo
mailto:mimibarbour66@gmail.com